THE LAST GUNFIGHTER

The Devil's Legion

BOOK YOUR PLACE ON OUR WEBSITE AND MAKE THE READING CONNECTION!

We've created a customized website just for our very special readers, where you can get the inside scoop on everything that's going on with Zebra, Pinnacle and Kensington books.

When you come online, you'll have the exciting opportunity to:

- View covers of upcoming books
- Read sample chapters
- Learn about our future publishing schedule (listed by publication month *and author*)
- Find out when your favorite authors will be visiting a city near you
- Search for and order backlist books from our online catalog
- Check out author bios and background information
- Send e-mail to your favorite authors
- Meet the Kensington staff online
- Join us in weekly chats with authors, readers and other guests
- Get writing guidelines
- AND MUCH MORE!

**Visit our website at
http://www.kensingtonbooks.com**

THE LAST GUNFIGHTER

The Devil's Legion

William W. Johnstone

with J. A. Johnstone

PINNACLE BOOKS
Kensington Publishing Corp.
www.kensingtonbooks.com

PINNACLE BOOKS are published by

Kensington Publishing Corp.
850 Third Avenue
New York, NY 10022

All Kensington titles, imprints, and distributed lines are available
at special quantity discounts for bulk purchases for sales promo-
tions, premiums, fund-raising, educational, or institutional use.

Special book excerpts or customized printings can also be
created to fit specific needs. For details, write or phone the
office of the Kensington special sales manager: Kensington
Publishing Corp., 850 Third Avenue, New York, NY 10022,
attn: Special Sales Department; phone 1-800-221-2647.

PINNACLE BOOKS and the Pinnacle P logo are Reg. U.S.
Pat. & TM Off.

ISBN 0-7860-1632-9

First printing: October 2006

10 9 8 7 6 5 4 3 2 1

Printed in the United States of America

Chapter One

Because of the thick growth of trees on the ridge, Frank Morgan smelled the smoke before he saw it. He reined the big Appaloosa called Stormy to a halt, and beside him, the wolflike cur known only as Dog stopped as well and sat down, ears cocked forward alertly.

Frank sniffed the smoke and didn't like the smell of it. Wood, without a doubt, but there was an undercurrent of something else in it, something that made the hairs on the back of Frank's neck prickle and an icy finger trail along his spine.

Something ugly.

"Come on," he said to Stormy as he lifted the reins. "Let's go see about this." He rode through the trees, followed by Dog.

Whatever was happening, it was none of his business. He hadn't been in Arizona Territory for a good long while, and he didn't have any real reason for being here now. As could be expected from a man called by many The Drifter, he had ridden aimlessly in this direction after wrapping up that ruckus over in New Mexico Territory, where his son Conrad was building a railroad.

Frank Morgan didn't look like a rich man. He wore dusty range clothes and a somewhat battered old hat.

But he had more money than you could shake a stick at in bank accounts in Denver and San Francisco, and he was a partner in that railroad, along with various other enterprises. Cash flowed into his accounts on a regular basis.

Frank didn't much care. As long as he had enough coins in his pocket to keep him in bacon and beans and flour and salt and sugar, to buy oats for Stormy when they came to a settlement, to maybe pick up a good soup bone from a butcher shop for Dog, and to see to it that there were plenty of bullets for the Colt .45 on his hip and the Winchester snugged into a saddle boot, Frank was happy.

At least, as happy as a man could be when he had seen way more than his share of death and suffering and folks tried to kill him on a semiregular basis.

Tall, broad-shouldered, and lean-hipped, with graying dark hair under his Stetson, Frank reached the edge of the pines and rode out to where the ridge dropped off to a broad valley. The Mogollon Rim loomed darkly, off to the northeast. Stretching southwestward were miles and miles of prime ranching country, lush valleys between ranges of thickly wooded mountains and hills. The grass in these high-country pastures was thick and tall and green.

The scene would have been truly beautiful had it not been for the column of black smoke rising from the burning cabin in the valley below Frank.

His mouth tightened into a grim slash as he studied the layout. The burning cabin had been small and crudely built, probably used as a line shack by punchers who rode for whatever spread controlled this range. Off to one side was a pole corral where three horses milled around nervously. They were so spooked they would probably bust down one side of the corral and run off pretty soon.

Frank wasn't worried about the horses. They were far

enough away from the fire so that they weren't in danger from the flames, and if they got loose they would go back where they came from, in all likelihood the ranch headquarters.

He was more concerned with the two bodies sprawled motionless in front of the cabin door.

Three horses, two men, he thought. The third man was unaccounted for, but the smell in the air that put Frank's teeth on edge told him where that hombre was. It was the smell of burning flesh.

The third man was still in the cabin.

The fire was burning so fiercely that Frank knew there was nothing he could do for the man inside the shack. But one or both of the other two might still be alive. "Let's go," he said to Stormy, and he guided the Appaloosa over the brink and down the steep slope of the ridge.

Stormy handled challenges such as this as if he were part mountain goat, picking his way down the incline with relative ease. Frank let the horse have his head. He knew that Stormy could be trusted. After a few minutes they reached the floor of the valley. Frank heeled the Appaloosa into a fast trot toward the blazing cabin.

When they got there, he reined in and swung down out of the saddle almost before Stormy stopped moving. Frank's right hand hovered near the well-worn walnut grips of his Colt as he approached the nearer of the two men on the ground. The man lay on his belly, and now Frank could see the large red stains on the back of his vest. A pool of blood had collected underneath him as well. The man had been shot through the body five or six times, maybe more. There was no way he could still be alive.

Heat from the flames beat at Frank's face as he hurried over to the second man. This one lay on his side, curled up almost as if he were simply sleeping. His shirt was bloody, too, but there didn't seem to be as much gore. Frank knelt, his eyes narrowing in discomfort from the heat, and felt for a pulse in the man's neck.

He found one, faint and thready but still there.

The fire was close enough so that the wounded man's eyebrows and some of his hair had been singed off. That added to the stink in the air. Frank hooked his hands under the man's arms and pulled him farther away from the flames, not stopping until a cool breeze blew over them both. In his delirium, the man muttered something that Frank couldn't make out.

Frank eased the man's head to the ground. There was a bloodstain on his left side, another on his right shoulder, yet another on his right thigh. He had been hit three times. Frank pulled up the man's shirt to check the wound in his side. It was a deep one, angling in, and there was no exit wound on his back. The slug was still in him somewhere. It had probably struck a rib and splintered, shattering the bone in the process and doing God knows how much other damage. Frank didn't figure the fella had much time left.

He whistled, and Stormy came trotting over. Frank straightened and got his canteen off the saddle. He knelt again, uncorked the canteen, and held it to the man's lips, letting a little water trickle into his mouth. The man sputtered and coughed and came awake. He sucked greedily at the canteen for a second or two before weakness overcame him and his head fell back.

"B-Bragan?" he gasped.

Frank glanced at the dead man. "If that was one of your pards, I'm afraid they've crossed the divide, fella. One's shot up real bad in front of the cabin, and the other is still inside."

The wounded man closed his eyes and let out a groan. "Sandeen," he said, and Frank realized that was what he had said a few moments earlier, as Frank was dragging him away from the inferno that until recently had been a line shack.

"Is that who did this to you?"

"His . . . riders. Am I gonna . . . be all right?"

"I don't know," Frank said honestly. "I'm not a doctor. It doesn't look good, though."

"Them . . . sons o' bitches! They shot . . . Wardell . . . through the window . . . set the shack on fire . . . me'n Bragan stood it as long as we could . . . then we come out shootin' . . . bastards was waitin' for us . . . cut us down . . ."

That was what Frank figured had happened here, and now the guess had been confirmed. He had known from the start that white men had done this. In the past, Apaches had burned plenty of isolated cabins in Arizona Territory, but Geronimo, the last of the war chiefs, had surrendered to the Army seven or eight years earlier, effectively ending the Indian threat in the territory.

But there were still plenty of other dangers around here. The grisly scene Frank had come upon was proof of that.

"What's your name, son?" Frank asked quietly. The wounded man wasn't much over twenty years old.

"I'm called Rufe . . . Rufe Blake."

"Anybody you'd like for me to write to?"

"You mean . . . to tell 'em . . . I'm dead?"

"Just in case," Frank said, although he was more convinced than ever that this young puncher had only minutes to live.

"My ma . . . and sister . . . live in Flagstaff. Ma's name is . . . Alma Blake. My sister is . . . Tess." A bloodstained hand lifted and clutched at Frank's arm. "I got wages comin' . . . from the Lazy F. Spread's owned by . . . Howard Flynn."

"I'll see to it that your ma and sister get what's coming to you, Rufe. Don't you worry."

The cowboy's fingers tightened on Frank's arm. "I'm . . . obliged . . . One more thing . . ."

"What is it, Rufe?"

"If you ever see . . . Ed Sandeen . . . plug the mangy varmint!"

Rufe Blake's back arched slightly and his voice strengthened as he delivered that plea for vengeance, but as soon as the words were out of his mouth, he sagged back on the ground and a long sigh came from him. His eyes began to grow glassy as they stared up at the blue Arizona sky, as if he were watching his departed soul ascend toward Heaven.

Frank sighed, too. His long years of roaming the West had been filled with people dying. He had been forced to kill many of them himself. He had gotten used to death—but he had never grown to like it. He hoped he never did.

Leaving Rufe Blake's body where it lay, Frank stood up and went to the man he knew only as Bragan. He dragged Bragan's body over next to Rufe's. As for the man still inside the cabin—Wardell, Rufe had called him, Frank remembered—he would have to wait until the fire burned down and the ruins cooled off some before he could recover that body. He was sure it wouldn't be a pretty sight. A corpse never was.

In the meantime, he could start digging the graves. There wasn't much danger of the fire spreading, he judged. The area right around the line shack had been trampled down by horses and men until there wasn't much vegetation left on it to burn. Besides, there had been plenty of rain here in the Mogollon country in recent months, and everything was green. Still, Frank planned to keep a close eye on the fire to make sure no glowing ashes floated away to cause trouble.

He had a folding shovel in the pack that was lashed onto Stormy's back behind the saddle. As he went to get it, he thought about what he had learned in the past few minutes. Rufe Blake and his two companions had ridden for the Lazy F, a spread owned by a man called Howard Flynn. And gunmen who worked for Ed Sandeen, obviously an enemy of Flynn's, had torched the line shack and killed the three cowboys.

Frank had ridden into the middle of a range war.

He had encountered such things before and heard about many others, epic, bloody conflicts that could consume an entire range in killing. Often they continued until one side or the other was completely wiped out. As a younger man, Frank had taken part in range wars. Now he wanted nothing to do with this one—although the brutal way in which Rufe, Bragan, and Wardell had been killed rankled at him. Trapping men in a cabin, burning them out, and shooting them down like dogs was a coward's way of doing things. Frank could respect somebody who went at trouble straight up and head-on, even when he didn't agree with him. But this . . .

This was nothing short of murder.

He had barely hung his hat on the saddle horn and started digging when Dog suddenly growled, a low, rumbling sound of menace and warning from deep in his throat. Frank pushed the blade of the shovel into the ground so that it would stand up and turned to see what had raised Dog's hackles. He heard what the big cur's keen hearing had picked up a few seconds earlier, a swift rataplan of hoofbeats. Frank saw several riders emerge from some trees on the far side of the valley and gallop toward him.

He suspected they were more riders for the Lazy F, who had spotted the smoke from the burning cabin and were coming to check it out. They could take over this burying chore, he thought. Once he told them what Rufe had said, he could ride on.

Things weren't going to be quite that simple, though, he realized a moment later when one of the men racing toward him shucked a repeating rifle from its saddle sheath and opened fire, sending bullets whipping through the air toward Frank.

Chapter Two

Luckily, the hurricane deck of a galloping horse was just about the worst place in the world for accurate shooting. One of the slugs came close enough for Frank to hear the whistling whine of its passage, but the others were even farther off the mark. Leaving the shovel where it was, he walked unhurriedly toward Stormy and pulled out his own Winchester. He levered a round into the chamber, laid the barrel across the saddle to steady it, and drew a bead. The Appaloosa stood stock-still, knowing from experience what was about to happen. When Frank pressed the trigger and the rifle cracked, the hat on the head of the man shooting at him suddenly jumped into the air. That hombre started sawing on the reins, trying to bring his mount to a halt. The men with him hauled in their horses, too.

Frank worked the rifle's lever again and then stood there waiting while the four riders milled around, obviously confused and unsure what to do next. He would let them call the play. If they came a-shootin' again, the odds were that he could pick off all of them before they got close enough to stand a good chance of hitting him.

Now, if they dismounted and opened fire with their

rifles, that would be a different story. He would have to hunt some cover if that happened.

Instead, after a few minutes of heated conversation, the four men started forward again, but they walked their horses this time and didn't shoot at him. Frank watched them come. When Dog growled, he said, "Take it easy, old-timer. I reckon they want to parley."

When the riders were about fifty yards away, they stopped again, and one of the men—not the one who had been shooting earlier—shouted, "Hold your fire, mister! We just want to find out if our pards are all right!"

"Come ahead!" Frank called back. "But keep your hands where I can see 'em!"

The men advanced slowly. They were close enough now so that Frank could make out their rugged, unshaven faces. They looked rough as a cob and probably were, but for the moment at least, they weren't shooting. The one who had popped off those rounds earlier had a particularly unfriendly look on his face. He had slid his rifle back in the saddle boot, though, and as long as he didn't reach for it again, Frank was willing to let him live.

When they came to a stop again, they were about thirty feet away. The spokesman peered past Frank at the two bodies and said grimly, "That looks like a couple of our friends."

"One's Rufe Blake, and the other's called Bragan," Frank said. "That's all I know about him. Wardell's still in the cabin."

The men turned their heads to look at the shack. The roof had fallen in by now, and one of the walls was about to. The fire wasn't burning as strongly as it had been earlier, but it still gave off plenty of heat.

"What happened here?"

"I rode up and found the cabin on fire and those men lying out here. They'd been shot as they ran outside."

The trigger-happy hombre scowled at Frank and said

loudly, "He's lyin', Buckston. I'll bet a hat he's the one who killed them boys."

"I'm telling it like it happened," Frank said, his voice hard as flint. "And I don't much cotton to being called a liar. I'd be willing to bet that Rufe Blake wouldn't have liked it, either."

The one called Buckston, who seemed to be in charge, frowned and asked, "What do you mean by that, mister?"

With his left hand, Frank flicked a gesture toward Rufe's body. "I mean that young puncher was still alive when I rode up. He's the one who told me what happened here. And before he died, he said that men who ride for somebody called Ed Sandeen were responsible for it."

"Sandeen," one of the other punchers said. He made it sound like the worst curse that could ever come out of his mouth.

"I reckon you men ride for the Lazy F," Frank went on. "That'd be Howard Flynn's spread?"

Buckston's eyes narrowed even more. "You seem to know a hell of a lot about what's goin' on in this part of the country for somebody who just rode in."

"All I know is what Rufe Blake told me, and what I can see with my own eyes," Frank said with a shrug. "It's pretty obvious that there's some sort of range war going on between Flynn and Sandeen. And judging by what happened here, Sandeen's men fight dirty."

Buckston leaned over and spit deliberately in the dust. "That's because Sandeen's a polecat, and he hires men just like him . . . gunslingers, hired killers, men who been ridin' the hoot-owl trail. I'm convinced Sandeen used to ride that trail his own self, before he come here to the Mogollon country and tried to act all respectable-like. But once a polecat, always a polecat."

The man who had shot at Frank earlier was still having a hard time controlling his temper. "Damn it, Buck, why are you sittin' here jawin' with this fella? Can't you see he's gotta be one of Sandeen's men? Look at that thonged-down Colt! He's a gun-thrower, sure as hell."

"If I was working for Sandeen, why would I still be here?" Frank asked. "Why didn't I ride off with the rest of his men?"

The hothead sneered at him. "You prob'ly stayed behind to see what poor ol' Rufe and Bragan had in their pockets. Damn scavenger."

Anger welled up inside Frank. He felt like yanking the hothead down from his saddle and teaching him a lesson, but he knew that the first sign of violence would probably lead to gunplay. These men were keyed up, ready to shoot somebody, and even Buckston, who seemed to be the most levelheaded of the bunch, looking like he was ready to slap leather at the slightest provocation.

So Frank kept a tight rein on his own temper and said, "You're free to search them. I haven't taken anything from them."

Buckston rubbed his jaw with his left hand and frowned in thought. He was a lanky man with a drooping black mustache, obviously plenty tough, but he didn't look like a gunfighter, more like a top hand who could also handle a six-shooter if he needed to.

While Buckston pondered the situation, the fourth man, who hadn't spoken yet, stared intently at Frank. After a few moments, he said abruptly, "By the Lord Harry, I know who this hombre is! Thought I recognized him. I've seen his picture on dime novels. Boys, that's Frank Morgan!"

That announcement made the other men stiffen in their saddles. "Is that true?" Buckston demanded. "You're the gunslinger they call The Drifter?"

"My name is Frank Morgan," Frank admitted. "What folks call me is their business, not mine."

"Damn it, Buckston, now you gotta know I'm right

about him!" the hothead said. "Think about it. What would a hired killer like Morgan be doin' around here, if he didn't come to work for Sandeen? You know Sandeen's put out the word that he's lookin' for men, and payin' fightin' wages!"

Buckston nodded slowly. "That's true." He looked at Frank. "What you got to say for yourself, Morgan? You come here lookin' to hire out to Sandeen . . . or is he already payin' you?"

"I never heard of the man until about fifteen minutes ago," Frank said, "and I'm getting a mite tired of being accused of things. I've told you what happened here, and that's all I've got to say." He slid the Winchester back in the saddle sheath and snagged his hat from the horn. As he put it on, he said, "Since these fellas were your pards, you can have the chore of burying them, or you can take them back to the Lazy F, or whatever you want to do with them. But I'm out of it, understand?"

"You can't just ride away," the hothead said. "I still think you were part o' the bunch that done this."

"What's your name?" Frank asked.

The question surprised the man. "If it's any business o' yours, which it ain't, my name is Dennis Houlihan. Why'd you wanta know?"

Frank just smiled thinly and didn't answer.

Houlihan took offense. "Looky there, Buck!" he said excitedly to Buckston as he pointed at Frank. "He's threatenin' me! He just as much as said that he figures on shootin' me!"

"Calm down, you fool," Buckston said. "A man like Morgan ain't gonna shoot nobody unless there's some profit in it for him."

That hurt, Frank thought. Despite the stories that were told about him, he didn't hire out his gun to just anybody and never had. In every fight he had ever been part of, he had either been forced to use violence to save his own life, or he had been sticking up for somebody who couldn't protect themselves. He was no knight in shining armor, but he wasn't a cold-blooded murderer like Deacon Jim Miller, either.

At the moment he had other worries more important than hurt feelings, though. He didn't like the way that fourth man, the one who had recognized him, was looking at him. The hombre was fairly young, about the same age as Rufe Blake had been, and he had visions of glory dancing before his eyes. Frank knew the look. It said that the man who gunned down the notorious Drifter would then be even more famous.

It was a look that had gotten way too many glory-hungry young men killed.

As if to confirm Frank's worry, the young man said to Houlihan, "We can take him, Denny. Look at him. He's an old man, 'bout ready for the rockin' chair."

"You a damn fool, Crenshaw," the other older puncher said. He was a middle-aged black man with considerable gray in the hair under his floppy-brimmed hat and the beard stubble on his jaw. "Don't you know that an old lobo wolf is just about the most dangerous kind?"

"Shut up, Glover," Crenshaw snapped. "If you're scared, you can ride back home."

Glover started to turn his horse toward Crenshaw's, but Buckston put out a hand to stop him. This group of four cowboys had split down the middle, with the two older men, Buckston and Glover, on one side, and the pair of young firebrands, Houlihan and Crenshaw, on the other. They had even edged their mounts physically apart.

"Crenshaw, Houlihan, you listen to me," Buckston said. "You keep your hands away from your guns. If you want to fight Morgan, you go back to the ranch and draw your time first, so you won't die as Lazy F riders. I don't want to feel compelled to throw my life away just because you went and got yourself killed."

"But Buck, this is crazy!" Crenshaw protested.

"Morgan's a hired gun, we all know that. He's gotta be workin' for Sandeen!"

Frank just shook his head wearily. He put his foot in the stirrup, grasped the saddle horn and reins, and got ready to swing up onto Stormy's back.

"He's gonna get away, Denny!" Crenshaw said in an urgent voice.

"I'm takin' him!" Houlihan yelled suddenly. He jammed his spurs into his horse's flanks and sent the animal surging forward. At the same time he clawed an old Remington revolver out of a cross-draw holster on his left hip.

Frank was in an awkward position, half in and half out of the saddle. He dropped the reins and stood in the left stirrup, straightening so that he could draw. In what was a rarity for one of his gunfights, his opponent got off the first shot. Houlihan's Remington roared, but less than a heartbeat later the Colt in Frank's hand bucked as flame geysered from its muzzle.

He was trying to shoot Houlihan in the shoulder. It didn't seem that a misunderstanding was enough of a reason for a man to die. But fate conspired against that, as the slug from Houlihan's gun spanked across Stormy's rump. The big Appaloosa was trained to stand still when guns started to go off, but the pain of the bullet burn made him jump forward a little—just enough so that Frank's bullet hit Houlihan at the base of the throat. Blood spurted in the air as the man was driven backward off his horse by the slug's impact.

As always at moments such as this, time seemed to slow down slightly for Frank. He saw that Crenshaw had hung back after goading Houlihan to start the ball. That gave Crenshaw a chance to get his gun out and aimed. He fired, but his aim was off a little. The bullet buzzed past Frank's head.

Frank's return shot slammed into Crenshaw's chest. He shot to kill this time, with cold anger inside him.

Crenshaw had played on Houlihan's reckless impulsiveness, not caring if Houlihan got killed as long as that improved Crenshaw's chances of downing the famous Frank Morgan. That sort of callousness didn't sit well with Frank.

Besides, when somebody was trying to kill you, it was hard not to return the favor.

As Crenshaw toppled out of his saddle, too, Frank kicked free of the stirrup and dropped to the ground. Dog was about to go after either Buckston or Glover, but Frank called out, "Dog! No!" He didn't want this fracas to go any farther.

"Hold it, Morgan!" Buckston shouted. He and Glover had backed up their horses and shucked their saddle guns. The Winchesters were trained on Frank, and although he knew he could knock both men off their mounts, at least one of them was likely to get him, too.

Frank lifted his hands, the Colt still in the right one.

"Drop that gun!" Buckston commanded.

"Not hardly."

"I'm foreman of the Lazy F," Buckston grated. "You don't think I'm gonna let you ride away after you killed two o' my men, do you?"

"They brought it on themselves," Frank said. "You're not blind, Buckston. You saw it. For what it's worth, though, I didn't aim to kill Houlihan. My horse jumped just as I fired."

"What about Crenshaw?"

"He called the tune," Frank said coldly. "He had to dance to it."

Grudgingly, Glover said, "Crenshaw did sort of nudge Houlihan into drawin'."

"Yeah." The barrel of Buckston's Winchester dropped a little. "What're we gonna do about this?"

"Take Morgan to the boss," Glover suggested. "Let Mr. Flynn decide."

"Yeah," Buckston said with a nod. "I reckon that would

be best." The rifle barrel came up again. "If you're not gonna drop that gun, Morgan, at least holster it. Otherwise, there'll be more powder burned here and now."

Frank lowered his arms and slid the Colt back into leather.

"Mount up," Buckston continued. "We're goin' to the Lazy F."

"And what do you think will happen when we get there?"

"I don't know. Mr. Flynn's a fair man. We'll tell him what happened, and let him decide what to do with you."

Frank didn't hesitate. He knew he would be riding into a bad situation, where he would likely be surrounded by tough cowboys who would be glad to ventilate him if their boss gave the order.

But he also knew he hadn't done anything wrong, and he wanted to tell Howard Flynn as much, right to his face. When passing out the qualities that made up a man, the Good Lord hadn't put any back-up in Frank Morgan.

He stepped up into the saddle, nodded coolly to Buckston, and said, "Let's ride."

Chapter Three

Glover hung back to tie the bodies of Houlihan and Crenshaw on their horses. He also got the horses from the corral and loaded up the corpses of Rufe Blake and Bragan, too. By now all the walls of the burning line shack had collapsed, but it would still be a good while before the body of Wardell could be recovered. Somebody would have to come back with a wagon to do that. For now, Glover led one riderless horse and four carrying grim, grisly burdens as he rode after Frank and Buckston.

"For what it's worth," the foreman of the Lazy F said, "I sort of believe you, Morgan. I've heard a lot of things about you, but never that you went in for bushwhackin' or petty thievery."

"It happened the way I told it," Frank said.

"If that's true, then Houlihan and Crenshaw were in the wrong when they drew down on you. Not to mention damned foolish."

"Yes, but will your boss agree with that?"

Buckston shrugged. "Around here, men ride for the brand, right or wrong. We'll see, I reckon."

Buckston rode with his Winchester across the saddle in front of him, but despite that it would have been child's play for Frank to shoot him and Glover. He could have killed both of them before they knew what was happening. But he didn't want to live down to the opinion they had of him, and he wanted to be able to live with himself. That meant he kept riding.

"Tell me about the trouble in these parts," he said, deciding to indulge his curiosity.

"Between Mr. Flynn and Ed Sandeen, you mean?"

"That's right."

Buckston wiped the back of a hand across his mouth. "Mr. Flynn come to Arizona Territory thirty years ago, durin' the War Between the States. He was one o' the first settlers under the Mogollon Rim. Had to fight Apaches for years, and when he wasn't fightin' Apaches, he was fightin' rustlers and badmen. His wife died of a fever, and he lost their two boys, too, one of 'em to an Apache arrow, the other to a stampede."

Life on the frontier was hard and dangerous, even in these days when some folks thought the West was starting to get civilized. Frank had heard plenty of stories like Howard Flynn's before.

"Flynn got any family left?"

"A niece," Buckston said. "An old maid from back East who come to live with him when her own folks passed on. Don't think she quite knew what she was gettin' into, though."

"What about Sandeen?"

Buckston grimaced. "He showed up 'bout five years ago and bought the Saber spread. It wasn't right next to the Lazy F. There was one little ranch between 'em. But the fella who owned it sold out to Sandeen a year later, and that made Sandeen and Mr. Flynn neighbors. Sandeen bought up some other little holdin's, until his spread was the biggest in these parts except for the Lazy F."

"So then he set his sights on Flynn's ranch," Frank guessed. It was an old story, repeated many times and in many places throughout the West. Man's greed knew no geographical limitations.

"Well . . . not exactly," Buckston said. "He set his sights on Miss Laura, more'n he did the ranch."

A frown creased Frank's forehead. "You're talking about Flynn's niece?" he said.

"Yeah."

"I thought you said she was an old maid."

"She is. Must be twenty-five years old, if she's a day. I ain't asked, o' course, since that wouldn't be the proper thing to do. You see, Miss Laura was a schoolteacher when she lived back East, and she knows a heap about art and opera and books 'n' such. I might've mentioned that Sandeen wants folks to think he's some sort o' respectable gentleman, and I reckon he figured it'd be a good thing if he got himself some culture. Miss Laura's the closest thing to it around these parts. And I don't mind admittin', she ain't hard on the eyes, neither, in spite o' being a mite past prime marryin' age."

Frank found his interest growing, almost in spite of himself. "So Sandeen set out to court Laura Flynn?"

"Yep. And at first, she was a mite tooken with him. He's the sort that ladies seem to find handsome, and when he works at it he can charm the stripe off a polecat's back. It was all an act, though, and after a while Miss Laura figured that out. She must've told Sandeen to go climb a stump. Whatever she said, he didn't take it too well. *That's* when he decided to move in on the Lazy F. Maybe he figures that if he takes over her uncle's ranch, Miss Laura won't have no choice but to knuckle under and marry up with him."

"How's he trying to go about it?"

"Well, we started out losin' some cows here and there to rustlers. We had dammed up one o' the creeks to make a little lake, and somebody blowed that dam to pieces with dynamite. The flood from that drowned some stock in the pastures downstream from the dam. More than once, somebody's shot at our hands while they were out ridin' the range." Buckston's voice became grimmer as he went on. "A couple o' the boys were killed, and several more were wounded. We've had other line shacks burned, too, but never when any of our hands were around. Until today."

"What's Sandeen got to say for himself?"

"He denies that he's got anything to do with it, o' course. Says *we're* the ones who're tryin' to start a range war. But it's all a pack o' lies. He's behind it, all right."

Frank frowned in thought again. More than once in his adventurous life, he had run into situations that weren't exactly what they appeared to be on first glance, where some cunning schemer was playing two sides against each other so that he could step in eventually and make a big cleanup. Although Buckston seemed completely convinced that Ed Sandeen was behind the trouble in the Mogollon Rim country, Frank wondered if the same thing could be happening here.

He might not be around here long enough to find out. He would talk to Howard Flynn, explain to the man that he'd had nothing to do with the burning of the line shack and the killing of the three cowboys and that he had been forced into the shootout with Houlihan and Crenshaw . . . and then he would be on his way. Maybe he would ride down to Phoenix. He could wire one of his banks for money from there, get himself a decent hotel room, and maybe spend a while playing poker and taking life easy . . . until he got fiddlefooted again and had to move on.

It was a good plan, but it depended on Howard Flynn being a reasonable man. That was a big question mark.

With Glover and the assortment of dead bodies bringing up the rear, Frank and Buckston rode for the next hour across some of the best range Frank had seen in quite a while. He could understand why men might go to war over country like this. Wooded hills and lush pastures were well watered by several creeks that flowed fast and cold and clear, fed by springs in the mountains to the north. Arizona had its burning deserts to the south and its red-rock wastelands north of the Grand Canyon of the Colorado, but this fertile strip that slanted across the territory from northwest to southeast was prime country indeed.

They came to a valley nestled between two ranges of low hills, with a creek running through the middle of it, and the thin curl of smoke that rose into the blue sky told Frank they were nearing the headquarters of the Lazy F. That smoke had to be coming from a chimney. Sure enough, a few minutes later they came in sight of a big house sprawled on a bench just above the creek. The two-story center section of the house was built of stone, but several wings constructed of logs had been added. Quite a few outbuildings were scattered around the place—a long structure that was probably the bunkhouse, a cookshack and smokehouse and blacksmith shop, several barns, and plenty of corrals. The Lazy F was an impressive place. Howard Flynn certainly hadn't been lazy during the years when he had built this spread into one of the finest in the territory.

Several dogs ran out to greet the riders, barking exuberantly. Trotting along next to Frank, Dog growled in response to the display. "I expect you to behave yourself," Frank told him sternly. "No fighting with these ranch dogs."

"That critter looks like he's part wolf," Buckston commented.

"Might be. He won't cause any trouble, though."

"Unless you tell him to."

Frank chuckled. "A good dog stops more trouble than he starts, just by being around."

"What's his name?"

"Dog."

It was Buckston's turn to laugh a little. "And I reckon that Palouse you're ridin' is called Horse?"

"Nope," Frank answered solemnly. "His name is Stormy. I used to have a horse named Horse, though."

Buckston just shook his head.

The commotion created by the dogs had alerted people on the ranch that someone was coming. A long porch ran across the front of the main house. A white-haired man stepped out onto it and gazed toward them. His pose was casual at first, with his hands tucked into the back pockets of his jeans. But then, as he saw what the horses Glover was leading were carrying, he straightened and took his hands out of his pockets. Frank saw him turn his head sharply and say something to someone still in the house. A second later another man emerged from the house and hurried toward the bunkhouse, the long dark braid of hair hanging down his back flapping as he ran.

"That the cook?" Frank asked.

"Yeah. The boys call him Acey-Deucy, because that's what he likes to play all the time."

"And the white-haired hombre is Howard Flynn." Frank wasn't asking a question this time. The man on the porch stood there with an unmistakable air of command about him.

"That's right," Buckston said. "And here come some o' the boys from the bunkhouse, so don't get any funny ideas, Morgan."

"I don't intend to," Frank said. "Believe it or not, Buckston, I'm sorry about the way things turned out. I just want to clear this up and ride on."

Buckston just grunted, as if to say, *We'll see.*

At this time of day, most members of the ranch's crew would be out on the range, but there were usually a few cowboys around headquarters all the time, for one reason or another. Four men came out of the bunkhouse and strode quickly toward the main house, followed by the Chinese cook. By the time Frank and Buckston got there, the four punchers had formed a line in front of the porch and stood there with their hands resting on the guns they carried.

"What the devil is this, Buck?" Howard Flynn asked in a loud voice as Buckston and Frank reined to a stop. "Who's that with you, and why are those boys facedown on their saddles?"

"They're dead, Mr. Flynn," Buckston answered. "Blake, Bragan, Houlihan, and Crenshaw. Wardell's dead, too, but he's out at what's left of the east line shack. It's been burned."

"Son of a bitch!" Flynn exploded. He was about sixty years old but still hale and hearty despite his age. Deep lines seamed his weathered face, but his blue eyes sparkled with vitality. He looked like he could ride the range from dawn to dusk, work from can to can't, and be the last to quit a chore and the first to buy the beer. A damned fine hombre, in other words. Frank liked him right away, instinctively.

Flynn went on. "You still ain't told me who this hombre is."

"He says he's Frank Morgan, Boss."

Flynn's bushy white eyebrows went up in surprise. "Morgan! The gunfighter?"

"One and the same."

Flynn switched his gaze to Frank. "Damn it, did that blasted Sandeen hire you, Morgan? I wouldn't put it past that skunk to bring in a hired killer!"

Frank's lips thinned. "I never heard of Sandeen before today, Flynn, and I'm sure as hell not working for him. I don't know anything about this range war between the two of you except what your foreman here has told me."

Flynn leveled a finger at the bodies as Glover rode up leading the horses. "You didn't have anything to do with those boys bein' dead?"

Buckston opened his mouth, but before he could say anything, Frank said, "I killed two of them. Crenshaw and Houlihan."

Flynn's already florid face turned an even darker shade of red. "And you've got the gall to sit there and brag about it?" he roared. "Grab him, boys! We're gonna string us up a gunslinger!"

Chapter Four

Frank's hand flashed to his Colt, the movement too fast for the eye to follow. One second he was sitting there casually in the saddle, his hands empty. Less than a heartbeat later, he had his six-gun leveled at Flynn, and his finger was taut on the trigger.

"Back off, Flynn," he said stonily. "I don't intend to let anybody lynch me, especially not some hotheaded cattle baron who acts before he thinks."

The Lazy F punchers in front of the porch hesitated, not sure what they should do next. They were all armed, but their guns were still in their holsters. None of them could hope to draw before Frank could put three or four rounds right through their boss. So for now they just stood there tensely and didn't do anything.

"You come on my ranch and dare to point a gun at me?" Flynn said as he glared indignantly at Frank. "You might as well go ahead and shoot me now, Morgan, because if you don't, sooner or later I'll kill you!"

From beside Frank, Buckston said, "Morgan, you gotta know that if you pull that trigger, you're a dead man. I figure you pack five rounds in that smokepole, with one chamber left empty for the hammer to sit on. There's six of us. You can't get us all."

Frank allowed himself a thin smile. "Not unless I get two of you with one bullet. Might be an interesting challenge."

"The gall of the man!" Flynn exploded. "I've never seen the like."

The tense tableau held for another couple of seconds, and then it was disturbed abruptly by the opening of the door behind Flynn. A woman stepped onto the porch and asked, "Uncle Howard, what's going on here? I heard angry voices."

Frank couldn't study her closely because he still had his gaze fixed on Howard Flynn, but he saw enough in a glance to realize that the woman was blond and quite attractive. Buckston had said that she wasn't hard on the eyes, but Frank thought that was an understatement. Laura Flynn—and that was obviously who she was, based on her calling Flynn "Uncle Howard"—had a great deal of fresh, wholesome beauty about her.

"Laura, get back in the house!" Flynn snapped. "It ain't safe for you to be out here."

Laura noticed now that Frank was pointing a gun at her uncle. Her blue eyes widened with fear and surprise. "Good Lord!" she exclaimed. "Is that man going to shoot you?"

"Not if he knows what's good for him," Flynn growled.

"I don't plan on shooting anybody unless I have to, miss," Frank said to her, still without taking his eyes off Flynn. "But your uncle here threatened to have me lynched, and I don't plan on sitting still for that."

"Lynched! Is he telling the truth about that, Uncle Howard?"

"He killed two of our hands," Flynn said as if that simple answer explained everything. "And he's a gun-fighter, a notorious killer. What he did was the same as murder."

Buckston rubbed his jaw and said, "Don't know if I'd go so far as to say that, Boss. Houlihan fired the first shot, and Crenshaw got a round off, too, before Morgan plugged him."

"Mr. Houlihan and Mr. Crenshaw are dead?" Laura asked in a hollow voice. "That . . . that can't be."

"And Bragan and Wardell and the Blake kid, too," Flynn told her. "Morgan's bound to be workin' for Sandeen, so he probably had somethin' to do with killin' them, too."

Frank felt a surge of anger and frustration. "Is there something in the water in this country that makes everybody deaf as a post? How many times do I have to say that I didn't have anything to do with burning that line shack and killing those three punchers?"

"You admitted gunnin' Houlihan and Crenshaw," Flynn said.

"Because they drew on me first."

Buckston put in, "That's sure enough true, Boss. I told those boys to settle down, but they wouldn't do it. Told 'em if they were bound an' determined to brace Morgan, they ought to come back here and draw their time first, just so we wouldn't have a problem like this."

"My men ride for the brand," Flynn said harshly, "and I back them all the way."

"That's an admirable quality," Frank said. "Why don't you try using some common sense with it?"

Glover had pulled his mount and the other horses to a stop about forty feet behind Frank and Buckston. Now he swung down from his saddle and said wearily, "Somebody come get these horses and help me with the bodies. Things happened out there the way Morgan and Buck say they did, so I don't see that there's any call to string up Mr. Morgan."

"Now it's *Mr.* Morgan, is it?" Flynn asked. "Since when did you start givin' the orders around here, Glover?"

"I just don't like lynch talk," the cowboy said. "It don't seem right."

One of the other cowboys laughed. "What do you expect a darky to say, Boss?"

Glover stiffened, and his big, work-roughened hands twitched like they wanted to close into fists. Instead of throwing a punch, though, he said, "Black or white, it don't matter. I'm just talkin' fair, that's all. Morgan didn't do nothin' 'cept defend hisself."

Laura said, "I don't like the idea of a man being lynched, either, Uncle Howard. If something like that is necessary, the law will do it."

The old rancher sighed in frustration. "The law!" he said. "When I come out here, girl, the only law was right here." He slapped the butt of his pistol. "It got enforced, too, until this country settled down some. And sometimes it's still needed."

"But not today," Morgan said. He lowered the heavy Colt and slid it back into leather. "I'm tired of this, Flynn. You're not going to lynch me or tell your men to shoot me, or you'd have already done it before now. I've told you what happened. I'm riding away now. I'm out of this."

"Wait a minute!" Flynn said quickly. "You say Sandeen burned the line shack?"

"His men, anyway. That's what Rufe Blake told me before he died. I don't know if Sandeen was there personal-like."

"Poor Rufe," Laura murmured.

"Sandeen probably wasn't there," Flynn said. "These days he likes to pay other men to do his dirty work. Men like you, Morgan."

"I don't have any interest in working for Sandeen." Frank lifted his reins. "Fact is, I'm just passing through this part of the country. Thought I'd ride on down to Phoenix."

"You do that," Flynn said sullenly. "Best you keep movin', because I ain't gonna forget that you pointed a gun at me. Next time I see you, I'm liable to kill you."

Not likely, Frank thought, but he didn't say it. Flynn had settled down a little, and there was no point in goading him into a rage again.

Frank turned Stormy and said, "Come on, Dog." As he rode away with the big cur trotting alongside him, the skin in the middle of his back crawled a little, as if a bull's-eye had been painted on it. He didn't think a man like Flynn would stoop to shooting somebody in the back, but he knew he was betting his life on that hunch.

A sudden rattle of hoofbeats made him glance over his shoulder. Buckston was riding after him. Frank reined in for a moment and let the foreman catch up to him.

"I told the boss I'd see to it that you got off of Lazy F range," Buckston said.

"But what you're really doing is making sure that nobody tries to drygulch me, right?"

Buckston shrugged. "Nobody who rides for the Lazy F would do a low-down thing like that, least of all the boss."

"Well, I'm glad for the company, anyway."

The two men rode on in silence for several minutes. When the ranch house was a good half mile behind them, Buckston asked, "Did you mean that about ridin' down to Phoenix?"

"I did," Frank said. "If there's a settlement somewhere around here, though, I wouldn't mind stopping there for a night or two. I'd like to replenish my supplies and maybe give my horse a little rest." With a smile, Frank patted Stormy's shoulder affectionately. "He's like the rest of us . . . not as young as he used to be."

"He looks like he's still got plenty of sand," Buckston commented. "So do you, Morgan. A word of advice . . . the boss meant what he said. If he ever runs into you again, he's liable to slap leather."

"I hope it doesn't come to that."

"I do, too, because you'd kill him, and then you'd have every waddy who ever rode for him on your trail, tryin' to even the score. There ain't a finer man in Arizona Territory than Howard Flynn."

"I can believe that," Frank said. "I liked him as soon as I saw him."

Buckston looked over at him, eyes narrowing in disbelief. "Is that so?"

"Of course. Oh, he had his back up because five of his men were dead. I'd think less of him if he *hadn't* been mad enough to chew nails and spit out thumbtacks. He just directed some of his anger toward the wrong man."

"Meanin' you."

"I'm sorry about Crenshaw and Houlihan. But they didn't leave me much choice."

"No, I don't reckon they did," Buckston said as he jogged his horse along next to Stormy. "But I ain't over-fond of you my own self. Those boys were too proddy, but they were still Lazy F."

"I know what you mean," Frank said quietly. "Is that your way of saying the same thing Flynn did? That you'll try to kill me if you ever see me again?"

"If it's on Lazy F range . . . I'd have to think long and hard on it."

"Fair enough." Frank couldn't ask a man not to feel loyalty toward his friends. "What about that settlement? Is there one around here?"

Buckston nodded. "Yeah, a little place called San Remo. It don't amount to much, but you can buy some supplies and get a drink and a night's sleep there, if you're of a mind to. It's just the other side of the Verde River, maybe five miles from here. If you need to go someplace bigger, you could ride up to Prescott. It ain't too far. But that'll take you in the wrong direction to go to Phoenix."

"San Remo will probably do."

Buckston pulled back on his reins. Frank did likewise. "I reckon this is far enough for me to go, then," the Lazy F foreman said. "You just keep to this trail we been fol-

lowin', and it'll take you to San Remo. You ought to be
there by nightfall."

"Are we off Flynn's range now?"

"No, but close enough." Buckston lifted a hand.
"*Hasta la vista,* Morgan. I hope our trails don't never
cross again."

"*Vaya con Dios,*" Frank said in return. He hipped
around in the saddle enough to watch Buckston ride
back toward the ranch headquarters.

The thought crossed his mind briefly that Buckston
could have ridden along with him solely to keep him occupied so that he wouldn't notice more of Flynn's men
getting ready to ambush him. Frank discarded the idea.
He hadn't lived as long as he had without becoming a
good judge of character, and he knew that while Buckston could be a rough, dangerous man when he wanted
to, the foreman was also fundamentally honest. Otherwise, Flynn wouldn't have trusted him to ramrod the
crew of the Lazy F.

Frank watched until Buckston had vanished around a
bend in the trail. Then he lifted Stormy's reins and said,
"Let's ramble on, hoss."

As Buckston had predicted, Frank reached the little settlement of San Remo before night fell, but it was late in
the afternoon before he got there. Calling the place a
town would have been generous. A wooden bridge
crossed the fast-flowing Verde River, and beyond it San
Remo consisted of one block of business buildings and a
dozen or so cabins. There were a couple of stores, a blacksmith shop, a saddlemaker's, a café, a Baptist church at
one end of town and a Catholic mission at the other, and,
not surprisingly since it was located in the middle of a
ranching region, four saloons where the cowboys from
the surrounding spreads could come to blow off steam.

Although Frank liked a cold beer from time to time and
could appreciate a shot of fine whiskey, he wasn't really interested in the saloons at the moment. The café was more

what he was looking for. A home-cooked meal and a cup of hot, strong coffee sounded mighty fine right about now. There was no hotel as far as he could see, but he had spotted a corral and a livery barn behind the blacksmith shop. If push came to shove, he could sleep in the hayloft of that barn and be reasonably comfortable.

With those thoughts in his mind, he wasn't paying much attention to the Verde Saloon as he rode past it. The sudden blast of shots intruded on his musing, and as he twisted in the saddle, he saw a man burst through the batwings at the saloon's entrance, guns blazing.

Chapter Five

Frank's hand had started toward the Peacemaker on his hip before he realized that the man on the board-walk in front of the saloon wasn't shooting at him. Instead, the man had writhed around so that he was blasting back through the flapping doors into the saloon. Both hands were filled, and smoke from the flame-spouting irons wreathed the figure on the walk.

The fusillade lasted only a couple of seconds. Then inside the saloon a shotgun roared. Its double charge of buckshot slammed into the gunman on the walk, shredding his midsection into a bloody horror and throwing him backward almost a dozen feet to land on his back in the dust of the street. That put him almost under the Appaloosa's hooves. Stormy shied away from the gory spectacle. Frank tightened the reins to bring the horse under control. He said, "No, Dog," as the big cur stepped closer to the wounded man and sniffed delicately at him.

With a jingle of spurs, a man pushed the batwings aside and stepped out onto the walk. He held in his hands the Greener that had just been fired. The weapon was broken open now so that he could slide fresh shells into the barrels. He snapped the shotgun closed and looked up at Frank, managing to seem both alert and bored at the same time. He was lean and dark and well dressed, wearing a black, flat-crowned hat over a white shirt, black vest, and gray whipcord trousers stuffed into high-topped black boots. A black string tie was around his neck.

"You see something interesting, friend?" he asked mildly.

"Well, it's not every day you see a man blown nearly in two with a Greener," Frank said. "You going to check and make sure he's dead?"

"Oh, he's dead, all right. His guts are laying all over the street."

That was pretty much true. No one could survive a wound like that.

"You know, I was almost in the line of fire. If that buckshot had spread out a little more, some of it might have hit me or my horse or my dog."

"That would've been too bad. I might've been a little more careful about where I was shooting if that bastard hadn't been trying to kill me at the time."

"I know the feeling," Frank said. He hitched Stormy into a walk again, heading once more for the café. He had seen sudden death plenty of times in his life; once more wasn't going to bother him. But even he had to admit that the way in which the two-gun pistolero had died was pretty shocking.

"Come back down to the saloon later, I'll buy you a drink," the shotgunner called after him. Frank just waved a hand in acknowledgment of the offer without looking back.

By the time he swerved the Appaloosa to the hitch rack in front of the café, a small crowd was beginning to gather around the dead man. The shotgunner had gone back into the Verde Saloon. A man with a hand-drawn cart trundled it from the direction of the black-smith shop toward the sprawled corpse. Probably the blacksmith also served as San Remo's undertaker, as well as running the smithy and the livery stable.

Frank dismounted and looped Stormy's reins around the hitch rail. Normally he would've seen to the horse's needs before his own, but if his guess about the black-smith was correct, the man would be busy for a while with the dead man. Frank hadn't pushed Stormy hard during the ride from New Mexico Territory. It wouldn't hurt the Appaloosa to wait a while to be unsaddled, rubbed down, and grained.

A man sat on the front porch of the café, puffing on a pipe. As Frank stepped up onto the porch, followed by Dog, the man said, "Howdy, mister. That your dog?"

"He's his own dog," Frank said, glancing at the big cur, "but we travel together most of the time."

The man took the pipe out of his mouth and slapped his knee in amusement. He was probably sixty years old, with a short, grizzled beard and gray hair under a bowler hat. One eye was a little off-kilter. He wore a brown tweed suit that had seen better days.

"I like that answer, mister," he said. "You sound like a man who knows dogs."

"This one, anyway." Frank added, "Dog, sit. Wait out here for me."

The man pointed the stem of his pipe at Dog as Dog sat down. "He does what you tell him?"

"Most of the time. Unless it disagrees too much with his idea of what ought to be done."

The man lumbered to his feet and stuck out his hand. "Willard Donohue," he introduced himself. "Local char-acter and hanger-on."

Frank chuckled at the man's dry humor. He shook hands with Donohue and introduced himself. "Frank Morgan. Just passing through."

Donohue put his pipe back in his mouth, clamped his teeth on the stem, and said around it, "Morgan? The shootist from over Texas way?"

"Not that many people remember that I come from Texas."

"Oh, I've read every yellowback ever written about you, Mr. Morgan. Man cultivates a life o' leisure like I do, he has time to read and learn a lot." Donohue removed the pipe and used it to point with again. "Take that little incident down the street as you were ridin' into town. I know who those fellas are and why they were doin' their damnedest to kill each other. It's an interestin' story."

Frank realized that the man was hinting. He said, "Why don't you come inside and tell me about it? Since it's nigh on to supper time, I'd be happy to buy you a meal."

"Well, that's mighty nice of you, Mr. Morgan. That's another thing I know about you . . . you've got a generous nature."

Frank slapped him on the back, grinned, and said, "Come on, old-timer. I've got a feeling there's a steak in here with your name on it."

Donohue licked his lips and smiled.

As soon as Frank opened the door of the café, a blend of delicious aromas drifted out. Often the food in these cow-town hash houses was terrible, but every so often a fella found one with an exceptional cook. Clearly, the owner of this place took pride in more than its food, too, because the floor was swept clean, the tables were neatly covered with red-checked tablecloths, and several lamps were already lit, casting a warm glow over the room.

A counter with several pies on it sat to the right. Willard Donohue glanced at them and licked his lips again. He flinched, though, as the middle-aged black woman behind the counter said sharply, "Mr. Donohue, what you doin' in here? I told you, I ain't feedin' you on the cuff no more. You got to pay what you owe before you get another bite!"

"Now, now, Mary Elizabeth, don't get in such an

uproar," Donohue said. "This kind gentleman here has offered to stand me to a meal."

The woman frowned at Frank. "You let this ol' rapscallion hornswoggle you into buyin' his supper? No offense, mister, but you look smarter'n that."

"Mr. Donohue's going to sing for his supper," Frank explained. "Or at least tell me a story."

"About the shootin' down at the Verde," Donohue supplied.

The woman snorted. She wore a crisp blue calico dress with a white apron over it. "I heard the shots, but I don't want to know nothin' about it. You two sit down. Steak or pot roast?"

"Steak," Frank said, and Donohue nodded in agreement.

"Two steaks with all the trimmin's, comin' up." The woman went through a door behind the counter, into a kitchen.

Frank and Donohue were the only customers at the moment, so they had their choice of where to sit. Without really thinking about what he was doing, Frank took a table in the corner and sat down so that his back was to the wall. He wasn't as fanatical about sitting that way as Wild Bill Hickok had been, but it was an old, cautious habit Frank had no interest in breaking. He had been in Deadwood, up in Dakota Territory, nearly twenty years earlier when the legendary pistoleer Hickok had broken his custom and wound up being shot in the back of the head by Jack McCall. That was all the lesson needed by the observant young man Frank had been at the time.

"Miss Mary Elizabeth Warren is the salt of the earth," Donohue said. "And probably the best cook between El Paso and San Francisco. You don't know how lucky you are to have stopped here, Mr. Morgan, but you'll soon find out. That is, if you don't mind eatin' a colored woman's cookin'."

"It's pretty hard to tell the color of the cook by the taste of the food," Frank said.

"Very true. You'll think Mary Elizabeth's food was cooked by angels. Caleb Glover is a damned lucky man. He keeps company with Mary Elizabeth. Probably marry her one of these days and take her off to some ranch, and that'll be a sad day for those of us here in San Remo who've come to depend on her."

"This fella Glover rides for Howard Flynn's Lazy F?"

Donohue grunted in surprise. "You know Howard?"

"We've met."

"Then you probably know about the trouble between him and Ed Sandeen."

Frank nodded slowly but didn't say anything about the violent incident at the Lazy F line shack. "I've heard some talk."

"Those two hombres who shot it out in the Verde . . . they both work for Sandeen. Moses *worked* for Sandeen, I should say, since from the looks of it the only wages he'll be drawin' from now on will be in Hell."

"Jack Moses?" Frank asked, his eyes narrowing. Something had struck him as familiar about the dead man's face, and now he recalled it. Jack Moses was a hired gun he had last seen up in Idaho, a good ten years earlier. Frank hadn't known that Moses was even still alive.

"Yeah, that's right. Man with the shotgun is Vern Riley. I expect you've heard of him, too."

Frank nodded. Riley was reputed to be middling fast with a six-gun, but the Greener was his weapon of choice. Frank should have realized who he was.

"If they were both working for Sandeen, why did they start shooting at each other?"

"The way I heard it, they had an old grudge against each other. Riley was here first, rode into these parts several weeks ago and signed on with Sandeen's Saber spread. Sandeen's been hirin' men who are good with their guns."

"So I've heard," Frank said grimly.

"Well, Jack Moses showed up a few days ago and hired on, too. I guess him and Riley tried to put their hard feelin's aside while they were both drawin' wages from Sandeen, but I reckon it didn't last. One of 'em probably said something that the other one didn't like, and before you know it all hell broke loose. They forgot that they were supposed to be on the same side. Don't know how Sandeen's gonna feel about that. He lost a good man in Moses. Or a bad man, might be a better way of puttin' it." Donohue looked intently at Frank. "I don't reckon a fella like you would have any trouble signin' on to replace him, Mr. Morgan . . . if you're lookin' for a job, that is. For all I know, Howard Flynn's already hired you. Howard's gonna have to start fightin' fire with fire, if you know what I mean."

"I'm not working for anybody," Frank said. "Just riding through on my way to Phoenix."

"Uh-huh," Donohue said, but he didn't sound like he believed it. "We got us a hellacious range war about to break out in these parts, and The Drifter just happens to show up."

"Believe what you want," Frank told him, "but it's the truth."

"Maybe so . . . but how long do you think a man like you will be able to stay out of it once the bullets really start to flyin'?"

Frank was saved from having to answer that question by the arrival of Mary Elizabeth Warren with their suppers. She expertly balanced two big platters of food, each with a large steak, a mound of hash-browned potatoes, and two fat, fluffy biscuits on it.

"I got a bowl of greens and some gravy for soppin' them biscuits," she said. "I'll bring 'em right over. Coffee for the both of you?"

"Yes, ma'am," Frank said.

"Ain't you the polite one, now. Dig in, gentlemen."

She delivered the greens and gravy to the table, as promised, along with a pot of strong black coffee and a couple of cups. Frank hadn't realized how hungry he was until he started eating and discovered that the food tasted as good as it smelled. The coffee was just the way he liked it, too, with a faint hint of peppermint to it from the stick of candy that had been dropped in the pot for sweetening. He knew when he tasted it that Mary Elizabeth had had experience making coffee for cowboys. She sure knew her way around a pot of Arbuckle's.

Now that the hour was a little later, more customers began to come into the café. By the time Frank and Donohue were finished with their meal, most of the tables in the place were occupied. Donohue saw Frank looking around and said, "Mary Elizabeth does a good business, sure enough. I figure either Howard Flynn or Ed Sandeen would hire her to cook for them in a minute. Howard's got a leg up, though, since Caleb Glover rides for the Lazy F. I'm hopin' that once him and Mary Elizabeth marry up, he'll let her keep the café open, but I reckon it ain't likely."

"Are folks around here worried about the problems between Flynn and Sandeen?" Frank asked, deciding to indulge his curiosity since Willard Donohue was obviously the sort of fella who liked to talk.

"Wouldn't you be? They both like to ride high on the hog, so I reckon it was inevitable that there'd be trouble betwixt 'em. When a couple of big skookum hewolves like that start after each other, innocent folks almost always get caught in the middle."

"Has anybody given any thought to bringing the law in?"

"What law? The Saber and Lazy F spreads are so big they lay in several different counties. Do we send for help to Sheriff Buckey O'Neill in Yavapai County or Sheriff Glenn Reynolds in Gila County? The sheriff in Maricopa County might want to get in on it, too. Problem is, they're all just as likely to say that it's the other fella's worry, not theirs, as they are to help out."

Frank knew what the old-timer meant. Boundary lines were sometimes tenuous things, and jurisdictional disputes were difficult to settle. By the time the various authorities involved got everything squared away among themselves, it might be too late for them to do any good.

"How long do you think it'll be before the whole thing boils over?"

"Probably not very long now," Donohue said. "Sandeen must have forty guns workin' for him. If he ain't ready to make a move, I don't reckon he ever will be."

Frank nodded slowly. Donohue's assessment agreed with his own. It might not bode well for San Remo and the surrounding part of the territory, but in all likelihood the burning of the line shack and the killings of Rufe Blake, Bragan, and Wardell were the opening salvo in what would soon be a bloody, full-scale war.

Chapter Six

Frank and Donohue finished off the fine supper with apple pie for dessert, washed down by a final cup of coffee. After living off his own trail cooking for a while, Frank thoroughly enjoyed the meal. Donohue seemed to as well, and he said, "I surely am obliged for your generosity, Mr. Morgan."

"Call me Frank. I enjoyed your company, and I have a clearer picture now of what's going on around here."

"It ain't a *pretty* picture, though, is it?"

Frank shrugged. "No, but luckily, it's none of my business."

"It could be," Donohue said with a shrewd gleam in his eyes.

Frank told himself not to ask the question, but he did it anyway. "What do you mean by that?"

"It just so happens that I'm the mayor of San Remo."

Frank's eyebrows rose in surprise.

Donohue chuckled. "Yeah, it's a hell of a note, ain't it, when a layabout like me gets put in charge of anything. I guess folks decided I had the time to devote to takin' care of the town, since I don't do much of anything else." He waved a pudgy hand. "But that ain't neither here nor there. As I was sayin', I'm the mayor o' this here burg, and as such, I'm offerin' you the job of town marshal of San Remo, Frank. The whole country may go to hell around us, but I got a hunch you could keep order here and keep the town from gettin' caught in the cross fire."

A frown creased Frank's forehead. "I don't normally wear a badge."

"You have before, though, so it ain't like I'm askin' you to do something you've never done."

"I'm on my way to Phoenix," Frank said stubbornly. "I've been mixed up in enough shooting scrapes in my life."

"I can see why you feel that way, but the plain fact o' the matter is, we need you here, Frank."

Donohue made a good case, but Frank shook his head. "Sorry. If I was you, I'd write to the sheriffs of all three counties involved and ask them to send in some deputies. Surely you'll get some help that way."

Donohue sighed. "Well, maybe. Don't know if it'll be in time, though."

"Maybe it will be," Frank said, but he knew from the feeling of tension in the air that gripped the whole Verde River basin that serious trouble might erupt at any second. It might have already started, for all he knew.

"You sure? The pay wouldn't be much, but I can maybe talk Mary Elizabeth into feedin' you for free. . . ."

"Sorry," Frank said again.

Donohue grunted and scraped his chair back. "Well, I tried. I'm obliged to you for listenin' to me, at least, Frank."

"Why don't you meet me here in the morning?" Frank suggested as Donohue got to his feet. "We'll have breakfast together before I ride out."

"Sounds like a mighty fine idea. I'll see you then."

Donohue nodded and walked out of the café, waving farewell to Mary Elizabeth as he left. She was hurrying from table to table, serving meals, but she paused long enough to call after him with genuine affection, "You take care o' yourself, you ol' scoundrel."

The prices for meals were chalked on the board behind the counter. Frank dug out enough coins to pay for his and Donohue's supper and stacked them on the table, then drained the last of the coffee in his cup and reached for his hat. Mary Elizabeth paused as she was going past the table and asked if she could get him anything else.

Frank shook his head. "No, that was mighty fine. Maybe you can tell me, though. . . . Is that livery barn behind the blacksmith shop the only one in town?"

"Yes, sir. Fella who runs it is named Jasper Culverhouse."

Frank stood up and settled his hat on his head. "Thanks." He smiled at the woman and headed for the door, aware that some of the men in the room were watching him, as they had been while he and Donohue were eating. He was a stranger in town, which made people take interest in him, and some of them might have recognized him, which would make them pay even more attention. He pretended not to notice the eyes following him.

Dog waited patiently on the porch. Frank signaled for him to follow, then untied the reins and led Stormy down the street toward the blacksmith shop. Jasper Culverhouse proved to be the man Frank had seen earlier, trundling his cart toward the scene of the shooting. Now he had the gory remains of Jack Moses stretched out on a table behind the blacksmith shop and was already knocking together a crude pine coffin by the light of a lantern. Culverhouse was short and mostly bald, with the thick-muscled frame of a man who worked with hammer and anvil all the time. As Frank led the Appaloosa around the corner of the building into the rear yard, Culverhouse looked up from his work and gave him a friendly nod.

"Something I can do for you, mister?"

"I need to put my horse up for the night," Frank said.

"Sure thing. Got half-a-dozen empty stalls in the barn right now. Just pick the one you want. Grain's in the bin. I'd take care of it myself, but I've got a chore that's a little more pressing right now." Culverhouse inclined his head toward the corpse. "Since you'll be doin' all the work, how about I just charge you two bits for the night?"

"Sounds fair," Frank agreed. "I need a place to leave the dog, and some food for him, too."

"Sure, I can take care of him. Does he bite?"

"Not if I tell him not to."

"No charge for that, then. I'm a man who likes a good dog, and he looks like a fine one. Maybe not quite tamed . . . sort of like his master."

Frank ignored that comment, figuring that the black-smith had recognized him as the notorious Drifter. "Is there a place to stay in this settlement?"

"A couple of the saloons rent out rooms, especially if you want a gal to go with it." Culverhouse waved a thick hand with short, stubby fingers at the barn. "Or you can sleep in the hayloft, which prob'ly has less bugs in it than the beds in them saloons. That'll be another four bits, though."

"Again, fair enough." Frank had no desire to spend the night in a saloon that probably stank of tobacco smoke, unwashed flesh, stale beer, and urine. Right now he wasn't interested in bedding down with a soiled dove, either. He took six bits out of his pocket and handed the coins to Culverhouse, who dropped them in one of the pockets on his blacksmith's apron. Frank nodded toward the corpse and added, "I hear that's Jack Moses, the gunfighter."

"Yeah. I'll clean him up a mite, drape a sheet over his middle where that buckshot tore him up so bad, and prop him up on a board in front of the place in the morning. Folks like to take a look at somebody even a little bit famous, especially if he's gotten himself killed. Burial won't be until the middle of the day tomorrow, so everybody ought to have time to come by and take a gander at him."

Frank nodded. Such displays were a grisly but common custom on the frontier. He sometimes wondered if he would wind up that way himself, propped up on a board so that people could stand around and gawk at his corpse. The undertaker would probably charge admission for folks to look at him. He had even heard a story about how the corpse of some famous gunman had been stuffed, so that the fella who had it could drive around with the body in his wagon and show it off while trying to sell patent medicines. That would be a hell of a way to end up, as a drawing card for some snake-oil peddler.

Frank shoved that thought out of his mind. He wasn't dead yet, after all, so there wasn't any point in dwelling on what might happen. He just enjoyed each day that came to him as much as he could.

And to that end, once he had put Stormy in one of the stalls in the barn and tended to the Appaloosa's needs, he decided to stroll down to one of the saloons and have a short beer before he turned in. Vern Riley had promised to buy him a drink, Frank recalled.

He heard the raucous music coming from the Verde Saloon before he got there. It was a warm night, so the doors were open, with only the swinging batwings blocking the entrance. Frank pushed between them and walked into the saloon.

The polished hardwood bar ran down the right side of the big room and then turned to run across the back wall as well, underneath the second-floor balcony. Stairs at the end of the bar led up there. The left-hand wall had a player piano, a faro layout, and a roulette wheel spaced along it. The area in the middle of the room was occupied by tables, and most of those tables were occupied by men in range clothes. Frank had noticed that the hitch rails in front of the saloon were crowded with horses, so he wasn't surprised to see that the place was doing a booming business. He hadn't checked the brands on those horses, but he figured most of them carried the Saber brand. That would mean that most of the men playing poker and tossing back drinks and fondling the saloon girls who moved among them were Ed Sandeen's men.

The ones who had burned down that line shack and killed those three men might be in here right now, Frank thought.

But he had no way of knowing, and anyway, he reminded himself, it wasn't his fight.

He was heading for the bar when he heard his name called. When he turned to look, he saw Vern Riley sitting at a table toward the back of the room with two other men. One of them wore the rough clothing of a saddle tramp, but the other was well dressed, in a dark, sober suit that made him look almost like a preacher. No, Frank corrected himself, the hombre looked more like a schoolteacher than a minister. He had sleek dark hair and a narrow mustache.

Something told Frank that he was looking at Ed Sandeen.

Riley had his hand up to signal Frank over to the table. Frank angled in that direction, and as he reached the table, Riley stood up and said, "Have a seat and join us, Morgan. I'll buy you that drink I promised you earlier."

Frank rested his left hand on the back of the table's lone empty chair. "I don't recall introducing myself when we spoke earlier."

Riley grinned and said, "Hell, you think I don't recognize the notorious Frank Morgan? A few years back, I saw you clean out a saloon where some of Vanbergen's gang had holed up. I didn't take a hand, since it was none of my affair either way, but I haven't forgotten it, either."

Frank's mouth tightened. The time Riley spoke of had been a bleak, tragic one for him. He had been reunited with his first wife, only to lose her to an outlaw's bullet. He had learned that he had a son, only to have that son turn his back on him. Things hadn't gone much better since then, either. He had married a second time, only to have Dixie die violently, just as Vivian had. For a while, plagued by guilt and sorrow, he had climbed into a bottle, and it had taken the friendship of the Texas Ranger Tyler Beaumont, to drag him out again. Then a face from even farther out of his past, Mercy Monfore, had come into his life again, and Frank had been faced with the possibility that Mercy's daughter Victoria was his child, too. And Victoria, bless her heart, was now paralyzed from a stray bullet that had hit her during one of Frank's gunfights. Again and again, the unwanted reputation that followed him had caused pain and suffering not only for him but also for those around him, those he loved.

But in recent months he had started to feel that maybe he had turned a corner of sorts. He still seemed to wander into gun trouble pretty regularlike, but he had mended some fences with his son Conrad and had passed some pleasant time with a few pretty ladies, none of whom had gotten themselves killed. Frank hoped that his luck had changed.

So he didn't want to dwell on the past. He shrugged off Riley's comment and said simply, "That was a long time ago."

"Sit down, sit down. I'm Vern Riley."

"To tell the truth," Frank said as he pulled out the chair, "I recognized you, too, Riley."

The gunman patted the shotgun that lay on the table. "It's hard to miss this baby, and most people know it's what I prefer. I reckon it's almost like a calling card for me." Riley gestured toward the roughly dressed man. "This is Carl Lannigan."

Frank shook hands with the man, who had a rusty wedge of a beard on his blunt jaw, and said, "Lannigan."

"Morgan," the man returned, equally taciturn.

"And this is my boss," Riley went on.

"Edward Sandeen," the well-dressed man said before Riley could give his name. "It's a pleasure to meet you, Mr. Morgan. I've heard a great deal about you."

His hand was smooth, the fingers manicured. It had been a while since he had done any hard labor. But his grip was still quite strong. Frank nodded to him, being polite but not overly friendly.

A bottle and three glasses sat on the table. Riley said, "I'll get another glass." He lifted a hand to catch the attention of one of the bartenders. Three men were working behind the hardwood tonight.

"That's all right, I'd just as soon have a beer," Frank said.

Riley glanced at him. "You're sure?"

"I'm sure."

Sandeen picked up the bottle and poured himself a drink. "It's a wise man who doesn't muddle his brain with whiskey." He tossed back the fiery liquor, in apparent contradiction of what he had just said. He chuckled and added, "Luckily, I wasn't wise to start with, so I have nothing to lose."

"I wouldn't say that, Boss," Riley put in. "You're just about the smartest man I know."

"If I was so smart," Sandeen said, his voice hardening, "I wouldn't have hired two men who hated each other's guts, now would I?"

Riley splashed whiskey in his glass. "Moses had it comin'," he said. "Carl can tell you. He was here and saw the whole thing."

Lannigan grunted. "That's right. Moses started it. He was to blame for what happened."

Frank had a feeling that if the gunfight had turned out the other way, Lannigan would be singing the praises of

Moses and blaming the whole thing on Riley. He knew how to take advantage of a situation, whatever it might be.

"Well, regardless of all that, I'm short-handed now," Sandeen said, and as he turned to look at Frank, Frank understood that the conversation probably had been worked out ahead of time, so that Sandeen would have a good excuse for offering Frank a job at fighting wages. Gunfighter's pay . . .

Before Sandeen could do that, an angry voice spoke up, interrupting him. It said, "Morgan? Morgan, it *is* you, damn your hide! I thought I recognized you. And now I'm gonna kill you, you son of a bitch!"

Chapter Seven

Frank didn't react suddenly. He just turned his head toward the sound of the angry voice and saw a man standing at the bottom of the stairs, gazing at him with murderous hatred in his eyes.

As far as Frank could remember, he had never seen the man before.

The shout had brought silence into the room as everyone turned to see what was going to happen next. Into that quiet, Frank said, "Take it easy, mister. I don't know you."

The man lifted his left hand and pointed a finger. It shook a little from the depth of the rage that gripped him. "Maybe not, but I know you! I been keepin' an eye out for you ever since you killed my old man five years ago in Wichita!"

"Damn it, Hanley," Sandeen put in, "can't you see I'm talking to Mr. Morgan?"

"Sorry, Boss," the man called Hanley said. "I got a score to settle with him that goes back 'way before I was ridin' for Saber."

Frank cast his mind back over the years, trying to remember shooting someone named Hanley in Wichita. The name didn't ring any bells. . . .

Then suddenly it did, and he said, "Was your father Lester Hanley?"

"You know damn well he was!"

"I didn't kill Lester Hanley," Frank said. "I put a bullet through his arm, all right, when he called me out and wouldn't let it go, but that didn't kill him. Later that night he got drunk, fell in a water trough, and drowned."

Several men laughed, but abruptly fell silent when the man at the foot of the stairs swung his furious gaze toward them. A girl in a short, spangled dress was on the first step, right behind him, and obviously they had just come down from one of the upstairs rooms. Hanley was a rawboned man with long, dirty-blond hair. The disreputable old hat he wore had the brim turned up in front. He wore a buffalo coat, too, even though it was a warm evening, and Frank could smell the thing from a dozen feet away.

"That's a damn lie!" Hanley said as he looked at Frank again. "I heard all about how you shot my pa in the back!"

"What you heard were lies," Frank said. "I'm willing to overlook what you just said, Hanley, if you'll just let it go."

"Let it go, hell! I'm gonna kill you, Morgan!"

Frank stood up smoothly, seeing that talk wasn't going to do any good. "You've got it to do, then," he said calmly. Panic never helped a man survive a gunfight.

He heard chairs scrape behind him and knew that Sandeen, Riley, and Lannigan were getting out of the line of fire. Likewise, the girl with Hanley turned and scurried back up the stairs, and men cleared out along the bar. The bartenders ducked under the level of the hardwood.

Hanley hesitated, and for a second Frank thought that he might change his mind about this. But then his face contorted in a snarl and his hand stabbed toward the butt of the gun on his hip. "You bastard!" he howled.

His hand had closed around the revolver's grips and

he had it halfway out of the holster before Frank's hand ever moved. Then, in an eyelash of time, the Colt Peacemaker was up and leveled. Flame geysered from the muzzle as it roared. Frank's first shot slammed into Hanley's chest and drove him back several steps. He staggered against the end of the bar. The impact turned him as well, so that the second bullet entered his right side, smashed a couple of ribs, and bored through his right lung before it struck the heart that had already been punctured by the first slug. Hanley's gun slipped from his fingers and thudded to the floor. He turned some more and faced the bar, leaning far forward over it. He braced his hands against it, trying to hold himself up. Blood drooled from his mouth and dripped on the polished hardwood. He lifted his head, groaned once, and then toppled over backward, dead when he hit the floor.

Grim-faced, Frank shook his head. He had fought too many of these battles. Wherever he went, there was always someone who wanted to even a score or make a name for himself by killing The Drifter. And so far, they were always the ones who died instead.

Frank was about to open the Colt's cylinder and replace the spent shells, when Vern Riley said, "I wouldn't do that, Morgan. Hanley had a brother."

A rush of heavy steps from the balcony made Frank glance up. He saw a burly, gun-toting man in long-handled underwear reach the railing and stare down in shocked horror at Hanley's body as it lay there on its back, the bloodstains slowly growing on the filthy shirt under the buffalo coat. The man on the balcony roared a curse. His eyes darted toward Frank, who still stood there with a smoking gun in his hand, and clearly he had no doubt who was responsible for his brother's death. He jerked the revolver in his hand toward Frank and fired.

The bullet whipped past Frank's ear and hit the table where he had been sitting with Sandeen, Riley, and Lannigan before the trouble broke out. Frank crouched slightly and returned the fire, triggering twice and hitting the man with both shots. Because of the angle, the bullets took him low in the belly and ranged upward through his body, wreaking havoc on his innards. Screaming in pain, he toppled forward against the flimsy railing and broke through it. The man turned a complete somersault in midair as he plummeted from the balcony to land with a crash next to the body of his brother. He twitched a couple of times and then lay still.

"Damn it," Sandeen said into the gun-smoke-scented hush, "that makes three men I've lost today, for no good reason."

"Sorry for the one I accounted for, Boss," Riley said. "Like I told you, though, Moses had it comin'. And I don't see what else Morgan could have done, other than stand there and let the Hanley brothers fill him full of lead."

Sandeen sighed. "I know. I couldn't ask any man to do that. Mr. Morgan, are you all right?"

Frank nodded curtly. "Are there any more of them?"

"No, that's all."

"Maybe I can reload this time, then."

He swung the Colt's loading gate open, punched out the empties, and refilled the chambers with cartridges from the loops on his gun belt. Then he holstered the Peacemaker and turned toward Sandeen. "I'm sorry, too," he said. "They wouldn't listen to reason."

"That sort never does. Even though they rode for me, I hold no grudge, Mr. Morgan."

"I appreciate that."

"However, now that I'm even *more* short-handed, maybe you'd care to entertain a proposition I have for you."

Frank faced Sandeen and shook his head. "You don't even have to make the offer," he said. "I'm not interested in working for you, Sandeen."

The cattleman's eyes narrowed and hardened, but he

maintained the affable expression on his face. "Why not?" he asked. "From everything I've heard about you, you've done the sort of work I have in mind before."

"Maybe you haven't heard the whole story."

Frank hadn't gotten that beer he was after, but he wasn't all that thirsty anymore. Nor did he care for the company. Even if he hadn't been predisposed to dislike Sandeen by the things he had been told about the man, the fact that Sandeen was gathering an army of gunmen and killers who were little better than outlaws was enough to make Frank want nothing to do with the man.

Sandeen wasn't ready to give up, though. He said, "Listen, Morgan, we've obviously gotten off on the wrong foot—"

"Two of your boys tryin' to kill him might've had something to do with that," Riley said, his voice dry with amusement.

Sandeen glared at him. "Stay out of this, Vern. This business is between Morgan and me."

"We don't have any business to talk about," Frank said. He started to turn away from the table. At that moment, Jasper Culverhouse came into the saloon, looked around, and then headed toward the bloody corpses lying on the floor in front of the bar.

"Busy night," he said to no one in particular.

Sandeen reached out and gripped Frank's arm, stopping him. Frank stiffened and looked down meaningfully at Sandeen's hand, but the rancher didn't remove it.

"At least have the courtesy to listen to what I have to say, Morgan," Sandeen grated. His pleasant façade was just about gone by now. "There's a problem I want handled—"

"Howard Flynn?" Frank cut in.

"The man has it in for me," Sandeen said. "He's spreading lies and vicious rumors about me. I suspect his men have rustled some of my stock. Flynn's trying to run me off my range, and I won't have it! He has to be made to stop."

"By killing him?" Frank asked coldly.

"By any means necessary," Sandeen replied, his voice equally icy.

Frank jerked his arm loose without any great difficulty, even though Sandeen's grip was still tight. "Don't ever lay hands on me again," he said in a low, dangerous voice. "And don't make the mistake of thinking that you can hire me to murder somebody. We're done here, Sandeen."

As Frank and Sandeen faced each other tensely, Riley poured a drink and said in a casual voice, "I've already told you I'll take care of that little problem for you, Boss."

"A job like that is more in Morgan's line," Sandeen snapped. "He's less likely to foul it up."

Riley's eyes turned into angry slits, but he didn't say anything, just tossed back the drink instead.

Frank turned toward the bar. Jasper Culverhouse was recruiting men to help him carry the bodies out to his cart. Frank didn't feel like volunteering. He had already done his part by killing the two vengeance-crazed gunnies.

"I don't like it when people tell me no, Morgan," Sandeen said behind him. "This isn't over yet."

"That's where you're wrong," Frank said without turning around. He stalked out of the saloon, every sense alert. If Sandeen or anyone else behind him tried to draw, he would hear them start to make their move.

No one tried to stop him, though, and once he was outside he paused and drew in a deep breath of air that was considerably cleaner than that inside the saloon. He never got the shakes or anything like that after a shooting, as some men did; he had been through too many of them to ever react that way again. But it still felt good to be out of that place, out where the air was a little fresher and a man could breathe a little deeper.

He was headed for the livery stable, intending to turn in, when a voice spoke from the shadows, saying, "Hello, Frank. I hear there was a shootin' inside the Verde. Couple of Sandeen's men got theirselves killed."

"Damn it, Donohue," Frank said, "don't sneak up on a man like that."

The old-timer chuckled. "Sorry. I just thought maybe you'd like to come down the street to the Mogollon with me and have a drink."

Frank's thirst reasserted itself. He had noticed the Mogollon Saloon earlier. It was a much smaller, quieter place than the Verde. When he looked at it now, he saw that there were only a couple of horses tied up at the hitch rack in front of it.

"Well, I didn't get the beer I went in there for. . . ."

"Come on, then," Willard Donohue said. "I think I can promise you there won't be no trouble."

Frank didn't see how the old-timer could guarantee that, but he was willing to chance it.

When they walked into the Mogollon Saloon, a chorus of voices greeted Donohue. Frank saw several men at the bar and a couple more at one of the tables. Donohue gestured toward that table and said, "Let's sit down here. I want you to meet these fellas."

Frank suddenly realized that he was being set up again. He decided to play along, though, to see exactly what Donohue had in mind. He thought he knew, but he wanted to be sure.

"This is Simon Wilson, who owns one o' the mercantiles," Donohue said as he and Frank took the two empty chairs at the table. "And Ben Desmond, who owns the other one."

"Business rivals, eh?" Frank said as he shook hands with both of the men.

"Yes, but tonight we're on the same side," Wilson said. He was a big man with a pugnacious jaw.

Desmond was smaller and more dapper. He said by

way of explanation, "Simon means we both want what's best for San Remo."

"That's right," Donohue said. "Those fellas at the bar feel the same way. That's Tom Williams, Jimmy McCain, and Alonzo Hightower." The men nodded to Frank as Donohue introduced them. "'Lonzo owns the Mogollon here, and Tom and Jimmy have the other saloons in town. Next to them is Vincente Delgado, the saddle maker, and Homer McCrory, pastor o' the Baptist church."

Frank's eyebrows rose. "You got a Baptist preacher to come into a saloon?" he said with a smile.

"The Lord associated with sinners for a good cause, Mr. Morgan," Homer McCrory said. "I can do no less."

"The other two are Roy Thurman and Jase Winslow. They own small spreads near here," Donohue went on.

Frank nodded. "Quite a gathering. Just why have all these solid citizens gotten together here tonight?"

Before Donohue could say anything else, the door of the saloon opened and Jasper Culverhouse hurried in. "I got those Hanley brothers laid out, but I got to get back to 'em pretty soon," he said. He looked at Frank and added, "You asked him yet?"

"Dadgummit, Jasper," Donohue groused, "you got all the tact of a locoed bull."

"I just don't have a lot of time to waste," Culverhouse said.

"Neither do I," Frank said. "Is this about that marshal's job again?"

"You don't know what it means to us, Mr. Morgan," Simon Wilson said. He waved a hand at the gathering. "The men in this room are all the business owners in San Remo except for Miss Warren, and she assured me personally that she supports our efforts. She just didn't feel comfortable coming into a saloon. She's a very religious woman."

"I can attest to that," Pastor McCrory put in.

"And Roy and I represent the other fellas who own small ranches around here," Jase Winslow said. "We need your help, Mr. Morgan, and we need it bad."

"*Si, señor,*" Vincente Delgado added. "All hell, she is about to break loose."

"You men want me to take that marshal's job and tamp down the feud between Howard Flynn and Ed Sandeen?" Frank asked. He knew that was what they were getting at, but he wanted someone to come out and say it.

Ben Desmond said, "Somebody's got to. Look around, Morgan. We're good men, but we're not gunfighters. Nobody's going to listen to us. We can't go up against Sandeen's army of hired guns. Howard Flynn's a good man, but he's blinded by hate and anger right now, and his crew, even though they're not hard cases like Sandeen's, is a mighty salty bunch. If open warfare breaks out, no one in this part of the territory will be safe."

"You've seen for yourself the kind of men Sandeen has working for him," Culverhouse said. "But they'd put a lid on their fight while they were here in town if you were the marshal, Morgan. They wouldn't have any choice."

Frank looked around and said slowly, "I think you're overestimating me a mite. You can't believe everything you read in those dime novels."

"Enough of it is true," Donohue said. He reached inside his old tweed coat and brought out a battered tin star. He set it on the table and slid it toward Frank. "What do you say? Will you take the job, Frank? If you don't, sooner or later that street out there is gonna run red with blood. The whole Mogollon range will."

For a long moment, Frank didn't move. Then he took a deep breath and reached out to pick up the badge.

"You've got yourself a marshal," he said.

Chapter Eight

He surprised even himself with that answer. He had suspected even before they reached the saloon that Donohue was going to ask him again to take the job. When he had seen so many of San Remo's leading citizens gathered here, he had been sure of it. And he had been equally sure that he was going to refuse again.

But now he saw that he couldn't. These people needed help, and although Frank Morgan was a lot of things, someone who could turn his back on folks in trouble wasn't one of them. He realized now that from the time he had ridden out of those trees and seen that burning line shack earlier in the day, he had been involved in this. Thinking that he could just ride away from it had been foolish.

Donohue looked surprised, too, as if he had expected Frank to refuse. He got over it quickly, though, and with a big grin on his bearded face, he said, "That's fine, Frank, just fine. I can't tell you how much we're obliged to you for your help. I guess we'd better start callin' you Marshal Morgan now."

Carefully, Frank pinned the badge on his faded blue shirt. Having it there felt strange.

"Don't you want to know how much the wages are?" Simon Wilson asked.

None of the townspeople knew that Frank was actually a wealthy man. He didn't think about it all that much himself. Now he just shook his head in reply to Wilson's question and said, "As long as some free meals over at the café are included, like Mayor Donohue mentioned earlier, whatever you folks can pay me will be fine."

Donohue chuckled. "We'll all be poolin' our funds to come up with your wages, Marshal, and Mary Elizabeth has already agreed to feed you for her part."

"What are *you* contributing?" Frank asked curiously.

Donohue hooked his thumbs in his vest and grinned. "My persuasive and diplomatic skills, o' course. And you may not know it, but I'm also the only attorney-at-law in these parts and the magistrate o' San Remo."

"So you're not just the town bum, like you claimed."

"He didn't *say* that," Ben Desmond put in. The comment drew laughter from everyone in the saloon, including Willard Donohue.

"All right, Marshal," Donohue said, "what's your first order of business?"

Frank looked at the blacksmith/undertaker/liveryman and said, "Mr. Culverhouse, when you get done preparing the bodies of Jack Moses and the Hanley brothers, don't display them. Don't give Sandeen's gunthrowers any more notoriety than they already have."

Culverhouse shrugged in acceptance of the edict. "That don't make no nevermind to me, Marshal. It ain't like I charge folks to look at 'em or anything like that. I'd just as soon put 'em in the ground and be done with it."

Frank nodded and said, "That's exactly how I want folks to feel about it. There's nothing glamorous about a gunfight." He pushed back his chair and got to his feet. "Now I think I'll take a walk back over to the Verde."

"That's Saber's hangout," Alonzo Hightower warned. "Sandeen and his bunch are used to getting their own way around here. They won't like it that there's law in San Remo."

"Then the sooner they find out about it, the better," Frank said. He glanced down at the badge on his chest. "Just out of curiosity, where'd you boys get this tin star?"

"San Remo had a marshal up until a few months ago, when Sandeen began hirin' so many hard cases," Donohue explained. "He never had much law work to do before that, since these parts have been pretty peaceable since Geronimo turned himself in to the Army. But one night in the Verde that fella Lannigan picked a fight with Marshal Crawford and gunned him down. Crawford drew first, so there wasn't much anybody could do about it. Lannigan may look like a saddle tramp, but he's pretty fast on the draw, Marshal."

Frank nodded. "I'll remember that. Now, you gents go on back to your businesses or your homes and go on about your life. I'll have a talk with Sandeen and let him know that any trouble here in town won't be tolerated."

Donohue rubbed his bearded jaw and frowned. "That's just what we wanted you to do, Marshal, but danged if I ain't a little worried about it now. We maybe asked you to bite off too big a chunk for any man to handle." Several of the other men nodded in agreement and looked nervous, as if they had started something that they now wished they hadn't.

"Well, there's one thing for sure." Frank smiled thinly. "It shouldn't take too long to find out if that's true."

The hitch rails in front of the Verde Saloon were still full as Frank walked toward the place, so he knew that Sandeen's men were still inside. He stepped up onto the boardwalk and paused for a second to square his shoulders. The street was quiet behind him. The citizens of San Remo who had hired him to protect them and their settlement had taken his advice and gone home.

He put his hands on the batwings, pushed them aside, and walked into the saloon.

At first there wasn't much reaction. But then one man at the bar noticed Frank, saw the badge on his chest, and nudged the man standing next to him. That man fell silent and nudged his neighbor, and on down the line. That spread to the men at the tables, and although the player piano kept plinking out a tinny tune, the buzz of conversation in the room gradually died away. Somebody finally reached over and threw the lever that stopped the piano's cylinder from revolving.

In the rear corner of the room Ed Sandeen, Vern Riley, and Carl Lannigan still sat together. Riley and Lannigan looked surprised to see Frank, especially with a lawman's tin star pinned to his shirt. Sandeen regarded him through narrow, contemplative eyes.

Frank saw a thick layer of sawdust on the floor where blood had leaked out of the Hanley brothers. That was going to leave a stain . . . but it wouldn't be the first such stain the planks of this floor had known.

And likely it wouldn't be the last.

"Since I seem to have everybody's attention," Frank said in a loud, clear voice, "I'll go ahead and tell you that I've just accepted the job of marshal here in San Remo. That means there's law in this settlement again, and I expect it to be obeyed and respected."

From the table where he sat with Sandeen and Lannigan, Riley asked mockingly, "You're not going to order us to give up our guns, are you, Marshal?"

"Not unless Mayor Donohue tells me to."

Sandeen snorted. "That old windbag. You've made a mistake by playing along with him, Morgan. This will just cause more trouble."

"No," Frank said, "as of now, there won't be *any* trouble in San Remo. I won't stand for it."

Lannigan leaned over, his cheek bulging, and rattled a spittoon with a gobbet of tobacco juice. "This is a damned joke," he said harshly. "Imagine a gunslinger like Frank Morgan packin' a badge. You're no town-tamer, Morgan. You're just like us. We're the fellas the lawmen don't like."

"Don't compare me to the likes of you, Lannigan," Frank said coolly. "And don't try to prod me into drawing on you like the last marshal did."

"That was a fair fight! Crawford drew first."

"I won't," Frank said. "I won't need to."

Lannigan's nostrils flared angrily. "That's mighty big talk. I didn't know you were a braggart, Morgan."

"It's not bragging if you can back it up."

The legs of Lannigan's chair scraped on the floor as he shoved it back and stood up. He turned more toward Frank and said, "Why, you—"

Sandeen leaned forward and said sharply, "Stop it, Carl. We don't want any trouble here tonight."

"Maybe you don't," Lannigan blustered, "but it seems to me that Morgan does!"

"I just want everybody in here to understand." Frank raised his voice. "Everybody. There won't be any gunfights or brawls in San Remo. If you run into Lazy F punchers on the street, let them go on past in peace. You're welcome in town as long as you conduct your business quietly."

"Has anybody said that my men conduct themselves otherwise?" Sandeen asked.

"Not to my knowledge," Frank admitted.

"And do you intend to issue this same warning to Howard Flynn and his men?"

"As a matter of fact, I do."

Sandeen shrugged. "Then I have no complaint, Marshal. As long as you treat us fairly, you won't have any trouble from us."

Lannigan spit again. "Speak for yourself, Sandeen."

"I speak for Saber!" The words lashed out from

Sandeen. "And the men who ride for me had damned well better listen when I speak."

"Then maybe it's time I draw my pay and ride on! I won't let this bastard push me around! Morgan thinks he's got me buffaloed, but he's wrong."

Frank said, "If you don't like me, Lannigan, I'm willing to make an exception and settle it with you."

Lannigan's lips drew back from his teeth and his hand curled over the butt of his gun, ready to hook and draw. "Now you're talkin'," he breathed.

"But not with guns," Frank went on. "Tell you what I'll do. I'll take off this badge for a few minutes, and we'll step outside and settle this, man to man."

"You want to fight me?" Lannigan laughed. "Hell, Morgan, I got fifty pounds on you, and I'm at least ten years younger."

"I'll take my chances."

Lannigan's hands went to the buckle of his gun belt. "Damn right you will!" He took off the gun belt and dropped it on the table. "Man to man, just like you said!"

Frank nodded. He unpinned the badge and slipped it into the pocket of his jeans. Then he unbuckled his own gun belt and looked around for something to do with it.

"I'll hold that for you, Marshal," a familiar voice said behind him.

He glanced around to see that Willard Donohue stood in the doorway of the saloon. The mayor of San Remo had an old Henry rifle tucked under his arm. On the boardwalk behind Donohue were several more of the townsmen, all of them holding rifles or shotguns.

A grim smile tugged at the corners of Frank's mouth. He had underestimated these men. They hadn't gone home to hide while he confronted Sandeen. They had just gone to arm themselves, and now they were ready to back his play if they needed to.

"Thanks, Mayor," Frank said. He handed his coiled gun belt to Donohue as he stepped out onto the boardwalk.

Behind him in the saloon, Sandeen ordered, "All you Saber men stay out of this! It's between Lannigan and Morgan."

As Frank started out into the street, he heard the heavy clump of Lannigan's boots on the boardwalk. Suddenly one of the townsmen called, "Marshal, watch out!"

Frank turned and saw that Lannigan had charged him from behind with no warning. He didn't have time to get his feet set and brace himself before Lannigan slammed into him. Frank's hat flew off his head from the impact as Lannigan drove him off his feet. Both men crashed to the ground, but Lannigan was on top and his weight drove the air from Frank's lungs as it landed on him.

As he gasped for air, Frank's instincts warned him that he couldn't let Lannigan get him in a bear hug. Frank was taller, but Lannigan was heavier and more powerful. If he trapped Frank in his brutal embrace, he would probably break Frank's ribs.

Twisting, Frank drove the heel of his hand up under Lannigan's bearded chin, forcing his head back. That loosened Lannigan's grip enough so that Frank was able to writhe free and roll over a couple of times, putting a little distance between them. He came up on hands and knees and then surged to his feet just ahead of Lannigan, whose greater bulk made his movements slower and more lumbering.

Frank stepped in and threw a hard right that caught Lannigan on the jaw. Despite his generally slender frame, Frank packed a lot of deceptive strength in his whipcord muscles. The blow landed solidly and drove Lannigan's head to one side, throwing him off balance. Frank moved closer and hooked a left to the man's midsection. Lannigan was stocky but not soft. Hitting those slabs of muscle over his belly was almost like punching a wall. He shrugged them off without any effect and launched a roundhouse punch at Frank's head.

If that blow had connected, it probably would have

ended the fight then and there. But Frank was able to duck under it and bore in again, this time landing a whistling right uppercut. Lannigan staggered backward, and Frank sensed a weakness in him. Lannigan might not have a glass jaw, but Frank had already figured out that he could pound away at the man's midsection all night long without doing any real damage. If he was going to win this fight, he was going to have to concentrate on Lannigan's head.

That was why he peppered a couple of swift left jabs into Lannigan's face while he had the chance. The second one made blood spurt from Lannigan's nose. Lannigan howled in pain and anger. Obscenities spewed from his mouth as he caught his balance and swung wildly. Frank was able to avoid most of those punches, but one of them landed on his chest and had enough power to take his breath away again. Then Lannigan's other fist clipped him on the side of the head and made the world spin crazily for an instant.

Lannigan must have thought that Frank was hurt worse than he really was. He let out an exultant yell and rushed in to finish off his opponent. Frank met him with another stinging left to the face that slowed him, and then threw a right that landed in the same place on Lannigan's jaw as the earlier punch. Lannigan staggered.

Frank didn't give him a chance to recover. He pressed his advantage, slugging with a left, a right, and then another left, all of them aimed at Lannigan's jaw. Lannigan stumbled backward, pawing feebly at Frank but unable to hold off those crashing fists. With a last-ditch effort, he reached out and grabbed Frank's shirt, then went over backward, pulling Frank with him.

Going back to the ground was the last thing Frank wanted to do. Once they were down again, the fight turned into a wrestling match, and his speed didn't do him any good there. He tried to tear himself loose as

Lannigan's big hands closed on him, but the tide of battle was turning again.

Instead of tugging against Lannigan, Frank suddenly went with him as the man tried to pull him in. He lowered his head and butted it into Lannigan's face. Lannigan hadn't expected that. His grip slipped, and Frank came free. He pushed himself upright. Lannigan followed, but he was wobbly. Frank brushed past his defenses, hit him with a left, then launched a piledriver right that knocked Lannigan completely off his feet. Lannigan crashed down onto his back, arms and legs loose, and didn't move as he lay there, out cold.

While the fight had been going on, Frank had been vaguely aware that shouts of encouragement were coming from all around them, mostly from Sandeen's men as they urged Lannigan to cripple or even kill him. Now a stunned hush fell over the street. Frank's chest rose and fell as he tried to catch his breath. He wiped the back of a hand across his mouth and looked around, glad to see that the townsmen weren't celebrating his victory or gloating over Lannigan's defeat. Instead they stood there watching quietly and soberly, making sure that no one interfered with the fight or tried to come after Frank now that it was over.

Sandeen stepped out onto the boardwalk, looked at Lannigan's sprawled figure, and shook his head in disgust. "Pick him up and put him on his horse," he ordered a couple of his men. "We'll take him back to Saber with us."

"I thought he drew his time, Sandeen," Frank said.

The rancher waved a hand. "That was just talk. Carl still works for me."

"Better keep a tight rein on him."

"I keep a tight rein on all my men," Sandeen said, "until it's time to let them go."

With that, he motioned for his riders to mount up and take Lannigan with them.

Willard Donohue and Jasper Culverhouse came over to Frank. "That was one hell of a fracas," Donohue said. "Sandeen and his men know you mean business now, Marshal."

Frank grunted. "I hope so." He flexed his fingers, frowning at the pain that went through them as a result of the battering they had taken.

Culverhouse grinned and said, "I got some liniment down at the barn that you can soak those hands in, Marshal. It'll fix 'em right up. You'll be fine by mornin'."

"I hope so," Frank said.

After all the violence this day had brought with it, from the attack on the line shack to this grudge match in the street, he didn't like to think about what tomorrow might bring.

Chapter Nine

True to Jasper Culverhouse's prediction, Frank's hands weren't in too bad a shape when he got up the next morning. The knuckles were somewhat sore and swollen, and the fingers were a little stiff. But Frank could use his hands without any trouble, and that was all that really mattered. That liniment of Culverhouse's was good medicine—even if it was meant for horses and not people.

Frank had other aches and pains as he rolled out of the pile of hay in the loft where he had slept. Some came from the bruising fight with Lannigan, while others were just the result of his age. He had heard it said that it wasn't really the years that aged a man, but rather the miles that he put on his body. In his case there had been plenty of both—years *and* miles.

He pulled on his boots, buckled on his gun belt, and settled his hat on his head, then climbed down the ladder to the hard-packed dirt floor of the barn. Culverhouse was nowhere in sight. Frank looked in on Stormy, who appeared to be fine, and rubbed Dog's head as the big cur nuzzled his leg. "Stay here, and I'll bring you back something to eat," he told Dog, then left the barn and walked toward the café, eager to find out if Mary

Elizabeth Warren's breakfasts were as good as the supper he'd had the night before.

Judging from the crowd inside the café, they were. Several of the men he had met in the Mogollon Saloon were there, sitting at the tables with platters full of food and steaming cups of coffee in front of them. Frank didn't see any of the saloon owners, but that came as no surprise; saloons were nocturnal enterprises, and the men who ran them tended to sleep late.

Willard Donohue was at one of the tables, though, along with Simon Wilson and Ben Desmond, the two merchants. Donohue raised a hand in greeting and said, "Come and join us, Marshal. We thought you might be along."

Frank took the empty chair at the table and nodded pleasantly to the three men. "Mornin'," he said.

"How are you feeling, Marshal?" Desmond asked. The dapper little storekeeper smiled. "A bit sore, I imagine."

Wilson commented, "A man would have to be, after a tussle like that one with Lannigan."

"I'm fine," Frank told them. "A little stiffer than usual, maybe, but nothing to worry about."

"Lannigan won't forget what happened, you know," Wilson went on. "You'd better have eyes in the back of your head from now on, Marshal."

"I've got pretty good instincts," Frank said dryly. "And why don't all of you call me Frank? I'm not much of one for standing on ceremony."

"All right, Frank," Desmond said. "I imagine you *do* have good instincts to have lived this long, a man in, ah, your profession."

"I didn't set out to make gunfighting my life's work. It just sort of happened that way."

"Of course. I didn't mean any offense."

Frank smiled. "None taken. And you're absolutely right, Ben. I have to know when trouble's coming. Most of the time I do."

Mary Elizabeth brought over a cup of coffee and a plate stacked high with flapjacks, bacon, scrambled eggs, and hash-brown potatoes. As she set the food in front of a somewhat puzzled Frank, Donohue chuckled and said, "You don't order breakfast here, Frank, you just eat what Mary Elizabeth brings you . . . if you're smart, that is."

The food and coffee smelled wonderful. Frank took a sip of the strong black brew and nodded appreciatively. "Mighty good," he told the woman, who smiled back at him.

"You eat up and enjoy your meal, Marshal," she said. "You know it's on the house."

"And I'm much obliged for that." Frank dug in.

This arrangement might work out pretty well, he thought. After Frank had taken the marshal's job, Jasper Culverhouse had refused any payment for taking care of Stormy and Dog, and he wouldn't hear of accepting money for letting Frank sleep in the hayloft. Frank could eat for free at the café, and he supposed he could go down to Pastor McCrory's church for spiritual comfort and guidance any time he wanted to. He was taken care of, body and soul.

And all he had to do in return was keep the peace in San Remo and try to prevent a bloody range war from engulfing the whole country hereabouts. Just a simple little chore, he thought wryly.

Donohue, Wilson, and Desmond finished their meals before Frank, but they lingered over cups of coffee and kept him company while he ate. Frank took advantage of the opportunity to question them, asking them to fill him in on all they knew about Howard Flynn and Ed Sandeen.

As one of the first settlers in the region, Flynn was known by everyone in these parts and liked by most. That wasn't to say that he hadn't rubbed a few people the wrong way over the years. Like a lot of cattlemen, he was accustomed to getting his own way, and he had been known to ride roughshod over anyone who defied him. He had never descended to outright violence against his enemies, though. His intimidating nature and tough crew of riders had been enough to get him what he wanted. The only people he had fought against were rustlers and Apaches. Those he and his men had battled ruthlessly.

Sandeen was a newcomer, having been in the Mogollon country only a few years. Nobody knew where he came from, because he was tight-lipped about his past. He was always well dressed and cultivated an air of culture and education, but despite that he impressed observers as a tough man who was probably dangerous to cross. From the start, he had hired an even saltier crew of riders than Howard Flynn, although it was only in recent months that cold-eyed killers like Vern Riley and Carl Lannigan had started showing up on the Saber payroll.

"Things might've been different if Laura Flynn had taken an interest in Sandeen when he tried to court her," Donohue said. "Might've postponed the trouble, anyway. Couple of hombres as full o' themselves as Flynn and Sandeen likely would've butted heads sooner or later, no matter what else happened. But we'll never know, because Miss Laura wasn't interested. I reckon she's got her cap set for Jeff Buckston."

"Flynn's foreman?" Frank asked.

"Yeah. She's fond of him, and I suspect he returns the feelin'. Leastways, I've seen him makin' calf eyes at her while they were both in town and Miss Laura was shoppin' for supplies."

"I hear she used to be a schoolteacher back East."

Wilson said, "Yes. She talked about starting a school here, but there aren't enough children around to do it, especially if you don't count the Delgado youngsters. None of them speak anything but Spanish, so Miss Laura would have a hard time teaching them."

"How does Sandeen get along with his other neighbors?"

"Pretty well," Donohue said. "But there ain't all that many of 'em anymore. Sandeen sort of gobbled up all the small spreads around him. Except for a little bit here and there, the other ranches in the area all border the Lazy F."

"The ranches that Sandeen bought," Frank said. "Was there anything improper about the way he acquired them?"

"You mean did he force those other fellas to accept his offer at the point of a gun?" Donohue shrugged heavy shoulders. "Nobody could ever prove it if he did. And I don't know if he actually did that. But I know some water holes went bad and a few barns got burned. Those things happen, you know. Might've been pure coincidence that those ranchers decided to sell out not long afterward."

Frank didn't doubt for a second that Sandeen had forced those men to sell. Despite his suave exterior, rapaciousness lurked in Sandeen's eyes. Frank had seen it for himself, and he'd had no trouble recognizing it. He had run into many men over the years who were the same way.

"Has there been any trouble here in town between Sandeen's men and the Lazy F riders?"

"A few ruckuses, but no real gunplay. One mornin' one of Howard's punchers was found out behind the Verde Saloon, dead. He'd been stabbed in the back. He'd been in there the night before and won some money in a poker game, but his pockets were empty when his body was found. He could've been robbed and killed by a drifter. We have some of them come through here now and then."

"Or he could have been killed by Sandeen's men and robbed to make it look like they didn't have anything to do with it," Frank said.

"Yeah. It could've happened that way."

Frank finished the last of the food, which had been

excellent all around, and reached for his coffee cup. "Who owns the Verde Saloon?" he asked.

"Sandeen does," Donohue said. "He bought it from the previous owner, a gambler name of Ford Fargo, about a year ago."

Frank's eyebrows rose. "That's interesting. So Sandeen is a saloonkeeper as well as a cattleman. He's making himself into a real power in these parts."

"Yeah. He has a fella named Mitch Kite who looks after the Verde for him. Sandeen still spends most of his time out at Saber, but it ain't uncommon to see him in town."

"Do you think if things escalate into open warfare between Flynn and Sandeen, it'll spill over into the settlement?"

"How can it fail to?" Desmond asked. "The businesses here all depend on Saber and the Lazy F. There'll be gunfights and God knows what else going on."

Frank sipped the still-warm coffee and leaned back in his chair. "So in order to really do my job of protecting the settlement, I have to make sure that Flynn and Sandeen don't go to war against each other."

With a faint smile, Desmond said, "There's an old saying about an irresistible force and an immovable object, Frank. That may be what you're up against here."

"More like a rock and a hard place," Donohue put in.

"Whatever you call it, I've got it to do," Frank said. He drank the last of the coffee and reached for his hat.

Wilson said, "You've put Sandeen on notice already. What's your next move, Frank?"

"I thought I'd ride out to the Lazy F and have a talk with Howard Flynn."

"He won't be glad to see you," Wilson warned.

Frank just smiled. Wilson was right about that—and the storekeeper didn't even know about the run-in Frank had had with Flynn and his men the day before.

* * *

That same morning, across the border in New Mexico Territory, a man walked into a sleepy little cantina in a sleepy little village. Tall and lean, he had red hair and a rawboned face and wore a black hat and a black frock coat. The drowsy man behind the makeshift bar looked up at the stranger, didn't recognize him as anybody who had ever passed through this nameless village before, and said, "Sí, *señor.* What can I do for you?"

"Too early to get a drink?" the gringo stranger asked.

The proprietor of the cantina, whose name was Rivas and who was the only one in the place at this hour, chuckled. "Never too early for that, Señor. Tequila? Pulque? Mescal?"

The stranger rested his hands on the bar and said with a smile, "Don't you have any American booze, you damned greaser?"

Rivas took no offense. He had been called many things in his life, and his theory was that as long as the men calling the names had plenty of money and were willing to part with it, the words that came out of their mouths mattered not at all.

"I have whiskey," he said. He reached for the bottle under the bar and took down a glass from the shelf behind him.

"I don't need the glass," the stranger said. "Just give me the bottle."

He reached for it, and as he did, the cuff of his white shirt stuck out a little from the sleeve of the frock coat. Rivas noticed a few drops of red staining the shirt cuff. They stood out against the white fabric.

The stranger took the bottle, pulled the cork, and tilted it to his mouth. The whiskey gurgled a little as he swallowed a healthy slug of it. When he set the bottle down on the bar, he wiped the back of his other hand across his mouth, and Rivas saw the little red stains on that shirt cuff, too.

"If you want what is left in the bottle, Señor," Rivas said, "it will cost you two dollars."

The stranger reached inside his coat, but instead of getting some money from his pocket, he brought out a small, well-thumbed little book bound in black leather. At first Rivas thought it was a Bible, or at least a New Testament, but then the stranger rested it on the bar and opened it, and Rivas saw that some of the pages were blank and others were filled with rows of neat, precise writing.

Again the stranger reached inside his coat. This time he took out a pencil. "What's your name, hombre?" he asked.

Rivas was confused, but he said, "Antonio Rivas."

The stranger wrote in his book. "Where were you born?"

"Across the border in a village much like this one."

"Did it have a name?"

"San Elizario."

The stranger nodded and wrote that. "How old are you? Do you know your birthday?"

That was one thing Antonio Rivas did know. He told the stranger the day he was born, and the stranger wrote it down.

Rivas could read a little, and even though the writing was upside down from where he stood, he studied it and began to make out that the words were a list of some sort, name after name, some gringo, some Mexican, with varying degrees of information such as date and place of birth out to the side. The names had other, more recent dates beside them as well.

The name right above his was Rudolph Talmadge. Señor Talmadge ran the general store up the street. Talmadge's birth date was printed next to his name, and today's date as well, which was puzzling. It occurred to Rivas that this gringo with his list might be a little bit crazy.

"Are you going to pay me for the whiskey, Señor?" When dealing with potential lunatics, it was always better to get paid as soon as possible.

"In a minute. Are you married, Señor Rivas?"

"*Sí*, of course. My wife Carmen is asleep in the back."

The stranger smiled. "Young and pretty, is she?"

More unease stirred inside Rivas as he said, "*Sí, muy bonita.*"

"Good. It's been a while since I've had a woman. I'll enjoy her."

Rivas's eyes were no longer sleepy. They opened wide in shock and anger. "I think you should leave now, Señor," he said tautly. "Take the bottle. I do not even care if you pay me."

"Oh, I can't do that, not yet." The stranger closed his book, tucked it and the pencil away. "Not until after I've finished my business."

"You are finished here, Señor. Please go."

"Well, I suppose I could," the stranger mused. "I've already talked to Mr. Talmadge down at the store, and he told me what I needed to know. He said that the man I'm looking for came through here about a week ago, riding west toward Arizona Territory. That's enough. But somehow, even when I was through with Mr. Talmadge, I didn't feel like I was done here. Something was keeping me from riding on, and now I know what it was."

Definitely a lunatic, Rivas thought. He started to move his hand toward the old cap-and-ball pistol that he kept on a shelf right underneath the bar.

"Now I know that I wasn't meant to leave here until I'd had me some fun with your pretty little wife, Señor Rivas."

That statement was so shocking that it made Rivas hesitate as he reached for the gun, and that was his undoing. The stranger's hand came up and the early morning light flashed on something in it, and suddenly Rivas couldn't swallow and he felt faint, and when he looked down at the bar in front of him he saw the hot flood of crimson that poured from his throat. The stranger reached across the bar with his other hand, tangled his fingers in Rivas's thick black hair, and jerked his head up. Then the gringo slashed again with the knife, cutting so deep this time that the blade grated on the top of Rivas's spine and his head almost came loose from his body. When the stranger let go, Rivas fell forward loosely, landing on the bar with its pool of blood and then sliding off to land in the floor behind it.

The stranger came around the bar, wiped the blade on the dead man's shirt, and frowned when he saw that he had gotten even more blood on his cuffs. He had always been so fastidious in the past. Now that he was closing in on his quarry, he was getting eager, and that made him a little sloppy. He would have to get that under control before he caught up with Frank Morgan.

Everything needed to be nice and neat when he killed Morgan. Just because people died didn't mean that there had to be a mess.

Chapter Ten

Frank took a couple of flapjacks and some ham fat back to the livery stable for Dog. By the time he got there, Jasper Culverhouse was on hand, scooping grain from the bin into the troughs in the stalls that had horses in them.

"Mornin', Marshal," Culverhouse greeted him. "How are you today?"

"Not bad, considering. And you might as well call me Frank. I told some of the other fellas in town to." Frank tossed one of the flapjacks to Dog, who caught it deftly and wolfed it down.

"Been up to the café, have you?"

"That's right. Miss Warren's breakfasts are as good as her suppers."

"You're right about that. Reason I wasn't here earlier is that Pastor McCrory and I took the bodies of Jack Moses and the Hanley brothers up to the graveyard and planted 'em. Since you said you didn't want 'em put on display, Homer and I didn't see any reason to drag our feet about the buryin'."

"Anybody show up for the funeral?" Frank asked curiously.

Culverhouse snorted. "For gunmen like that? There

are no mourners at *those* funerals." As soon as the words were out of his mouth, he looked like he regretted them. He went on quickly, "But I didn't mean—"

"It's all right, Jasper," Frank said, stopping him. "When a fella rides the trails I do, it *is* a lonely life, no getting around it. A man doesn't make many friends. He never stays in one place long enough to do that." He smiled. "When my time comes, I expect that service will be pretty sparsely attended, too. Could be just me and El Señor Dios."

"Man could do worse," Culverhouse said with a scowl.

"Amen," Frank agreed. "Now, I reckon I'll get Stormy saddled up. I'm going to take a ride out to the Lazy F."

"Let me do that for you," Culverhouse said as he put down the scoop he had been using for the grain. "That's a fine horse you've got. We get along pretty well, but I'm glad you told him that I was all right. I wouldn't try to ride him or even mess with him too much when you weren't around, that's for sure."

"You'd regret it if you did," Frank said with a grin. Stormy was a one-man horse when it came to riding, although he would allow other people besides Frank to saddle him, groom him, and feed him—as long as he was in the right mood.

When the horse was ready to ride, Frank swung up into the saddle and said, "I'll see you later, Jasper." Culverhouse lifted a hand in farewell as Frank rode out of the barn.

Stormy's hooves rattled on the plank bridge over the Verde River, and Frank left San Remo behind as he headed east toward the Lazy F. It was a nice day, with a few clouds floating in the blue sky over the dark green hills and the even darker line of the Mogollon Rim.

As he reached the range claimed by Howard Flynn, he began to see cattle bearing the rancher's brand. He didn't know if Flynn actually owned all this land or just grazed his stock on it. In most places, the days of the huge, open-range spreads, where men owned a lot less land than what they actually used, were over and ranchers had to establish clear title to any range they wanted to use for grazing. Frank wasn't sure what the situation was here in Arizona Territory, though. Things hadn't had as much time to settle down here as they had in other parts of the country. In fact, it had been less than a decade since the days when no one was sure if the Army would ever be able to defeat the Apaches and make Arizona safe for settlement. The territory was still a raw land, bright with promise but also fraught with danger.

Frank estimated that he was only a couple of miles from the Lazy F ranch house when he saw a rider coming toward him. He had expected to run into some of Flynn's punchers before now. But as this rider trotted along the trail toward him, he realized in surprise that the approaching figure wasn't one of Flynn's cowboys at all. Instead it was the cattleman's niece, Laura.

Frank reined Stormy to a halt, and as Laura rode up to him, he lifted a hand to the brim of his hat and nodded politely. "Miss Flynn," he greeted her. "Good morning."

She wore pants and rode astride like a man, but there was no mistaking the fact that she was a woman. Her hat hung on her back from its chin strap, and that allowed her long, thick blond hair to tumble loosely around her shoulders. The man's shirt she wore didn't do much to conceal the thrust of her breasts, either.

If she was nervous about being in the presence of the man who had killed two of her uncle's men less than twenty-four hours earlier, she didn't show it. "Mr. Morgan," she said coolly. "What are you doing out here?" Then, before he could answer, her gaze stopped on the badge pinned to Frank's shirt and she said, "Oh, my goodness. You're a lawman?"

"Freshly minted," he said with a smile. "The mayor of San Remo offered me the job of marshal, and I took it."

"Willard Donohue is a disreputable old windbag. I'm not sure he was ever legally elected mayor. From what I gather, he just started calling himself that, and everyone went along with it to humor him."

"Maybe so," Frank said with a shrug, "but the other folks in the settlement seemed agreeable to the idea of me being the marshal. So I reckon it's official enough." His smile widened into a grin. "Mary Elizabeth Warren is even feeding me for free, as her part of my wages for the job."

The mention of Mary Elizabeth brought a smile to Laura's face, too, the first one Frank had seen on her. It made her even prettier. "Mary Elizabeth is a wonderful woman," she said. "I hope that Caleb will be able to talk her into marrying him one of these days."

"So that she can come out here and cook for your uncle?"

Laura laughed. It was a good sound. "No, so that she and Caleb will be happy, of course. But being able to eat Mary Elizabeth's cooking more often than just when we go into town would be nice, too, and I don't mind admitting it. I'm not one of those dainty, delicate Eastern ladies who pretends she doesn't like to eat. I might have been like that once, but the West is growing on me, I suppose."

Frank nodded. "It has a way of doing that to folks."

"You still haven't told me what you're doing out here, Mr. Morgan. Or should I call you Marshal Morgan?"

"Why not make it Frank?" he suggested. "As for what I'm doing here, I'm on my way to see your uncle and have a talk with him."

"A talk about what?"

Frank didn't see that it would do any harm to explain his errand to her. In fact, if he could make her understand what his goal was, she might be willing to help him convince Flynn to be reasonable.

"Since I've been hired to keep the peace in San Remo, it seems to me that the best way of doing that is to persuade your uncle and Ed Sandeen to give up the idea of a range war between them. Nobody really wins in one of those things. I know; I've been involved with them before. They just lead to a lot of bloodshed that doesn't solve anything."

A shadow had passed over her face at his mention of Sandeen, driving away the smile that had been there a moment earlier. She said, "I really don't see that what happens between Edward and my uncle is any of your business, Marshal. You don't have any jurisdiction except in San Remo."

Frank nodded. "That's true. But what happens out here on the range has an effect on the settlement." He added grimly, "Violence has a way of spreading."

"Yes, I'm sure that's true. But the man you need to talk to is Edward Sandeen, not my uncle. He's the one who's stirring up trouble."

"Because you turned him away when he came courting?" Frank ventured.

Anger flared in her eyes. "Who told you that?" she demanded.

"More than one person," Frank said with a shrug. "Isn't it true?"

From the way she was glaring at him, he thought for a moment that she wasn't going to answer him. But then she said, "I won't deny that Edward expressed . . . a romantic interest in me. I even considered his suit for a short time. I'm an educated woman, Marshal. I thought at first that Edward was . . . was a man of breeding and culture. He has the ability to make it seem like he is."

"You can put a suit on a polecat, but he's still a polecat," Frank said.

"I'm not sure I would have phrased it quite so bluntly . . . but it didn't take me long to realize that I didn't want to become romantically involved with Edward Sandeen." She shook her head. "Out here most people consider me an old maid, you know. But I'd rather be thought of that way than to become involved with the wrong man."

"Sounds pretty wise to me," Frank told her. He changed tack a little by saying, "I'm a mite surprised to find you out here riding by yourself this way."

"I'm armed," she said, patting the stock of the Winchester that stuck up from a saddle boot strapped to her mount.

"Can you use that rifle?"

"Of course! Well, at least to a certain extent. I've been practicing. Mr. Buckston is teaching me how to shoot."

"From what I saw of him yesterday, Buckston seems like a pretty good fella."

"He's a fine man," Laura said without hesitation. "A bit unlettered, of course, but a true gentleman at heart. A diamond in the rough, you might say."

Frank didn't really want to dig any deeper into Laura's feelings for Buckston, but he reminded himself of why he had ridden out here in the first place.

"Sounds like you're fond of him."

Laura's chin came up defiantly. "And why shouldn't I be?"

"No reason that I know of," Frank said. "I was just thinking that if war breaks out between your uncle and Sandeen, Buckston will be right in the middle of it. As foreman of the Lazy F, he'll be a prime target for any gunman who wants to curry favor with Sandeen."

Laura's pretty blue eyes blinked. "You think so?" she asked worriedly.

"I know so. Like I said, I've seen it before. Each side starts killing off the other, and it goes on and on until sometimes there's hardly anybody left to fight. That's usually how it ends, with a lot of death on both sides."

Laura looked even more worried now. Her teeth caught at her bottom lip as she considered what Frank had said. "Maybe it wouldn't be a bad idea for me to have a talk with Uncle Howard," she said after a long moment. "I . . . I don't really feel that I have a right to tell him what to do, though. He's been very kind to me. He took me in and gave me a place to live when he didn't really have to."

"In that case, I'm sure you don't want anything happening to *him,* either."

"Certainly not!" She gave an abrupt nod. "I'll do what I can to help you, Marshal. And I'll start by riding with you to the ranch house. It's probably not all that safe for you to be approaching the Lazy F by yourself today. Some of the men still hold a grudge against you because of what happened to Mr. Crenshaw and Mr. Houlihan."

"That gunfight wasn't my idea," Frank told Laura as she turned her horse so that she could ride alongside Stormy. "Those two hotheaded young punchers started shooting and didn't give me any choice but to defend myself."

"I know that," she said. They began riding at an easy pace along the trail, side by side. "Mr. Buckston explained the whole thing to me. But that doesn't change the hard feelings that some of the men have toward you."

"No," Frank said, "I reckon it doesn't."

They rode on toward the ranch for several minutes without saying anything else. As they passed a knoll that was thickly covered with pines, Frank glanced toward it and saw the late morning sunlight reflect off something in the trees.

That brief flash of light was all it took to make his instincts take over. He kicked his feet free of the stirrups and left Stormy's back in a dive that sent him toward Laura. She cried out in surprise as he crashed into her, wrapped his arms around her, and pulled her out of the saddle. His diving tackle sent both of them crashing to the ground.

But even as they were falling, Frank heard the crack of a rifle and the high-pitched whine of a bullet passing through the space they had occupied only a heartbeat earlier.

Chapter Eleven

The rifleman hidden in the trees on the knoll fired again as Laura's horse skittishly danced aside, forcing Stormy to move, too. The bullet kicked up dust in the trail scant feet from where Frank and Laura lay. Frank surged to his feet, hauling the shocked woman with him. Laura didn't seem to be hurt, but she was stunned and not very cooperative.

Frank hoped that lack of cooperation wouldn't get them both killed. He shoved her toward a stand of pines on the other side of the road and shouted, "Run! Head for the trees!"

Even as the words were leaving his mouth, he pivoted toward the knoll and drew his Colt. The Peacemaker seemed to leap into his hand of its own volition. The range was a little far for a handgun, but he wasn't trying to actually hit the bushwhacker as much as he was attempting to spook the man. He triggered three shots toward the pines that concealed the rifleman, then turned to run after Laura.

The rifle cracked yet again. She cried out and stumbled. Frank saw a bloodstain appear on the sleeve of her shirt. She was hit, but the wound didn't look too bad, maybe just a graze. His long legs covered the ground swiftly, and he caught up with her in a hurry as she continued to stumble. His left arm went around her waist, tugging her into a faster pace. He veered to the left with her.

Just as he did, he heard another shot and the wind-rip of a bullet past his ear. That one had been close, too damned close. But the trees were only a few steps away now. He lunged toward them and half-carried, half-dragged Laura with him.

As they entered the growth of pines, Frank slid to the ground and pulled Laura down, too. The hidden rifleman on the other side of the trail fired again, the slug smacking into the trunk of one of the pines. Frank pulled Laura deeper into the undergrowth and told her sharply, "Stay down as low as you can!"

The bushwhacker couldn't see them anymore, and the trees grew close enough together so that their trunks afforded quite a bit of cover. Several more shots blasted out, but the bullets didn't come close to Frank and Laura.

She whimpered in pain as she lay stretched out on her belly on the needle-covered ground. Her right hand clutched at her upper left arm where she had been wounded. Frank wanted to see how badly she was hit, but that would have to wait until the bushwhacker was no longer a threat.

The sound of those shots must have carried to the ranch house itself. Somebody had to have heard them and would be coming to investigate. Frank didn't think the bushwhacker would hang around much longer. The man was more likely to take off for the tall and uncut, rather than risk being discovered.

Another bullet whistled through the branches of the pines. Laura gasped in fear. From where he lay a few feet away, Frank said, "Take it easy. He can't see us, and among these trees like this, he'd have to be mighty lucky to hit either of us."

"Wh-who is it?" she choked out. "Who's trying to kill us?"

"Don't know. How bad is your arm hurt?"

"I . . . I'm not sure. All I know is that it burns and aches terribly."

That was actually a good sign, Frank told himself. If the bullet had hit bone or torn up the muscles too bad, chances are the arm would still be numb from the impact. The fact that it already hurt probably meant that the wound was superficial.

Somehow, though, he didn't figure that Laura would take much comfort from that knowledge right now, so he kept it to himself. Instead he said, "We'll get you taken care of real soon now."

"Are . . . are we going to die, Marshal Morgan?"

"Not hardly." There hadn't been any more shots for the past couple of minutes, and as Frank listened closely, he heard the thud of hoofbeats diminishing into the distance. "In fact, I think that bushwhacker is gone. We'd better wait a few minutes before we move, though, just in case he's trying to lure us out into the open where he can take another shot at us."

If Frank had been alone, he would have stayed where he was for at least another quarter of an hour, just to make sure the silence wasn't a trick. He didn't think he could afford to do that, though, what with Laura being hurt and all. After about five minutes, he holstered his gun and scooted over to where she lay.

"Let me take a look at that arm," he said.

Tears streaked her face, but she wasn't sobbing. She was making an obvious effort to control herself and to be brave. Frank ripped the shirt sleeve at its shoulder seam and slid the bloody fabric down her arm until he exposed the injury.

As he had thought, the bullet had barely clipped her, leaving a shallow trench a couple of inches long in her upper arm. Blood still oozed from it, but the flow had slowed considerably. If the wound was cleaned and bandaged, probably it would scab over and heal up without any trouble. Laura's arm would be stiff and sore for a few days, maybe a week, but that would be the extent of it.

"You're going to be fine," he told her reassuringly. He tore a strip off the shirt sleeve and tied it around the wound. Laura winced in pain as he pulled the makeshift bandage tight. "That'll hold you until we can get you back to the ranch," Frank went on. "Is there a doctor in San Remo? I don't recall hearing any mention of one."

Laura shook her head. "N-no, the nearest doctor is in Prescott."

"No matter. I'll bet your uncle has plenty of experience at patching up bullet wounds. If he can't take care of it, maybe the cook can. For that matter, I can do it myself, as long as I've got a bottle of whiskey and some clean cloth."

"This . . . this doesn't seem like the proper time for a drink," Laura said as she summoned up a wan smile.

Frank grinned at her. "You'd be surprised. A slug of Who-hit-John would likely make you feel a little better right about now." He got to his feet and reached down to grasp her uninjured arm. "Come on."

Her smile disappeared and she looked worried. "Is . . . is it safe?"

"There haven't been any shots for several minutes now, and I'm pretty sure I heard the bushwhacker riding off. Chances are your uncle or some of his men will be showing up any minute now to try to find out what all the commotion is about."

Frank helped her to her feet. She was a little unsteady at first, but she seemed to get stronger as he led her out of the trees toward the trail. The two horses were still there. By now they had drifted over to the far side of the trail and were cropping at the grass growing there. The shooting might have spooked Laura's horse enough to make it bolt, but evidently Stormy's presence had been a steadying influence. Stormy had smelled enough powder smoke over the years that such things were second nature to him by now.

As they reached the trail, Frank heard the swift rata-plan of hoofbeats from the direction of the ranch head-quarters. When he turned in that direction, he saw a rider sweep around a bend in the trail and gallop toward them. The strap of the rider's hat was taut under his chin, and the swiftness of his passage pushed the brim up. As the man caught sight of Frank and Laura, he leaned forward in the saddle, raked his mount with his spurs, and raced toward them even faster. Frank recognized the rugged, mustachioed face of Howard Flynn's foreman, Jeff Buckston.

Laura was still a little woozy from fear and loss of blood. Frank helped her to her horse and told her, "Hang on to the stirrup for a minute, until your head settles down. Then I'll help you get mounted."

He turned away from her and stepped out into the trail, lifting a hand in greeting to Buckston.

Frank expected the rider to slow down, but Buckston kept coming at a breakneck pace. By the time Frank realized that Buckston intended to ride him down, it was almost too late. He flung himself aside. Buckston's horse thundered by less than a yard away as Frank rolled at the side of the trail.

"What the hell!" Frank shouted in amazement as he came up onto his feet. "Buckston, have you gone—"

He intended to say "crazy," but he didn't get the chance. Buckston had yanked his horse to a sliding, skidding halt and was already out of the saddle. He charged toward Frank, fists swinging.

Frank barely had time to block the punches that Buckston flailed at him. "Stop it, you damned fool!" he shouted as he gave ground a little. He wanted to reason with Buckston, but the foreman was making it mighty difficult.

One of the blows slipped through, and Buckston's bony fist crashed against Frank's jaw. The impact made Frank drop his guard, and Buckston landed another punch. Frank grappled with him, trying to slow down the flurry of fists.

At close quarters like this, Frank heard Buckston mouthing curses, caught the name "Laura," and heard the phrase "hurt that girl!" He realized that Buckston had spotted the bloody bandage on Laura's arm and thought that *he* was responsible for whatever injury had befallen her. He said, "Damn it, Buckston, settle down! I didn't hurt her!"

The words didn't penetrate Buckston's enraged brain. He got his left hand on Frank's chest and shoved, putting enough distance between them so that he was able to land another sledgehammer right that rocked Frank's head to the side.

Enough was damned well enough, Frank thought. If he had to knock Buckston on his butt to make the man listen to reason, then so be it. He stepped in and slammed a left hook to Buckston's solar plexus.

It hadn't been much more than twelve hours since Frank had engaged in that brutal brawl with Carl Lannigan, and now here he was again, standing toe-to-toe with somebody and slugging it out. Frank and Buckston were more evenly matched as far as size and weight went, and both men had the rawhide strength and iron constitution that an active, outdoor life had bestowed on them. Buckston was younger, but Frank probably had the edge in experience and guile. He feinted, Buckston went for it, and an instant later Frank's looping right crashed solidly against Buckston's jaw. Buckston was driven down to one knee by the blow.

Frank could have kicked him in the face then, but he wasn't the sort of hombre who would kick a man when he was down. That hesitation gave Buckston the chance to tackle Frank around the waist and bring him down. Both men rolled in the trail, wrestling with each other.

They came to a stop with Buckston on top. His hands found Frank's throat and clamped around it, the thumbs digging in savagely. Frank knew he had only seconds to act before Buckston crushed his voice box. He scooped up a handful of dirt from the trail and dashed it into Buckston's eyes. Buckston roared in pain as the grit stung his eyes and made him recoil. His choking hands slipped off Frank's throat.

Frank arched his back and heaved, throwing Buckston off to the side. He went after the foreman, who was pawing at his eyes, and landed with a knee in Buckston's belly. That drove the air out of Buckston's lungs and left him gasping and helpless. Frank hit him again, just for good measure and to make sure that he stayed down.

"Blast it, Buckston!" he panted. "I told you to . . . take it easy!"

The sudden crack of a shot made Frank's head jerk up. He saw Laura Flynn standing several yards away, her Winchester in her hands. Smoke wisped from the rifle's muzzle. She worked the lever, jacking another round into the chamber.

"Stop it!" she screamed at Frank. "Stop hurting him!"

What about me? Frank wanted to ask. Buckston had landed several good punches, and Frank had already been bruised and battered from the fight with Lannigan. He wondered suddenly just what had possessed him to come to the Mogollon Rim country. Ever since he'd gotten here, folks had been shooting at him and punching him. It was enough to make a fella think that nobody wanted him around.

Laura was still wild-eyed and shaky. Frank kept a close eye on the barrel of the Winchester and said, "You'd better put that rifle down, Miss Flynn. You might shoot somebody without meaning to."

"If you hurt Jeff again, I'll mean to shoot you, all right!" she threatened. "Stand up and get away from him."

Frank did as she told him, hoping that would be enough to keep her calm. "Buckston misunderstood what he saw when he rode up," he said. "He thought I was the one who had hurt you. I tried to tell him, but he wouldn't listen."

"I . . . I know," Laura said, sounding a little more rational now. "It wasn't your fault, Mr. Morgan. But I still can't let you hurt him anymore."

The sound of more hoofbeats came to Frank's ears. "I don't reckon you have to worry about that," he said as he looked along the trail and saw half-a-dozen more riders come tearing around the bend. The big, white-haired figure in the lead was unmistakably Howard Flynn.

Flynn and the handful of punchers galloped up to the three people in the trail—Laura with the rifle in her hands, Frank dusty and disheveled, with blood leaking from the corner of his mouth where Buckston had clouted him, and the Lazy F foreman lying there coughing, still trying to catch his breath. Buckston rolled onto his side and shuddered.

Flynn's deep-set, blue-gray eyes took in the scene rapidly. He drew the pistol at his hip, leveling it at Frank and earing back the hammer. The men with him followed suit. The muzzles of six revolvers stared at Frank.

"You done good, Laura," Flynn rumbled. "Mighty good, in fact. Get mounted up and ride on back to the ranch now, fast as you can. Acey-Deucy'll tend to your arm."

"Wh-what are you going to do?" Laura asked.

Flynn stared grimly at Frank over the barrel of his gun. "We're gonna give this damned gunfighter his needin's once and for all, that's what we're gonna do."

Chapter Twelve

"Maybe you haven't noticed," Frank said in response to the cattleman's ominous words. "That's a marshal's badge pinned to my chest."

"I see it," Flynn snapped. "Where'd you steal it, gunfighter?"

"It's not stolen. The citizens of San Remo gave it to me. I'm working for them now."

Flynn's bushy eyebrows lifted. "*You're* the marshal of San Remo now? A man like you?"

Frank chuckled humorlessly. "Hell of a note, isn't it?"

Laura spoke up, saying, "Uncle Howard, you've got to listen to me. Mr. Morgan didn't hurt me. Someone shot at us. If anything, Mr. Morgan saved my life."

Flynn scowled and gestured toward his foreman, who was struggling to sit up. "What about Buckston? Looks to me like Morgan jumped him."

"It was the other way around," Frank said. "Buckston rode up and jumped to the same conclusion you did, Flynn. He thought I was responsible for your niece being hurt. So he tried to ride me down and then attacked me."

Flynn looked at Laura, who nodded and said, "That's the way it happened. I fired a shot into the air to break up the fight because I didn't want Mr. Buckston to be hurt badly, but Mr. Morgan's telling the truth about none of it being his fault. Marshal Morgan, I should say."

With a dubious grunt, Flynn said, "I still ain't sure about that part." But he lowered the hammer on his gun and slid the iron back into leather. Once again, the men with him followed his example.

Flynn went on. "All right, Morgan, I'm a big enough man to admit it when I was wrong. Don't expect me to apologize, though."

"I wasn't planning on holding my breath," Frank said. He looked around, spotted his hat lying on the ground a few feet away, and stepped over to it to pick it up. He knocked the dust off it and put it on.

Meanwhile, Flynn had dismounted and gone over to Laura. "How bad're you hurt?" he asked.

"Not bad. Marshal Morgan can tell you. He bandaged it."

Flynn glanced at Frank. "You did that?"

"Of course. When somebody bushwhacked us from that knoll over there"—he pointed to indicate where he was talking about—"Miss Laura got nicked by one of the bullets. But it just needs to be cleaned up, and it should be fine."

"Bushwhacked, eh? You see who done it?"

Frank shook his head. "Didn't even get a glimpse of him."

One of the Lazy F punchers suggested, "Maybe it was a trick, Boss. Maybe it was one o' Morgan's outlaw pards doin' the shootin', to make him look good by savin' Miss Laura."

"And what would the purpose of that be?" Frank snapped.

"Get me to trust you, maybe," Flynn said speculatively, "so you could get close enough to kill me and collect your payoff from Ed Sandeen."

"I'm close enough to kill you *now*, Flynn," Frank said in a quiet voice.

Flynn's jaw clenched angrily. "Yeah, but you'd never get away from my boys."

"Don't be too sure of that."

Several of the cowboys looked nervous, as if they thought the notorious Drifter was going to throw down on them at any second. Instead, Frank went on. "We're wasting time. You need to get Miss Laura back to the house so that wound can be tended to properly."

"Yeah, you're right about that," Flynn said. "All right, fellas. A couple of you help Buck get on his horse. Looks like Morgan whaled the tar out of him."

Buckston scowled at that. He had been almost friendly the day before, but Frank knew that likely wouldn't be the case in the future. Buckston would feel like he had a score to settle with Frank now.

Two of the men lifted Buckston to his feet. He shook them off and growled, "I'm all right, damn it." Somewhat shakily, he managed to get his foot in the stirrup, grasp the saddle horn, and swing up into his saddle.

Flynn helped Laura mount and then climbed onto his own horse. When he saw that Frank was mounted as well, he said, "Where in blazes are you goin'?"

"With you," Frank said. "I rode out here to talk to you, and I intend to do it."

"Even if I don't want you settin' foot on my land?"

"I'm stubborn," Frank said with a thin smile.

"Huh. As if I hadn't noticed. Well, come on, then. No point in sittin' around here jawin'."

The group of riders moved off toward the ranch house. Laura rode close beside Buckston, as if she wanted to be ready to reach out and steady him with her good arm if she needed to. She seemed to have forgotten about her own injury, although Frank knew her arm still had to hurt pretty badly. At the moment, though, she was more concerned with Buckston.

The Lazy F foreman was a lucky man, Frank mused with an inward smile. Laura Flynn was a beautiful, intelligent woman. She might not have been born and raised out here in the West, but she was doing her best to fit in.

Frank brought his horse alongside Flynn's and said, "I reckon you heard the shooting and rode out to see what was going on."

"That's right. Buck got there first because he was already part of the way in this direction, I guess." Flynn scowled. "You didn't have to beat the hell out of him."

"I did if I wanted to make him listen to me," Frank said. "He was the one who called the tune."

"Yeah, well, it may wind up bein' one you don't want to dance to." Flynn was silent for a moment, then he asked, "Do you think that bushwhacker you told us about was shootin' at you . . . or at Laura?"

Frank hadn't considered that Laura might have been the target. He couldn't think of any reason someone would want to harm her. Sure, she had rejected Ed Sandeen's advances, but Sandeen hadn't struck Frank as the sort of man who would try to kill her over that. Sandeen would be more likely to try to get back at Laura by ruining her uncle and taking over the Lazy F.

It was more likely that he had been the target, Frank told himself. He had insulted Sandeen's pride by refusing to go to work for him, then added injury to insult by killing the Hanley brothers and whipping Lannigan in that fight. Sandeen would want to settle that score. In addition, Sandeen wouldn't want a man like Frank entering the upcoming fight on the side of Howard Flynn. Sandeen might have decided that the best way to prevent that was to take Frank out of the picture entirely.

However you added it up, Frank believed that the shots had been intended for him. But there was no way of being sure about that until he found out the identity of the bushwhacker—which was something he intended to do.

They came in sight of the ranch headquarters and reached the big house a few minutes later. Flynn had sent one of his men galloping ahead to alert the cook to the fact that Laura had been wounded. Acey-Deucy was waiting for them on the porch when they rode up. He rushed down the steps and hurried to Laura's side, where he helped her dismount and held on to her good arm as they went into the house. "Don't worry, Missy Laura," he told her. "You be just fine. Acey-Deucy take good care of you."

Buckston dismounted and stumbled off toward the bunkhouse, muttering something about needing a drink. Flynn dismissed the other punchers with a flick of his hand, then turned to Frank and said, "Let's sit out here on the porch. If you've got something to say to me, you can say it there."

"Don't want me in your house, eh?" Frank said.

"Let's just say I don't have much use for gunslingers. I've never cottoned to your kind, Morgan."

Frank didn't feel like defending his life to this stiff-necked cattleman. Let Flynn think whatever he wanted to, he told himself. What mattered was making it clear to Flynn that under no circumstances would any range war be allowed to spill over into San Remo. Once Frank had gotten that message across, he could deal with the problem of the conflict between Flynn and Sandeen itself.

There were several old ladder-back chairs on the porch. Flynn sat down in one of them and took out the makin's. He didn't offer the tobacco pouch to Frank. Frank picked up one of the chairs and turned it around so that he could straddle it and rest his arms on the back. He said, "Laura told me that Willard Donohue wasn't ever elected the mayor of San Remo."

"That's true." Flynn licked the edges of the paper onto which he had spilled tobacco, pasted them together, and twisted the ends of the quirly. "So if Donohue's the one who gave you that badge, I ain't sure if callin' yourself a marshal is exactly legal."

"Everyone else in the settlement went along with it, so I reckon it's legal enough."

Flynn shrugged as he took a block of lucifers from his pocket, broke one off, and scratched it to life on the sole of his boot. He held the flame to the end of the cigarette and lit it.

"Do what you want," he said. "It don't make no never-mind to me."

"I'm going to proceed as if I'm the duly appointed marshal of San Remo," Frank warned him. "That means that if you or any of your men try to start trouble in town, I'll do my best to stop it."

"Why don't you go warn Sandeen?" Flynn snapped. "He's the one causin' all the trouble."

"I did warn him, last night. Which makes me wonder if whoever fired those shots at your niece and me this morning works for him."

Flynn's weathered forehead creased even more as he frowned. "If you've already had a run-in with Sandeen, he sure might've sent somebody after you. There's sure as hell no shortage of backshooters and cold-deck killers on Saber to choose from for a job like that."

"That's pretty much what I thought," Frank said with a nod. "I'm told that one of your punchers was murdered in town not long ago."

Flynn's scowl grew even darker. "Yeah. Joe Harrington. A pretty good kid, just a little wild and careless, otherwise he wouldn't have been playin' poker in the Verde Saloon without any other Lazy F men around. The story was that some drifter robbed and killed him, but I never believed that. Sandeen was responsible. He saw a chance to get rid of one of my boys and took it."

"We're in agreement on that, too," Frank said. "But you didn't try to strike back at Sandeen for it."

Flynn shook his head disgustedly. "Didn't have any proof, and I like to think I'm a fair man. It ain't like what happened yesterday. Rufe Blake *told* you before he died that Sandeen's men were behind that. That's good enough for me."

"But Blake and Bragan and Wardell were all inside the line shack when the shooting started," Frank pointed out. "A shot came through the window and killed Wardell, and Blake and Bragan were pinned down in there until the shack was set on fire. They were shot when the flames drove them out. That means they never really got a look at who killed them."

Flynn had been puffing furiously on the quirly as Frank spoke. Now he threw down the butt and ground it out savagely with his boot. "Damn it, are you sayin' maybe it wasn't Sandeen?"

"I'm saying you can't prove that, either. Personally, I believe that Sandeen ordered the shack burned and your men killed. I spoke to him in the settlement last night, and I didn't like the looks of him. But if you want to be fair, you can't take action against Sandeen based on what happened yesterday."

"Maybe you'd rather I wait until the bastard's got a gun to my head," Flynn growled. "It'll be too damned late then."

Frank inclined his head. "You've got a point there. Here's what I suggest. Keep your men close to home for a while. Don't let them go into San Remo and stir up trouble. I'll poke around some and see what I can find out, maybe get you the proof you need to go to the authorities."

"I been stompin' my own snakes for forty years."

"I know, and I understand how you feel. I'm just trying to keep this trouble from boiling over and spreading bloodshed all over the range."

Flynn snorted. "You're a fine one to talk, Morgan, considerin' how much blood *you've* shed over the years."

"I know," Frank said. "Maybe I'm trying to make up for some of that."

"Atonin' for your sins, eh? Been my experience that that don't really work."

"Mine, too." Frank shrugged. "But I figure it doesn't hurt anything to give it a try."

Flynn sat there for several moments, frowning in thought. Finally, he nodded and said, "All right, Morgan, I'll play it your way . . . for now. My riders will steer clear of San Remo. But if you come up with the proof that Sandeen is behind those killin's . . . well, I make no promise what I'll do then."

"Fair enough," Frank said. If Flynn kept his word, then Frank had accomplished his first goal, which was to protect the settlement. Now he could work on preventing the range war that might threaten it.

Flynn put his hands on his knees and pushed himself to his feet. "Grub ought to be ready soon," he said. "Come on in and eat with us."

"Your opinion of me must have gone up a little," Frank said, "for you to invite me to sit at your table."

"Yeah, well, nobody's ever gonna say that Howard Flynn ain't hospitable . . . even to low-down gunfighters."

Chapter Thirteen

The cook had cleaned and bandaged the wound on Laura's arm, and she had changed from her riding clothes into a simple but attractive dress. Her face was still pale and drawn from the pain, though, as she sat down at the table in the ranch house dining room with her uncle and Frank.

"How're you feelin', Laura?" Flynn asked her.

"I'll be all right," she said.

"We can hitch up the wagon and take you over to Prescott to see a real sawbones."

Laura shook her head. "No, I'm sure that won't be necessary. Acey-Deucy did a fine job of cleaning and dressing the wound."

"Just keep an eye on it," Frank advised. "I think it'll heal all right."

"You'd know about bullet wounds, wouldn't you, Morgan?" Flynn said.

"I suspect you've been nicked a few times yourself," Frank responded.

Flynn chuckled grimly. "Yeah, you're right about that. Now dig in. The Chinaman ain't as good a cook as that colored woman in town, but his food ain't bad."

Frank found that he agreed with that assessment. The

steak that Acey-Deucy served him wasn't quite as tender and flavorful as the one he'd had in Mary Elizabeth Warren's café the night before, but it was still more than passable.

When they had finished eating, Frank said his good-byes to Flynn and Laura and went outside. Flynn followed him onto the porch and said in a low voice, "Don't be too long about that pokin' around you're plannin' on doin', Morgan. I'll only wait so long before I take my men over to Sandeen's and clean out that nest o' vipers."

"I'll be in touch," Frank promised. He knew that if Flynn and his men attacked Sandeen, it wouldn't be as easy a victory as Flynn made it sound. In fact, it would probably be a bloodbath on both sides, and Frank suspected that Sandeen might actually win. He had the advantage in that many of his men were cold-blooded killers. They probably outnumbered Flynn's crew, too. Flynn might not realize it, but an attack on Saber would be like baiting a grizzly in the bear's own den.

Frank had left Stormy tied to a hitching post in front of the house. The horse was still there. One of Flynn's punchers lounged nearby. He said, "We were gonna take that horse o' yours over to the barn, Morgan, but the fool jughead wouldn't let us near him. Like to bit one fella's hand off. He'd have lost some fingers for sure if he'd been just a little bit slower."

"He's lucky," Frank agreed as he patted Stormy on the shoulder and gathered up the reins. "This big fella doesn't trust anybody until I tell him it's all right."

With that, he swung up into the saddle and turned Stormy toward the west. Before he could ride out, he heard someone call, "Morgan!"

Frank looked toward the bunkhouse and saw Jeff Buckston striding in his direction. Bruises were starting to form on Buckston's face, and there was still some dried blood here and there around his mouth. Although

Frank hadn't looked in a mirror recently, he figured he was sporting some fresh signs of battle himself.

"What do you want, Buckston?" he asked as the foreman came to a stop about ten feet away. Buckston had a gun on his hip, of course, and Frank hoped that he wouldn't try to draw it. There had already been too many killings in the past twenty-four hours.

"I know now you weren't the one who hurt Miss Flynn, Morgan," Buckston said. "Reckon I jumped the gun on that. Sorry."

The apology surprised Frank a little; he had Buckston pegged as a man who would be too proud to admit that he was wrong, especially this soon after the fact. But he nodded and said, "Fair enough."

"That don't mean there's no hard feelin's, though," Buckston went on, his voice hard and edged with anger. "You and me left things unsettled between us, and it can't end like that."

"They seemed pretty settled to me," Frank said coolly. He didn't aggravate the situation by pointing out the fact that the fight had ended with Buckston on the ground, helpless and gasping for breath.

"Just heed what I'm sayin'. . . . Sooner or later, you and me will have it out, Morgan."

"That's a fight I don't want."

"It's one you'll have, like it or not."

That was a challenge Frank couldn't allow to pass unanswered. He said, "It'll be up to you to start the ball, then, whenever you're ready."

"You'll know when the time comes," Buckston said. "I ain't no bushwhacker or backshooter."

"Never thought you were."

Buckston nodded. "We understand each other, then." Without saying anything else, he turned and walked back toward the bunk house.

Frank glanced over his shoulder and saw that Howard Flynn was still on the porch of the big house, watching the confrontation with interest. Laura had joined him, and she looked even paler and more worried than ever. Frank lifted a finger to the brim of his hat, gave them a nod, and heeled Stormy into a trot.

Buckston was right. Frank knew he was leaving unfinished business behind him as he rode away from the Lazy F. But there was nothing he could about it now, and he had other problems on his plate.

Like stopping a bloody range war . . .

A man could learn quite a bit about the country in which he found himself simply by riding over it. That was how Frank spent the afternoon, riding the range.

During his conversation with Jasper Culverhouse as he was soaking his hands in liniment the night before, he had asked about the boundaries of the Lazy F and Sandeen's Saber spread. The two ranches took up most of the land between the Mogollon Rim and the Verde River for a lengthy stretch along the stream. According to Culverhouse, the Lazy F was really the prime piece of real estate of the two; Saber lay to the south of Flynn's spread, and the terrain there was more rugged, not as well watered during the dry spells, and lacking in good grazing land when compared to the Lazy F. Saber certainly wasn't a *bad* ranch. It just wasn't as good as its neighbor to the north.

So after leaving Flynn's headquarters, Frank rode east for a ways, then left the trail and headed south, intending to have a look at Saber for himself. Several times during the afternoon, he saw riders in the distance and steered clear of them, not wanting any confrontations with either Flynn's or Sandeen's men.

As he penetrated deeper onto Sandeen's range, he saw that Culverhouse's assessment of it was correct. If Sandeen was the sort to feel jealous, he probably felt some envy of Flynn. But he could have made a perfectly good cattle enterprise out of Saber, if he'd been willing to work at it. A man like Sandeen couldn't stand to see someone else being successful, though. In order to be satisfied, he had to be better than everybody else. He had to ride higher on the hog and have everybody look up to him, or else resentment would eat away at his guts. Frank had known people like that before, and he would have considered them pathetic—if they hadn't been so dangerous.

When he felt like he had seen enough, he turned and rode west until he came to the Verde, then followed the river north until he came to San Remo again. The sun was about to dip behind the mountains to the west by the time he reached the settlement. He rode across the plank bridge and went to the livery barn behind the blacksmith shop.

Dog came bounding out to greet him, tail wagging and tongue lolling. As soon as Frank had dismounted, the big cur jumped on him. Frank grabbed Dog's ears and rubbed behind them. Dog's tail was wagging so fast now it was just a blur.

Culverhouse came out of the blacksmith shop and took Stormy's reins. "I'll put him up for you, Marshal," he said. "Give him a good rubdown, too."

"I'm much obliged, Jasper. Quiet day around here?"

"Yeah." Culverhouse jerked his head toward the Verde Saloon. "A few of Sandeen's men rode by a while ago and went to the saloon, but I haven't seen any Lazy F riders, so there ain't been any trouble."

"I had a good talk with Flynn," Frank said, not mentioning the ambush or the subsequent battle with Buckston. "He's going to keep his men out of town for the time being. That should let things quiet down a little."

"Huh. I'm surprised you got Flynn to go along with that. He's a stiff-necked old pelican who always thinks he's right."

Frank grinned. He couldn't have described Flynn any better himself.

Since it was nearly dark, he walked along to the café. Not surprisingly, he found Willard Donohue sitting outside, apparently waiting for him.

"Evenin', Marshal," Donohue said. "Haven't seen you around since early this mornin'. Did you take that ride out to Howard Flynn's ranch?"

"I did," Frank said with a nod. "I explained to him that I'm the marshal of San Remo now, and told him there wouldn't be any trouble tolerated in town."

"How'd he take that?"

"Well, he cast aspersions on the legality of this badge I'm wearing. Said you appointed yourself mayor, rather than being elected."

Donohue grunted. "He did, did he? I reckon it's true there wasn't exactly an election . . . but everybody in town thought we needed a mayor, and nobody objected when I said I'd take the job. That makes it legal enough as far as I'm concerned."

"Me, too," Frank said. "You had supper yet?"

"Nope. Waitin' for you."

"Let's go on inside, then. It's been a long day."

Frank had the pot roast for a change, and it was every bit as good as the steak he'd had the night before. When Mary Elizabeth brought the food, she said to Donohue, "You'll have to pay for your meal, Mayor. You ain't eatin' on the cuff like the marshal here."

"Add it to my tab, if you would, my dear," Donohue said.

Mary Elizabeth sniffed and rolled her eyes, but she said that she would.

Over supper, Frank told Donohue everything that had happened, including the bushwhacking, the wounding of Laura Flynn, and the fight with Buckston. Donohue asked worriedly, "Will that young woman be all right?"

"I think so," Frank told him. "It wasn't much more

than a scratch. Of course, it seemed worse to her, since she's not used to being shot at."

"And you are."

Frank shrugged. "It seems to happen a lot. Not saying I like it, but that's just the facts of the matter."

"Do you really intend to bring in outside authorities if you can prove that Sandeen is behind the attacks on Flynn's spread?"

"That's the only way this thing will truly be settled, short of open warfare. I know you said there are jurisdictional problems, but I'll drag the sheriffs of all three counties involved in here if I have to."

Donohue nodded slowly. "It wouldn't break my heart to see Ed Sandeen behind bars, that's for damned sure. I don't see how you're gonna get that proof you want, though, unless maybe you can lay your hands on one of Sandeen's men and convince him to testify against his boss."

"That's the very idea that's been lurking in the back of my head," Frank admitted. "I have to make one of them talk."

"I don't know how in blazes you'll manage that. All the men who ride for Saber are mighty tough."

"Any man's liable to turn on his boss, though," Frank said, "if it's the only way he can save his own neck."

Donohue frowned. "How do you mean?"

"Sandeen wants me dead. He's going to keep sending men after me. I just need to take one of them alive, so that he's faced with either testifying against Sandeen or going to the gallows for trying to kill me."

"Just *tryin'* to kill somebody ain't usually a hangin' offense. You've got to actually commit murder to get your neck stretched."

"I think I can convince a prisoner otherwise," Frank said with a faint smile.

Donohue looked at him intently for a moment, then chuckled. "You know, I think you're right, Frank. If you told me I had a date with the hangman, I expect I'd believe you." He rubbed a hand along his bearded jaw. "The only problem with this plan is that you got to sit back and wait for somebody who works for Sandeen to try again to kill you. That's just like paintin' a damned target on your back."

Frank sipped his coffee and then said, "It won't be the first time I've worn one."

Chapter Fourteen

Mary Elizabeth had peach cobbler for dessert, and Frank thought it was some of the best he'd ever had. There was something a little different about it, and when he asked her about it, she smiled and said, "That's because I got me a secret ingredient in there, Marshal." She leaned closer and went on quietly, "I add a little ginger to it. Gives the peaches a nice spicy taste."

"Well, it's mighty good," Frank told her.

"Good enough, in fact, that I think I'll have another serving," Donohue said.

Frank grinned and reached for his hat. "Not me. I'm full. I'll see you in the morning, Mayor."

"I'll be here."

Mary Elizabeth added caustically, "Where else is he gonna be?"

Still smiling, Frank left the café. He walked toward Alonzo Hightower's Mogollon Saloon, intending to stop in there for a quick beer before he went back to the livery barn.

Along the way, he got to thinking over Donohue's comment about having a target painted on his back. That was true, and it made the hair on the back of Frank's neck prickle a little. He was as accustomed to danger as a man could be, but even so, it was never a pleasant feeling to know that there were hombres around who wanted him dead. He heard a faint noise in the shadows as he passed the mouth of the alley between Wilson's Mercantile and Vincente Delgado's saddle shop, and his muscles stiffened and his nerves cried out for him to draw his gun and whirl toward the darkness, ready to fire.

He did neither of those things, but instead just kept walking. He glanced over his shoulder after a couple of steps and saw a scrawny cat saunter out of the alley and sit down and start washing himself. Frank grinned and gave a little shake of his head. He was glad he hadn't made a fool out of himself.

He had taken another couple of steps when he heard the faint scrape of boot leather on hard-packed ground behind him. This time when he glanced back, his keen eyes caught the barest reflection as a stray beam of silvery moonlight bounced off the barrel of a gun.

Frank threw himself to the side as Colt flame bloomed in the shadows and lead clawed wickedly through the night.

He landed on his shoulder in the street and rolled over, his hat coming off. The Peacemaker leapt into his hand as he came to a stop on his belly. He fired twice toward the mouth of the alley and then rolled again, winding up behind a water trough that gave him a little cover.

The gunman in the shadows squeezed off another couple of shots. One of the bullets thudded into the thick wood of the trough while the other splashed into the water itself. Then Frank heard the thud of running footsteps. For the second time today, someone had tried to bushwhack him, failed, and now was fleeing.

Frank surged to his feet and leaped onto the boardwalk in front of the saddle shop. He pressed his back against the wall of the building, which was dark now because Vincente had gone home to be with his wife and their multitude of youngsters. Frank slid along the wall, ready to fire if anybody came around the corner of the building. When nobody did, he ducked around the corner himself, crouching low to make himself a smaller target.

Hoofbeats pounded, heading north. The bush-whacker had reached the horse he had left hidden somewhere behind the buildings. Frank bit back a curse, whirled around, and dashed out of the alley and along the street. There was no time for him to fetch Stormy from the livery stable; if he tried to do that, the bush-whacker would be long gone before Frank could get mounted. He had only one slim chance of stopping the gunman.

The bridge over the Verde was the only good place to cross the river for several miles in either direction. If the bushwhacker rode past the bridge and continued north along the river, he would get away. Frank wouldn't be able to catch him.

But if he tried to cross the bridge, Frank might be able to stop him. It would be a difficult shot, in poor light, at long range for a handgun. But a chance was just that, and Frank wasn't going to give up just yet.

The rider bolted out from between Desmond's store and the Baptist church, at the north end of town. Leaning low over the horse's neck, he galloped toward the bridge. Frank came to a stop in the street, leveled the pistol, and steadied his arm by gripping his right wrist with his left hand. The rider reached the bridge and started onto it. Frank's mind calculated the angles and the elevation with lightning-fast speed as he drew a bead and fired. For a second he thought he had missed, but then the horse stumbled and its front legs collapsed, dropping the animal on the bridge and sending the rider sailing over its head.

Frank hated to shoot an animal, but the horse made a

lot bigger target than the rider and he didn't have much choice if he wanted to stop that bushwhacker. As soon as the horse went down and threw its rider, Frank sprinted forward again, heading for the bridge.

When he reached it, he saw the horse lying there, motionless, but there was no sign of the fallen bushwhacker. Frank slowed to a stop and frowned. He had been watching the bridge as he approached, and he hadn't seen the gunman get up and run off to the other side. Was it possible that when the horse had gone down, the man had been thrown completely off the bridge into the river? Frank hadn't heard a splash.

There was an open railing on each side of the bridge. It would have been simple enough for the bushwhacker to slide through there. And there were support beams underneath the bridge, Frank recalled, where a man could stand.

Quickly, he reloaded the empty chambers of his Colt, then cautiously started out onto the bridge. He tried to move as quietly as possible, but the heels of his boots made unavoidable clomping noises on the planks. His eyes moved constantly as he checked back and forth between both sides of the bridge.

A flicker of movement to the left caught his attention. He twisted in that direction and dodged quickly to the right at the same time, and as he did so flame stabbed from the muzzle of a gun down near the level of the bridge. The slug whistled past Frank's ear. Moving so swiftly had saved his life. As he returned the fire, he realized that the bushwhacker was hidden underneath the bridge, just as he had suspected.

The only cover out here was the corpse of the dead horse. Frank threw himself down behind the horse as another bullet screamed overhead. They were at a standoff now. From where the bushwhacker crouched on one of the support beams underneath the bridge, he couldn't get a shot at Frank. But neither could Frank hit him.

Over in the settlement, voices could be heard shouting questions. The shots had roused everyone in San Remo, and they wanted to know what was going on. Sooner or later, they would come up here to the bridge to investigate. That meant the bushwhacker couldn't afford to stand around and wait. He had to either try something different or cut and run, abandoning his attempt on Frank's life.

Frank listened intently and heard a grunt of effort, then a scraping sound somewhere below him. The bushwhacker was on the move, trying to work his way around to a better position where he could get a decent shot at his intended target. Acting on instinct, Frank rolled out from behind the carcass and reached the edge of the bridge. Cedar posts spaced every eight feet or so supported the railings along the sides. With his left hand he grabbed one of them at the bottom where it was nailed to the bridge, clamping his fingers around it in a grip of iron. Then he continued rolling and dropped off the side of the bridge.

Pain shot through his arm and shoulder as his weight hit them, but his grip held. He dangled there, his keen eyes searching the shadows under the bridge. He saw a deeper patch of darkness perched in the support beams about a dozen feet away, heard the startled exclamation as the bushwhacker ripped out a curse. The man twisted toward Frank, his six-gun again belching flame and death.

Frank fired twice, and then he couldn't hold on anymore. His grip gave way and he fell. Luckily, it wasn't far to the river, only about six feet. He plunged into the swift-flowing Verde, unsure whether his shots had struck the bushwhacker or not.

Just before his head went under, though, he heard a big splash and knew that it was caused by the gunman falling into the river, too.

The water was cold, since the river was fed by snow

melt and mountain springs, but not bone-numbingly frigid. Frank was able to push himself to the surface and strike out for shore. His boots touched the rocky streambed. He surged out of the water and sprawled on the bank. Despite being chilled, he knew he couldn't just lie there. He had no idea whether the bushwhacker was still alive, but it was certainly possible that the man was not only alive but still bent on killing his quarry.

Frank scrambled upright and looked along both banks of the river. The newly risen moon and the stars that had popped out in the arching black vault of the sky gave enough light so that he could see fairly well. He spotted movement on the same side of the river, on the far side of the bridge, and after a second that movement resolved itself into the shape of a man stumbling away.

Frank gave chase, splashing through the edge of the stream as he crossed underneath the bridge. That noise warned the bushwhacker, who threw a frightened glance over his shoulder and broke into a shambling run. Frank was fairly sure from the way the man was moving that he was wounded. He had also caught enough of a glimpse of the man's face that he was reasonably certain the bushwhacker was Carl Lannigan.

Now that he had turned the tables on Lannigan, Frank wanted to take the man alive. He wanted Lannigan's testimony that Ed Sandeen had sent him to San Remo to murder the town's new marshal. With that sort of evidence, the authorities wouldn't be able to ignore the situation in the Mogollon Rim country any longer. From what Frank knew of Sheriff Buckey O'Neill, the man would find a way to come in and clean up this mess, jurisdictional disputes be damned.

But that hope was predicated on capturing Lannigan and getting him to talk. That was why Frank didn't open fire again. Instead, he jammed his Colt back in its holster, slipped the seldom-used thong over the hammer, and gave chase as Lannigan fled up the bank of the river.

Both men were soaked, exhausted, beaten up, and Lannigan possibly was wounded. Neither of them was in any shape to run a race. But a race was exactly what it was as Frank scrambled up the bank and ran after Lannigan, who was headed for some trees about a hundred yards away. If he reached that thick growth of pines, it would be hard for Frank to find him. Frank knew he had to catch up to Lannigan before he reached the trees, if he was going to have a good chance of capturing him. Frank summoned up as much strength, speed, and stamina as he could.

The fact that Lannigan hadn't turned around and started shooting at him told Frank that Lannigan must have dropped his gun when he fell in the river. That was a lucky break, one that Frank intended to take advantage of. He drew closer, his long legs flashing now as he ran at top speed. Riding boots weren't meant for making such a dash, but Lannigan had that same problem. He slowed and began to hobble even more. Frank closed in.

When only ten feet or so separated the two men, Lannigan looked back over his shoulder and screamed, "Morgan, you bastard!" He stopped short. Frank, who was moving considerably faster than the stocky Lannigan, couldn't slow his momentum in time. Lannigan dropped down and flung himself at Frank's legs. The two men crashed together. Frank flew forward, out of control, his legs chopped from underneath him by Lannigan's diving block.

Frank slammed into the ground, rolled over, and came to a stop on his back. As he looked up, Lannigan's bulk blotted out some of the stars as the man loomed over him. Frank saw the glint of starlight on the knife in Lannigan's upraised hand. As Lannigan dove at him, Frank jerked his feet up and planted his boots in Lannigan's stomach. With a heave, he sent Lannigan flying up and over him. Lannigan yelled in surprise and alarm as he somersaulted in midair and crashed down beyond Frank.

Frank flipped over onto his belly, pushed himself onto hands and knees, and came up onto his feet. Lannigan lay a few feet away, apparently stunned. Frank's hand went to his Colt. He thumbed the rawhide thong off the hammer and palmed out the gun. As he covered Lannigan, he said, "Don't move, you son of a bitch. It's all over. You're under arrest, Lannigan."

The man still didn't move. Wary of a trick, Frank approached him carefully. When he heard Lannigan's strained, raspy breathing, he realized that something was wrong. He got a toe under Lannigan's shoulder and rolled the gunman onto his back.

The handle of the knife Lannigan had tried to use on Frank stood straight up from his chest. The blade was buried deep inside his body. Obviously, he had fallen on it when he landed.

Blood trickled blackly from both corners of Lannigan's mouth. Frank dropped to a knee beside him and said urgently, "Lannigan! Lannigan, can you hear me?"

The man's eyes flickered open. He stared up into the night, seemingly unable for a moment to focus on anything. Then his gaze found Frank, and he grated, "D-damn you . . . Morgan!"

"Looks like you're on your way out, Lannigan," Frank said bluntly. It was too late to be pulling any punches. "Did Sandeen send you after me? Don't let him get away with it, Lannigan."

"G-go . . . to hell!"

"That's where you're headed. If it was Sandeen's fault, he ought to be keeping you company, shouldn't he?"

Frank heard people moving through the grass behind him. He didn't dare take his attention off Lannigan, because the man might admit to Sandeen's involvement at any second. Anyway, Frank knew the people who were approaching were probably some of the townspeople from San Remo. That was good. Maybe they would hear Lannigan's confession. Maybe they would hear him implicate Sandeen. The more testimony against the rogue cattleman, the better.

But Lannigan just laughed hoarsely, and more blood bubbled from his mouth, and he said, "You . . . you bastard . . . Morgan . . ."

Then he took one last rattling breath, and his chest stilled. He was dead—and he hadn't admitted that it was Sandeen who had sent him to kill Frank.

"Marshal?" The worried voice belonged to Jasper Culverhouse. "Marshal, is that you? Are you all right?"

Feeling weariness wash through him, Frank stood up and holstered his gun. "I'm fine," he said as he turned to look at the group of men who had come up. He recognized Culverhouse, Willard Donohue, and a couple of the saloon keepers. "Too bad I can't say the same for Lannigan."

"He's dead?" Donohue asked.

"He's dead."

"Well, I reckon that avenges Marshal Crawford, anyway."

Vengeance was the last thing Frank cared about right now. He had lost a valuable potential witness against Sandeen. He was back almost where he had started, with the threat of a deadly range war looming over this part of the country. With Lannigan dead, Sandeen had one less gun on his side now, but in the long run that didn't matter. Sandeen could always hire more killers.

And that was exactly what he would do, until sooner or later the Mogollon Rim would look down on a range that ran red with blood.

Chapter Fifteen

Frank's clothes were soaked. He hoped he wouldn't catch a chill from that as he trudged back to the settlement with the other men. Culverhouse was going to fetch his cart and bring Lannigan's body back to the blacksmith shop, which also served as an impromptu undertaking establishment when needed.

Here lately, there had been more call for Culverhouse's services in that line of work than as a blacksmith or liveryman.

"Somebody will have to let Sandeen know what happened," Culverhouse commented. "Since Lannigan worked for him, Sandeen may want to pay for the buryin'. Otherwise, I guess I'll just take whatever's in Lannigan's pockets."

"Sorry I had to shoot his horse," Frank said. "If I hadn't, you could claim it."

Culverhouse laughed grimly. "I ain't in the buryin' business to get rich. It's just something that's got to be done, and most folks don't want to have anything to do with it."

"I may need some of that liniment of yours for my shoulder," Frank said as he worked his left arm around, trying to get some of the stiffness and soreness out of it.

"Feels like I almost jerked the arm out of its socket." He had explained to the other men how he had hung from the bridge by that arm in order to get a clear shot at Lannigan.

"Got plenty of it," Culverhouse said. He paused, then added, "Does trouble always follow you around like this, Frank?"

Frank chuckled, but there wasn't much humor in the sound. "Seems like it," he said.

Donohue and the other men went their own way when they got back to the settlement, while Frank and Culverhouse headed for the livery stable. Frank got dry clothes from his war bag and changed into them, then set his boots aside to dry. Then he sat down on a stool and cleaned and dried his Colt while Dog lay at his feet. Frank kept at the chore until he was satisfied that the gun was in perfect working order. Then and only then did he get some of Culverhouse's liniment and rub it into his shoulder, massaging the sore muscles and ligaments and letting the heat generated by the liniment work its way into them.

When he was finished with that, he climbed into the hayloft and crawled onto the makeshift bed he had formed by spreading his blankets over some of the loose hay. His pillow was his saddle, as it would have been if he were still on the trail. As he dozed off, he heard the creaking of the wheels on Culverhouse's cart and knew that he was back with Lannigan's body.

Tomorrow, Frank would ride out to Saber and let Ed Sandeen know that Lannigan was dead. It would be interesting to see what Sandeen's reaction was to that news. Frank had a suspicion that Sandeen was going to be mighty disappointed to see him riding up to the ranch house instead of Lannigan.

Sleep claimed him then, deep and dreamless.

* * *

The sound of hammering woke Frank the next morning. When he came down from the loft, he found that Culverhouse was already knocking together a coffin for Carl Lannigan. "Sorry if I disturbed you, Marshal," Culverhouse said as he paused in his hammering.

"No, that's fine," Frank assured him. "Some chores just won't wait."

"That's sure true in the undertakin' business. You headin' out to Sandeen's?"

"As soon as I've had some breakfast."

"Maybe some of us ought to ride with you," Culverhouse suggested. "Mayor Donohue and I were talkin' about it. If Sandeen wants you dead, you'll be puttin' yourself in a heap of danger by riding out to his ranch alone. He probably wouldn't try anything if there were several of us from town there with you."

Frank considered the idea. Culverhouse made a good point, but finally Frank shook his head. "I don't believe Sandeen's going to try anything. He'll be aware that all of you know I've ridden out there, and that if I disappear, suspicion will fall on him right away. The disappearance of a marshal might be enough to bring outside law in here, and Sandeen won't want that, at least not yet."

"You sure about that?"

"Last time I checked, nothing in life was a hundred per cent sure," Frank said with a smile, "but I'm not worried about Sandeen trying anything today."

Culverhouse shrugged. "Well, it's your funeral . . . but I'd just as soon not have to do the buryin'."

"Don't worry about that," Frank told him. "If Sandeen did succeed in killing me, the body would never be found. He'd see to that."

"That's sort of a grim way to look at it."

"A hazard of the profession, I guess."

"Of bein' a lawman, you mean?"

"Yeah," Frank said, although it was equally true of the

profession he had followed for years, that of a drifting gunfighter.

After he'd had his breakfast at the café and seen to it that Dog was fed, Frank saddled Stormy and got directions from Culverhouse on how to find the headquarters of Sandeen's ranch. He hadn't seen it the day before when he was riding the range on the Lazy F and Saber.

Today he followed a well-defined trail that paralleled the river for several miles and then swung southeast. The sun was shining, but there were clouds to the south that looked dark and threatening. There might be a thunderstorm that afternoon, Frank thought. He planned to be back in San Remo before any storm had time to break, though.

An hour after leaving the settlement, he came in sight of a scattering of buildings. The largest was a sprawling, one-story adobe dwelling, constructed in the Spanish style with red tile roofs and wrought-iron gates in the wall around an inner courtyard. Sandeen hadn't started this ranch but had bought it from someone else, and the place could have had other owners before that. From the looks of it, the original settler had probably been a *hacendado* from south of the border.

A building that Frank pegged as the bunkhouse was made of adobe, too, but the barns, smokehouse, cookshack, and a couple of other outbuildings were made of either logs or rough planks. There were large corrals behind the barns. Judged strictly on their headquarters, the Lazy F and Saber were pretty much equal. Sandeen's layout was impressive. But it wasn't quite as nice as Flynn's, Frank decided, and that fact had to gnaw at Sandeen's vitals, because he would be well aware of it, too. Just one more reason to be jealous of Flynn.

Someone had spotted him coming. Several men came out of the bunkhouse. A couple of dogs ran out to meet Frank, barking furiously as they loped along. They sounded like they wanted to intimidate him, but when he ignored them they quit carrying on so much.

One of the wrought-iron gates in the wall around the main house swung open. Sandeen and Vern Riley stepped out. Riley had his shotgun tucked under his arm, but Sandeen appeared to be unarmed. He wore whip-cord trousers and a white shirt open at the throat. He regarded his visitor coolly as Frank reined Stormy to a halt. The five men who had come from the bunkhouse—hard cases who were almost as cold-eyed and dangerous-looking as Vern Riley—stood to Frank's right, about fifteen feet away. They struck casual poses, thumbs hooked behind their gun belts, but Frank knew just how swiftly that casualness would vanish if trouble broke out. His eyes flicked quickly over the faces of the men, and somewhat to his surprise he found that he recognized all of them.

Quint Parker and Shad Dooley were from Texas, Luther Pettibone from Arkansas, John McCormick from Montana, and the final man, Eli Franklin, was from Kansas. All of them were fast on the draw, mighty fast. All of them had numerous killings to their credit. Frank would have felt confident against any one of them, prob-ably even two. With luck, he might have been able to take three of them. But not all five, and sure as hell not with Riley and that deadly shotgun of his on the other side.

Maybe, he thought with a grim inward chuckle, he should have taken Culverhouse up on that offer of help.

But for the moment, everybody was standing around peacefully. Sandeen had a curious expression on his face, but he didn't appear to be on the verge of ordering his men to open fire.

"Morgan," he said coolly, "something I can do for you, or are you just visiting?"

"I brought some news out here for you from town, Sandeen," Frank replied. "Carl Lannigan's dead."

Riley and the other five gunmen stiffened in surprise. More than one of the gunnies moved a hand slightly toward his holster. But none of them tried to draw. They were waiting to see how Sandeen took the news.

Frank had been watching Sandeen's face closely when he told the cattleman about Lannigan. He had seen anger flare in Sandeen's dark eyes, but no real surprise. It must have been obvious to Sandeen as soon as he laid eyes on Frank that Lannigan had failed in his mission.

"And why would that be of any interest to me?" Sandeen asked.

"Lannigan works for you, doesn't he? I thought since he was one of your riders, you'd want to see to it that he got a proper burial."

"I would," Sandeen said, "if he still worked for me." He slipped a fat cheroot out of his shirt pocket and put it in his mouth, then said around it, "I gave Lannigan his time a couple of nights ago, after he got in that fight with you in San Remo."

"You did?"

Sandeen nodded, his teeth clenching on the cheroot. "That's right. I don't want a man on my payroll who brawls with lawmen. Isn't that exactly what I told Lannigan, Vern?"

"That's right, Boss," Riley drawled. "That's what you told him."

Frank didn't believe that story for a second. He glanced at the other gunmen, thinking that they probably knew Sandeen was lying, but their faces were impassive. He couldn't read a thing in those stony visages. They would back up whatever play Sandeen wanted to make, just as Riley was doing.

Frank tried a bluff. "That's funny," he said, "because before he died, Lannigan told me that he was still working for you, Sandeen."

Sandeen's shoulders rose and fell casually. "He was lying," he said as he took the cigar out of his mouth.

"Simple as that. Carl probably had a grudge against me because I dismissed him. How did he die?"

Sandeen had been a little slow in asking that, Frank thought. Seemed to him like it should have been one of the rancher's first questions.

"He tried to kill me. We traded shots, and then during the ruckus that came after that, he fell on his own knife."

Sandeen bit off the end of the cheroot and spit it out. "Damned shame. But it's nothing to do with me, Morgan. You can bury Lannigan in a pauper's grave as far as I'm concerned."

"That the way you feel about all of your men when they fail at the errands you send them on?"

That was another shot in the dark, one intended to stir things up a mite among Sandeen's hired guns. If it did any good, though, he couldn't tell it by looking at the men.

Sandeen struck a match, puffed his cheroot into life, and then said, "You're whistling up the wrong tree, Morgan. I've told you that I didn't have anything to do with Lannigan trying to kill you. Now, if there's nothing else, I've got a ranch to run."

"No, that's all," Frank said.

"So long, then. Maybe I'll see you in San Remo."

Frank nodded curtly and said, "Count on it." Then he turned Stormy and rode slowly away from the ranch house. Again, he could feel that imaginary target itching on his back.

Nothing happened, though. He heeled Stormy into a trot and soon left the ranch headquarters behind.

Frustration seethed inside Frank. No sooner had he formed his plan of trying to capture one of Sandeen's killers and persuading the man to testify against Sandeen than the perfect opportunity to do just that had presented itself. Given enough time, he could have broken Lannigan's nerve; he was confident of that.

But bad luck had stolen that chance from him. Lannigan was dead and couldn't testify against anyone. Now Frank had to start over, trying to keep the peace in San Remo while at the same time getting the proof he needed to put Sandeen behind bars and head off the range war.

He decided to head back to the settlement by way of the Lazy F. He was curious how Laura Flynn was doing the day after she had been shot. If he stopped there, his presence might irritate Jeff Buckston, but the foreman would just have to control his temper.

A gust of cool wind from behind him nearly lifted Frank's hat off his head. He turned and saw that the cloud bank was moving faster than he had expected it to. It was almost overhead now, and it wouldn't be long before the dark gray clouds swallowed up the sun. Lightning flickered faintly in the distance, slender, pale-yellow fingers that clawed at the sky. Frank heard the low rumble of thunder.

Maybe it was a good thing he had planned to stop at Flynn's place. He didn't want to get caught out in a thunderstorm. With so many tall pines around, lightning was always a danger. And while many areas of Arizona Territory were bone-dry most of the time, up here in this rugged range country a storm could turn quickly into a downpour. Frank had gotten wet enough from that dunking in the river the night before; he didn't have any desire to get soaked by rain now.

"Come on, Stormy," he said, urging the horse on to a faster pace. "Let's find somewhere to get in out of this blasted weather."

The wind had picked up, blowing even harder now, and Frank could smell the rain on it. The air felt strange, as if heavily charged by some force. Frank estimated that he was still a mile or so away from the Lazy F ranch house. As the wind buffeted him and he had to ride with one hand on his head to hold his hat on, he begin to think that he wouldn't reach Flynn's before the storm hit.

He was right. He heard a soft thud as something hit the crown of his hat. A second later there was another impact and another. A big, fat drop of rain struck his shoulder so hard that it stung a little. Yes, sir, he thought, this was going to be a real gullywasher and toad-strangler before it was over.

The rain began to fall harder and faster. Frank's slicker was rolled up behind his saddle. He untied the thongs that held it on, shook it out, and pulled it on. His shirt was already damp, but the yellow slicker would keep him from getting completely soaked. At least he hoped so. He tilted his head forward so that water would run off the front brim of his hat rather than dripping down his neck.

Again, he wondered why he had ridden over to Arizona Territory in the first place. He could have just as easily gone north from New Mexico to Colorado. Someplace where people wouldn't shoot at him all the time and try to wallop the hell out of him and he could go two days without getting soaked for one reason or another . . .

The sound of the shot penetrated even the rushing noise of the rain. Frank's head jerked up. He hadn't been hit, and neither had Stormy. He didn't even know if the shot had been aimed at him. All he could be sure of was that the sharp report had come from in front of him somewhere. A second later it was followed by a heavier boom, the sound of a different gun, and then a quick pair of shots from the first weapon.

Somebody was in trouble up there, and Frank intended to find out what was going on. He dug his heels into Stormy's flanks and said, "Let's go, big fella!"

Stormy leaped into a gallop. Frank was riding on the side of a hill, on a fairly open shoulder with a wooded slope rising to his right. The shoulder curved naturally as it followed the hill, and as Frank rounded the turn he spotted movement up ahead. It was hard to see clearly through the sluicing rain, but as he drew nearer, a rider-less horse suddenly loomed up and bolted past him. In the brief look he got, Frank didn't see any blood on the saddle, but that didn't mean anything. It was raining hard enough to wash away any blood that had been spilled.

He rode in the direction the stampeding horse had come from. Up ahead was a deadfall at the edge of the trail. Frank saw a man standing behind the fallen tree, looking down at something. Frank couldn't make out any details except that the man wore a yellow slicker much like his.

The man must have heard Stormy's hoofbeats, be-cause he turned sharply toward Frank. Frank saw his hand come up with a gun in it. Frank leaned low over Stormy's neck and reached under his slicker for his own Colt as the revolver in the man's hand boomed.

Luck was against Frank for a change. Despite the downpour and the hurried shot, the bullet raked Stormy's neck and then clipped the top of Frank's left shoulder with stunning impact. Stormy jumped from the pain. Frank reeled in the saddle and almost fell, but he managed to hang on and lift his gun, triggering three fast shots toward the mysterious gunman. The man turned and ran, and from the way he scampered nimbly up the hillside, Frank knew none of his shots had found their target. He tried to turn Stormy to head up the rise after the gunman, but the horse's hooves slipped on the trail, which had been turned muddy by the torrential rain. As Stormy jolted to the side, Frank tried to grab for the horn with his left arm, but it was numb from the bullet graze on his shoulder. He felt himself falling, and instinctively kicked his feet free from the stirrups.

He was able to hold on to the gun as he slammed down into the mud. Looking up, he blinked against the rain that streamed into his eyes and tried to locate the man with whom he had traded shots. He couldn't see the no-good skalleyhooter anywhere. He thought he heard hoofbeats, though, which probably meant that the man had reached his horse and was fleeing.

The man had been looking at something behind that deadfall, Frank recalled. With a bad feeling inside him, he pushed himself to his feet and stumbled along the trail toward the fallen tree. His left shoulder and arm were still numb, but he could use his right hand and his gun if he needed to. Right now, that was all that mattered.

He came around the end of the big log and stopped short. A man lay there on his back, concealed from Frank's sight until now. Blood welled from the bullet holes in his chest, and the rain diluted the crimson into pink streams. The man's hat had fallen off, revealing thick white hair. His tanned, weathered face was contorted in deep trenches of shock and pain.

Frank was looking down at Howard Flynn. The man was either dead or soon would be.

More hoofbeats made Frank lift his head from the grim scene before him. He saw several riders pounding toward him from the direction of the Lazy F headquarters. He couldn't be sure, but he thought one of them was Jeff Buckston. The others were bound to be more of Flynn's crew.

And here Frank stood over the body of Howard Flynn himself, gun in hand, three bullets gone from the Colt's cylinder, three blood-leaking holes in Flynn's chest.

Colorado was looking better and better . . . but suddenly Frank had serious doubts that he would ever see the place again.

Chapter Sixteen

Stormy stood several yards away, reins dangling. Frank knew he could reach the horse and get mounted before the riders got there, but they were so close he wouldn't stand a chance of getting away. And once the men saw that Flynn had been shot, they would probably open fire on Frank and blow him out of the saddle.

Like it or not, Fate had conspired to put him in a very bad situation. He hoped he could convince Buckston to listen to reason. A couple of days earlier, when they first met, that might have been possible. Now, after the trouble between them, Frank didn't know if it was or not.

He slid his gun back in its holster and then pulled the slicker over it. When the riders galloped up to the deadfall and reined their horses to a stop, Frank stood there waiting calmly.

One of the riders was Buckston, all right, just as Frank had thought, and now that he could see the other men he recognized them from his visit to the Lazy F, too. One of them was Caleb Glover, the middle-aged black puncher who kept company with Mary Elizabeth Warren. All of them looked shocked and angry when they saw Flynn's body.

Buckston drew his gun and pointed it at Frank. "Don't move, you son of a bitch! Try anything and I'll blow your damn head off!"

It had been mighty difficult for Frank to just stand motionless while Buckston slapped leather. Every instinct in his body cried out for him to draw and fire. But part of knowing how to use a gun was knowing when *not* to use it, and Frank sensed that this was one of those moments.

"Take it easy, Buckston," he said, his voice loud and clear and powerful over the pounding of the rain. "I didn't shoot your boss."

"Then who in blazes did?" Buckston demanded. "You're the only one here!"

"Another man traded shots with Flynn. I rode up right afterward and saw him. He threw a shot at me and then headed for the tall and uncut. I was winged and took a tumble off my horse when it slipped in the mud, so I wasn't able to go after him."

Frank gestured toward the bullet-torn shoulder of the slicker as proof of the wound. Buckston just shook his head stubbornly and said, "Mr. Flynn could have grazed you. We heard shots from two different guns, and I recognized the sound of that old Remington of his."

Actually, there had been three different guns fired, Frank thought, but the killer had been using a Colt Peacemaker like his, so they had sounded the same. The report of the Remington had been the heavier, duller booms he had heard. Come to think of it, the shot that had winged him had been fired from that gun, which now lay beside Flynn with the rain pouring down on it. The killer had picked it up, fired it toward Frank, and then dropped it before he ran off. Frank put that chain of events together in his mind and knew it was the only explanation that made sense.

But why? What the hell was going on here?

He was in deadly danger, that's what was going on, he reminded himself. Flynn's men looked like they wanted to fill him full of lead, at the very least. Or they might just throw a lariat over a tree limb and string him up. Frontier justice for what looked to them like a clear case of murder, with the man whose brand they rode for as the victim.

"That other man shot Flynn, I tell you, not me," Frank insisted. "Why in the world would I want to kill him? We parted on decent terms yesterday, if you'll just remember, Buckston."

"Maybe," Buckston said. "Or maybe you been playactin' all along, Morgan, and really *are* workin' for Sandeen. You've got a rep as a gunfighter, and that kind of man usually rides for whoever's willin' to pay the most."

"That's crazy. Sandeen hates me because I refused to work for him. Not only that, but I killed several of his men, including Carl Lannigan last night."

Buckston's bushy eyebrows rose in surprise. Obviously he hadn't heard about Lannigan's death. But then he said adamantly, "You can talk all you want, but it don't change what I saw with my own eyes." He gestured with the barrel of his gun. "Shuck your hogleg and hand it over."

Frank hesitated. Once Buckston saw that three rounds had been fired from the Colt, he would be more convinced than ever that those were the three bullets in Flynn's body. But faced with these odds, there was nothing else Frank could do except cooperate. He pushed the slicker back, drew his gun slowly and carefully from the holster, and handed it up butt-first to Buckston.

Meanwhile, Caleb Glover had dismounted and knelt beside Flynn's body. He moved the cattleman's shirt aside to get a look at the wounds.

Buckston checked the cylinder of Frank's Peacemaker. "Three empty shells!" he said in a scathing voice. "Damn it, Morgan, if that's not proof—"

"I fired those three shots at the man who really killed Flynn—" Frank began arguing.

Glover cut them both off by exclaiming, "The boss ain't dead! He's still alive!"

That got everyone's attention. Frank turned toward Flynn and saw that the old man's eyes were open. They were unfocused, however, and he was only barely conscious. His head moved a little from side to side as his mouth opened and closed and he struggled to breathe. The rain had tapered off some, so it wasn't as loud now. Frank heard a whistling sound coming from Flynn and knew that at least one of the slugs had gone through a lung.

Glover leaned over him and said, "Boss! Boss, can you hear me?"

With a visible effort, Flynn turned his head toward Glover and tried to lock his eyes on the puncher's face. "Sh-shot!" he gasped.

Glover didn't offer Flynn any false hope or encouragement. All of the men knew that with three bullet holes through his chest, the cattleman wasn't going to make it. So instead, Glover asked, "Who shot you, Boss? Can you tell me? Who did this to you?"

"Sl-slicker . . . yellow slicker . . ."

Buckston, Glover, and the other Lazy F men looked at Frank, who stood there wearing a yellow slicker.

Knowing that he was probably wasting his time, Frank said, "The other man had on a yellow slicker, too, pretty much like this one. Hell, half the men in the country wear one when it rains! A couple of you are wearing them right now."

"Yeah, but we were all together," Buckston said. "That does it. I've heard all I need to hear. You're gonna swing for this, Morgan."

"I tell you—"

Buckston jerked his gun savagely. "Shut up! I don't want to hear any more of your lies." He turned his head. "Caleb, get back to the house as quick as you can and bring the wagon back for the boss. Maybe we can patch him up. . . ."

Buckston fell silent as he saw the way Glover was shaking his head. "No need for hurryin' now," the black cowboy said. "Poor Mr. Flynn's gone. Those were his last words."

Buckston took a deep breath and his face hardened even more. "A dying man's last words," he said. "You don't get any better proof than that."

"Except in this case you're wrong," Frank snapped. "And you're letting the real killer get away."

"I'm gonna enjoy seein' you dance at the end of a rope, Morgan," Buckston said, his eyes narrowing.

Frank's breath hissed between his teeth. Buckston wasn't going to believe him. Hell, he thought, if the situation had been reversed, he might not have believed a story like the one he had just told, either. So there was only one thing left for him to do.

As Glover wearily stood up from where he had knelt beside Flynn, Frank suddenly lunged behind him. The numbness had started to wear off in Frank's left arm, which meant it was beginning to hurt like hell, but the muscles still worked and he flung that arm around Glover's neck and tightened it as much as he could. At the same time, his right hand plucked the Colt from the holster on Glover's hip. The gun rose menacingly.

"Hold your fire!" Buckston yelled. They couldn't start shooting without running too big a risk of hitting Glover.

Frank hated like hell having to hide behind somebody. It went against the grain, went against everything that made him who he was. But right now he had no choice, because he realized that his only chance of clearing his name was to find out who had really killed Howard Flynn. He couldn't do that if he was locked up somewhere. He had to be free to move around and investigate.

"Drop your guns!" he ordered Buckston and the other Lazy F cowboys.

"Mister, you're makin' the worst mistake of your life," Buckston grated.

"No, the worst mistake would be letting you railroad me for something I didn't do. Now drop 'em, damn it!"

Glover said, "Don't you listen to him, Buck. He killed the boss. You go ahead and ventilate him, and don't worry about me."

Buckston's face worked as different emotions warred inside him. Finally, he said, "You know I can't do that, Caleb. For one thing, Mary Elizabeth would never forgive me if I got you killed." He sighed. "You heard Morgan, boys. Drop 'em."

He started by letting his own pistol fall to the ground. Slowly, reluctantly, the other men dropped their pistols. Frank told them to shuck their saddle guns, too.

"Now back your horses away," he ordered. "I want you at least a hundred yards up the trail before I turn Glover loose."

"You can't get away," Buckston warned. "We know every foot of this country. We'll hunt you down like the lobo wolf you are, Morgan."

"Just do what I told you, and nobody will have to get hurt."

"Too late for that," Buckston said with a meaningful glance at Howard Flynn's body.

"Back off," Frank said again.

Buckston and the other men backed their horses for several yards, then turned and rode along the muddy trail in the direction they had come from.

"That's far enough," Frank called to them. "Now dismount and stampede those horses!"

"Damn you, Morgan—" Buckston began.

Frank pointed the gun in his hand at Glover's head. "Do it!"

Threatening an unarmed man like that gnawed at his

vitals, too. When word of this got around, it wouldn't help his reputation. But again, it couldn't be helped.

The men swung down from their horses, shouted and waved their arms, and slapped the animals on the rump with their hats. The horses bolted, running off down the trail. Now the cowboys wouldn't be able to give chase as soon as Frank released Glover. They would have to round up their spooked mounts first, and that would take a while. With that much of a lead, Frank was confident that he could give them the slip on Stormy.

"Mr. Morgan, you're a dead man," Glover croaked past the arm that Frank pressed firmly to his throat. "I hope you know that."

"Listen to me, Glover," Frank said, his voice pitched low enough so that only the black puncher could hear. "I'm sorry I had to grab you like this. I'd rather face my troubles straight on. But Buckston wasn't going to believe me, no matter what I said."

"Why should he? Why should any of us?"

"Because I'm telling you the truth," Frank said. "I swear, Glover, I didn't shoot Flynn. It happened just the way I said. There was another man in a yellow slicker. He had a horse tied somewhere up the hill. I'd tell you to go look for the tracks, but the rain will have washed them all away by now."

Glover grunted. "Mighty convenient rain, ain't it?"

"Not for me. But one way or another I'm going to find out who killed Flynn, and I'll prove it. All I need is a little time. . . ."

"You won't get it," Glover said. "Buck meant what he said. Every man on the Lazy F is gonna be huntin' you now, Morgan. You won't get away. Be better if you just give up and take what you got comin' to you."

"I can't do that," Frank said. He whistled, and Stormy came trotting over to him. "I'm sorry about this, Glover. Believe that if you don't believe anything else I've said."

And with that he delivered a short, chopping blow

with the gun to Glover's head. The cowboy's hat absorbed some of the force, but Frank hit him hard enough to stun him, and a hard shove sent him sprawling on the ground next to Howard Flynn's body. Frank whirled away, stuck a foot in a stirrup, grabbed the saddle horn, and swung up into the saddle even as Stormy was breaking into a run. Behind him, Frank heard angry yells from Buckston and the other men. He knew they had seen him wallop Glover. When he glanced over his shoulder, he saw that they were already running after their horses, eager to get mounted and on his trail.

Frank slipped Glover's gun into his holster as he leaned forward in the saddle and sent Stormy up the hill toward the trees where the real killer had disappeared a short time earlier. He saw the angry red welt on the Appaloosa's neck where the same bullet that had nicked Frank's shoulder had grazed the horse. The rain, which by now was just a drizzle, had washed the wound clean of blood. Frank knew Stormy would be all right.

He couldn't say the same for himself, because in a matter of minutes he would have a group of angry cowboys coming after him, like a pack of hounds after a fox, eager to tear their prey to shreds.

But there was one big difference.

This fox was Frank Morgan, The Drifter.

Chapter Seventeen

It was a fuming mad Jeff Buckston who led the sorry procession into the yard in front of the big house around noon. Although the rain had stopped, the sky overhead was still heavily overcast, so that it was impossible to tell exactly where the sun was. Everyone was mounted again, and since they had found the boss's horse a few hundred yards down the trail, Flynn's body had been put on it and tied over the saddle.

That was after they had chased Frank Morgan for a while and found that the bastard had gotten away. At that time the rain was still falling hard enough to wash out any tracks Morgan had left, and anyway, it was difficult to follow a trail through those thick stands of pine. The carpet of fallen needles on the ground had a tendency to spring back up and conceal any evidence of someone passing that way.

That Appaloosa of Morgan's was fast and strong, too. Buckston and his companions had searched all over the hill and for a mile beyond it without finding a trace of Morgan. They had left Glover to watch over the body of their murdered boss, just in case any scavengers tried to bother it.

Now, as they rode in with Buckston leading the horse

that carried the grim burden, the foreman of the Lazy F thought about what Howard Flynn's death was going to mean. As far as Buckston knew, the boss's only living relative was his niece Laura. Flynn had made a will once, leaving everything to his wife and children, and Buckston happened to know that the document hadn't been changed after the deaths of the other members of Flynn's immediate family. He wasn't the nosy sort, but he had seen the will among some papers on Flynn's desk recently and had read enough of it to see the terms before he told himself to quit poking into things that were none of his business.

So as far as Buckston could see, that meant Laura Flynn was now the owner of the Lazy F. That was probably going to come as one hell of a surprise to her—along with the fact of her uncle's murder, of course.

Laura didn't know anything about running a ranch. She would have to rely on someone else, and Buckston knew who she would rely on—him. That thought made him uneasy. He liked Laura and knew she liked him, but he didn't want anybody thinking that he was trying to take advantage of her now that she owned the Lazy F. He wanted Laura to think that least of all. So he was going to have to be careful and make sure everything was done properly, open and aboveboard. That might make it harder in the long run for whatever had been developing between him and Laura to grow into a real romance, but if that was the case, then so be it. Jeff Buckston's honor meant more to him than almost anything else.

That was one reason he was so damned mad now. His instincts had told him at first that Frank Morgan was a good man, despite his reputation as a gunfighter. The first day they had met, Buckston would have almost said that he and Morgan were kindred spirits.

That sure had changed in a couple of days' time.

Now Morgan was the enemy, a kill-crazy gunman who had murdered the finest man Jeff Buckston had ever known. Buckston was going to hunt Morgan down and avenge Howard Flynn's death if it was the last thing he ever did.

As they drew rein in front of the house, Caleb Glover said quietly, "I sure don't envy you the job you got comin', Buck. That little gal and the boss were close, especially considerin' she ain't been out here all that long."

Buckston sighed and nodded. "Yeah, I know." He looked over at Glover. "How's your head?"

Glover lifted his hat, gingerly touched the spot where Morgan had clouted him, and winced. "Hurts like blazes. Got a nice goose egg up there, too. But I reckon I'll be all right. This ol' noggin o' mine is pretty hard. And if I didn't know better, I'd say that Morgan was bein' careful not to hit me too hard."

Buckston scowled. "Why would a gunslingin' bastard like that care who he hurt?"

Quietly, Glover said, "You know, Buck, he told me again that he didn't shoot the boss."

"You saw the evidence with your own eyes," Buckston said impatiently.

"Yeah . . . but sometimes there's more'n one way of lookin' at the things you see."

"Not to me," Buckston snapped. He swung down out of the saddle and whipped the reins around the hitching post. "Wait a few minutes to give me a chance to talk to Miss Laura, then a couple of you bring the boss's body into the parlor."

He went up the steps and into the house. He didn't know where Laura was, but he found her a moment later in the kitchen, where she was talking to Acey-Deucy.

"Hello, Jeff," she said as she turned toward him with a smile. She looked fetching in a white blouse and a long green skirt. Her left arm was cradled in a black silk sling. Buckston hadn't seen her that morning before he and the boys rode out to make their usual rounds of the high country pastures. As always, her loveliness almost took his breath away.

What he was about to tell her would drive that smile right off her face, he thought regretfully.

But postponing it wouldn't make things any easier, so he took a deep breath and said, "Miss Laura, I reckon you'd better sit down. I got some mighty bad news for you."

Her eyes widened, and sure enough, her smile disappeared. "My goodness," she said. "What is it, Jeff?"

He pulled out a chair from the table. "Sit first," he said.

She sank into the chair and stared up at him. Acey-Deucy looked pretty worried, too. Laura said, "You're scaring me, Jeff."

"Sorry," he said. "There ain't no good way to tell you this, so I'll just say it straight out. Your uncle's dead. Frank Morgan shot him."

Laura's wide blue eyes blinked a couple of times. They began to glisten with tears. "Uncle Howard?" she said in a hollow voice. "Uncle Howard is . . . dead?"

"I'm afraid so. We've got his body outside. Some of the boys will, uh, bring it into the parlor." Buckston looked at the cook. "Acey-Deucy, get a blanket and spread it on the divan in there. The boss's clothes are wet from the rain."

And the blood, Buckston thought, but he didn't say that.

Laura leaned forward slightly, brought her right hand up to her eyes, and began to sob. Buckston wanted to take her into his arms, hold her, and tell her that everything was going to be all right, that he would take care of her and protect her, but of course it would be way too forward of him to do that. He settled for awkwardly patting her shoulder a couple of times and saying, "I'm sure sorry, Miss Laura."

For the next few minutes there was considerable scrambling around in the house as Laura continued to sit in the kitchen and cry. Then Glover came in and said quietly to Buckston, "We got the boss laid out in the parlor, Buck."

Laura began to wipe her wet, red-rimmed eyes. "I . . . I have to see him," she said as she started to get to her feet. Buckston took hold of her right arm to help her, just in case she was unsteady. Even under these tragic circumstances, he was aware of the firm round warmth of her arm through the sleeve of her blouse.

Many of the ranch hands had crowded into the parlor and gathered around the divan where Flynn's body was laid out. He was wrapped in a blanket so that only his face was visible. The bloody ruin of his chest was hidden from Laura, and Buckston was glad of that. He led her over to the divan and stood beside her, still gripping her arm, being careful not to hold her too tightly.

"Oh, Uncle Howard!" Laura wailed as she looked down into the rugged, weathered face. Death had smoothed out Flynn's features somewhat; they weren't as contorted from pain as they had been at first. That was something else Buckston was grateful for.

Laura went on, "You . . . you gave me a home . . . and now you're gone. I . . . I'm so sorry." She turned to Buckston, and an edge of savage anger crept into her voice as she asked, "You said Frank Morgan did this?"

"We found him standing over the boss's body, the gun still in his hand."

"That doesn't sound like something Mr. Morgan would do. When I met him he didn't seem like a . . . a cold-blooded killer. But if you found him like that . . ." She stopped and drew a deep breath, and her voice was stronger as she went on. "I want you to find him, Jeff. I want you to find him and bring him to justice."

Buckston nodded and said, "That's just exactly what I plan on doin', Miss Laura."

* * *

For a saloon in a settlement like San Remo, a rainy day killed business. There weren't that many people in town, so the saloons depended on the cowboys who worked in the area for their customers. On a day like this, when there had been thunder and lightning and then a drenching downpour that finally settled into a steady drizzle, nobody wanted to get out and ride miles into town just for a drink or a roll in the hay with one of San Remo's three, count 'em, three soiled doves.

So Alonzo Hightower was pretty bored as he stood behind the bar in the Mogollon Saloon, lazily polishing the hardwood with a damp rag. He had sent his bartender home and was taking care of the saloon's two customers himself. One was a gambler named Farrell who had drifted into town a week or so earlier and probably would be drifting on pretty soon because the pickin's here were so slim. He sat at a table playing solitaire. The other customer was Mayor Willard Donohue, who hardly counted because he already had a tab that was a mile long and paid on it only once in a blue moon. Donohue stood at the bar, sipping now and then from a mug of beer. The atmosphere of boredom in the place was oppressive.

That was why Hightower looked up with interest as he heard a horse going by in the street outside, its hooves splashing softly in the mud. Maybe the rider was a stranger, or at least somebody interesting.

He was a stranger, all right, dressed in black from head to toe. He reined his horse to a stop in front of the saloon and just sat there in the saddle for a long moment, staring over the batwings into the Mogollon, as if he were trying to decide whether or not he wanted to come in. Since it was a gloomy day outside because of all the clouds, Hightower couldn't see the man's face very well. The broad brim of the black hat obscured the stranger's features even more. Hightower caught a glimpse of a hawk nose, and he thought the man had red hair but wasn't sure about that.

But even without being able to see the stranger very well, something about him struck a chord in Hightower, and the sound it produced wasn't a pleasant one. The rain had cooled things off considerably, but now an actual chill went through the saloon keeper, as if the temperature had dropped another twenty degrees in a matter of a second.

Or as if someone had just walked over his grave.

Then the stranger lifted his reins, clucked to his horse, and turned the animal away from the saloon. Slowly, he rode out of sight.

Hightower kept staring for a moment. There had been so much raw ferocity in the man that it seemed impossible he was gone. Something about him, an aura of sorts, seemed to linger in the air where he had been before slowly dissipating.

Hightower swallowed hard and looked over at Donohue. The mayor had swung around and was looking out the saloon entrance, too. His face was pale and he licked his lips nervously.

"You saw him, too, didn't you?" Hightower asked.

Donohue jumped a little, startled by Hightower's voice. "You mean that fella dressed all in black? Yeah, of course I saw him. Why wouldn't I have seen him? He was real, wasn't he? I mean, he wasn't some sort o' haunt or something, was he?"

"Seemed real enough to me," Hightower said. "Sure was a mean-looking fella, though."

"Yeah. Don't know what it was about him. He was just another hombre, but at the same time he was . . ." Donohue searched for a word.

"Spooky," Hightower supplied.

"That's right," Donohue said with a fervent nod. "That's it exactly. Spooky."

"Why do you reckon he just looked in the door and didn't come in here?"

Donohue rubbed his grizzled jaw in thought. Finally,

he said, "If I had to guess, I'd say he was lookin' for somebody . . . and I don't know about you, 'Lonzo, but I'm damned glad the fella he was lookin' for ain't in here."

Mitch Kite had been running the Verde Saloon for Ed Sandeen for about a year, ever since Sandeen had bought it from Ford Fargo, who had tired of Arizona and headed for California. Kite was a medium-sized, fair-haired man of indeterminate age who thought life in San Remo was boring as all hell. But no sheriff's deputies ever came around here, and for a man with reward dodgers out on him in four states and two territories—none of them Arizona—it made a good place to lie low. Still, Kite's restless nature was such that he knew he would have to move on eventually, even though it meant running the risk of having the law after him again.

The Verde wasn't much busier than the Mogollon, but he still had one bartender on duty, a balding gent named Speckler who had the biggest Adam's apple Kite had ever seen. Kite was sitting at a table drinking with a whore called Sweet Susie, whose sour disposition meant that she rarely lived up to her name. Kite was musing on the possibility of taking her to one of the rooms out back, but it almost seemed like more trouble than it would be worth.

That was when the stranger dressed in black pushed the batwings aside and walked into the saloon, pausing just inside the entrance to look around the room. When Kite saw that, he thought it looked exactly like a drawing he had seen once on the cover of a dime novel, and he almost laughed out loud at the melodramatic nature of the gesture, as well as the sinister all-black outfit.

But then the stranger's gaze touched him, and suddenly Kite was glad that he hadn't laughed. Very glad indeed, because something about the man said that he wasn't the type of hombre who would be happy about being laughed at.

After a moment, the stranger walked on over to the bar. Speckler came up to ask him what he wanted, and the two men talked quietly for a moment. Then Kite was surprised to see the bartender nod toward *him*. Speckler even pointed at him, for God's sake! The man in black nodded and turned toward the table where Kite sat with Sweet Susie. Kite's heart pounded in his chest. The man might be a bounty hunter, bent on claiming the reward from one of those dodgers that had Kite's face and a different name on them.

The stranger didn't appear too menacing as he walked toward the table, though, except for the cold glint in his eyes that reminded Kite of a rattlesnake's eyes. And the way that his hand never strayed far from the stag-butted revolver on his hip, under the long black coat. And the air of coiled violence just waiting to be unleashed.

Come to think of it, Kite realized as a chill went through him, the closer this son of a bitch got, the scarier he became.

But Kite could be a scary son of a bitch himself when he needed to be, so he steeled his nerves and said quietly to Sweet Susie, "Go ahead and get out of here."

The whore glanced nervously at the approaching stranger and said quickly, "You don't have to tell me twice, Boss." With that she was up and moving toward the bar, angling away from the stranger so that she wouldn't have to pass too close to him.

The stranger stopped by the table and said, "You're the fella who runs this place?"

"That's right," Kite said. "Something I can do for you?"

"I'm looking for a man."

If he said Gil Hunter or James Malone or Harry Sloan or any of the other names Kite had used in the past, Kite was going to twist his right wrist and cause the derringer under his sleeve to slip into his palm from its spring-loaded holster, and then he was going to plant a couple of .32 slugs right in this bastard's belly. That might not be enough to stop the stranger from drawing and killing him, but Kite was damned sure going to try.

"His name is Frank Morgan," the stranger went on.

Kite felt the tension go out of him. He smiled and said, "Sit down and have a drink, my friend. You've come to the right place. As of a couple of days ago, Frank Morgan is now the marshal of San Remo."

One of the red eyebrows quirked just slightly, but that was the only indication of surprise that the stranger allowed. "Is that so?" he said mildly.

Some manhunters—and there was no doubt in Kite's mind that was what this stranger was—might have been upset to discover that their quarry was packing a lawman's badge. But Kite had the feeling it wouldn't matter to the stranger that the man he had come to San Remo to kill now wore a tin star.

Not one damned bit.

Chapter Eighteen

Chilled, wet, and miserable, Frank huddled in a tiny cave in the hills as night fell. He had found the place around mid-afternoon. More of a niche in the side of a hill, tucked away underneath a cliff that bulged out above it, the cave was barely big enough for both Frank and Stormy. But they were out of the rain here, and more importantly, out of sight of anybody who came looking for them.

He knew he had given Buckston and the other Lazy F hands the slip earlier in the day. He had gotten up high enough to watch his back trail, and although he had spotted the riders twice, he could tell from the way they were wandering around that they didn't have any real idea where he was. He had waited until they were gone, then resumed his climb toward the Mogollon Rim.

Just because Buckston and the other men finally had turned back didn't mean that Frank was in the clear, and he knew it. Buckston would have wanted to get Howard Flynn's body back to the ranch house and tell the cattleman's niece what had happened. But Frank had a feeling that once Buckston had attended to that grim chore, the ranch foreman would be back out on the range again, searching for the man he believed to be Flynn's murderer.

After finding the cave, Frank had brought in a small pile of broken branches and moss from the trees that covered the hillside. At first the branches were too wet to burn, but he had been letting them dry all afternoon and now, as the light of day faded, he hoped they were dry enough to catch fire. He took a waterproof tin container that held matches from his saddlebags and knelt beside the branches. He made a small mound with some of the moss, which definitely had dried and would serve as tinder, and arranged some of the branches around it, leaning them against each other to form a tepeelike structure. Then he snapped one of the matches to life with his thumbnail and held the flame to the moss.

It caught right away, blackening and curling as a tendril of smoke rose from it. A few tiny flames leaped up and caressed the pine branches. Frank leaned over and blew gently on the fire, causing it to flare up a little more. Even the faint light that it gave off seemed bright in the gloom of the cave. More smoke twisted into the air. Flames danced around the branches. . . .

And went out.

Frank bit back a curse. Railing against the bad luck that had followed him ever since he rode into these parts wouldn't do any good. If a man didn't like how things were going, he took action and changed the course of events, even if it was something as simple as starting a fire. He poked more moss between the branches and struck another match. Again he lit the tinder and leaned over to blow on it.

This time one of the branches caught. Frank's lips drew back from his teeth in an expression that was half smile, half grimace of relief. He fed a little more moss to the tiny fire and made the flames dance higher and stronger. They spread to more of the pine branches. A bit of heat rose from the fire, but it was quickly swallowed up by the damp, chilly air inside the cave.

The Appaloosa let out a soft whicker and stirred restlessly. "Take it easy, big fella," Frank told him. "I know you don't like being this close to a fire, but we can't help it. The quarters are pretty cramped in here."

That was an understatement. He and Stormy both were practically on top of the small campfire. But Frank needed the flames, so he spoke in a soothing voice to the horse and continued to feed branches into the fire until he had a nice little blaze that wouldn't go out for a while. Nor would it be easy to spot from outside, and the gathering darkness could conceal the smoke that drifted from the mouth of the cave. Without any real ventilation other than the cave entrance, the air in the little niche in the hillside quickly became somewhat smoky, but Frank and Stormy would just have to put up with that annoyance.

Warmth filled the air along with smoke, and it soon made Frank feel better. He had taken off his slicker, but his damp clothing hadn't really dried much during the afternoon. Now it began to.

Earlier, Frank had worked the left shoulder of his shirt down so that he could take a look at the bullet wound. That hadn't been easy, since the blood had dried partially and the cloth wanted to stick. But he had been careful about freeing it and hadn't done any more damage. The graze was similar to the one Laura Flynn had received on her arm from the bushwhacker during the attack the day before. The raw welt on top of Frank's shoulder had bled quite a bit, but the bullet hadn't chipped the bone and he was grateful for that. Now all he had to do was see to it that the wound didn't fester, and since he didn't have any whiskey or anything else he could use to clean it, there was only one option.

He didn't normally carry a knife on his belt, but there was a sheathed one in his saddlebag. He took it out, slid the keen blade from its sheath, and hunkered beside the fire, holding the knife so that the flames licked around the blade. After a few minutes, the cold steel wasn't cold anymore. It glowed red with heat instead. Frank looked over at his injured shoulder, looked at the knife, and then took a deep breath. He lifted the knife from the fire and pressed the cherry-red blade to the wound. It made a faint sizzling sound.

His breath hissed sharply between his teeth at the pain that went through him. But he held the hot knife in place, burning away any possible infection and sealing the wound. The smell that rose from what he was doing made him gag slightly when he got a whiff of it. Finally, with a gasp of relief, he pulled the blade away from the wound and slumped back against the wall of the cave.

Stormy whickered again. "Yeah," Frank muttered. "It was bad, all right. I'm sorry, fella."

He apologized because he knew he had to do that same thing with the wound on Stormy's shoulder. With a grim look on his face, resigned to the task, Frank held the knife blade in the flames again and watched as it began to glow once more.

The Appaloosa bore the pain almost as stoically as his master had, but Frank was glad when it was over anyway. He sat down cross-legged by the fire, leaning against the wall again, and enjoyed the warmth that came from the flames. It made him a little drowsy, but the sharp hunger in his belly kept him from dozing off. He hadn't expected to be away from San Remo overnight, so he hadn't brought any supplies with him. He had nothing to eat except a bit of jerky left in his saddlebag from when he had been riding the trail before he ever reached the Mogollon country. He planned to get it out and gnaw on it later, but he wanted to wait as long as he could before he did that.

Something besides hunger kept him awake, as well. The wheels of his brain were spinning rapidly as he tried to sort out everything that had happened and what it was all going to mean. First and foremost, he was a fugitive now, and whatever course of action he followed, he would have to take into account the fact that Buckston and the other Lazy F punchers would be combing these hills for him. Frank suspected that they would shoot on sight, too, if they caught as much as a glimpse of him. Under the circumstances, he couldn't blame them.

Not that he was going to sit back and let them hunt him down and kill him. Not by a long shot. There had to be a way to find out who the mysterious gunman in the yellow slicker was and prove it.

Frank's gut told him that Sandeen was behind Howard Flynn's murder. Sandeen probably hadn't pulled the trigger himself, but one of his men almost certainly had. Frank closed his eyes and mulled it over. Sandeen hated him, no doubt about that, and had sent Lannigan to try to kill him. After Frank's visit to Saber, Sandeen could have put another of those hired killers on his trail, maybe one of the gun-throwers Frank had seen at the ranch or even Vern Riley himself. Say it was Riley, Frank thought. Riley could have followed him away from Saber and maybe circled around and gotten in front of him to set up an ambush.

But then, before Frank could come along to be bush-whacked, who had ridden up other than Howard Flynn himself, an even bigger enemy of Sandeen's than The Drifter. Riley, or whoever the gunman really was, had spotted Flynn and had also known that Frank was nearby, heading in that direction. So he guns down Flynn, in hopes that Frank would come along and be caught by Flynn's riders and blamed for the killing. . . .

That was too much to believe, Frank realized. No one could have guaranteed that Buckston and the others would ride up just then and jump to all the wrong con-clusions. More than likely, the bushwhacker had seized the opportunity to kill Flynn and planned to then drygulch Frank as well. But Frank had ruined that by coming along too soon and chasing him off. The shot with the Remington that had nicked Frank's shoulder hadn't been planned to be even more incriminating; it had just worked out that way when the gunman happened to pick up Flynn's revolver.

In fact, just about everything had worked out perfectly for the killer, whether it had been planned that way or not. He had shot Flynn and Frank had been blamed for it, through pure bad luck. Once again, Fate seemed to enjoy making life difficult for Frank Morgan.

Only one thing hadn't quite panned out for the gunman in the yellow slicker. Frank wasn't either dead or a prisoner, waiting to be hanged for killing Flynn. He was still free. Slightly wounded, sure, but he could live with that. And as long as he was free, there was a chance he would find the killer and turn this whole crazy situation on its head. . . .

All he had to do was avoid being captured or killed by the men hunting him. And it wouldn't be just Flynn's men who were after him, either. Once Sandeen heard that Frank was on the loose, he would send his own hired killers after the fugitive. Frank Morgan alive was still a threat and always would be. One way or another, Frank had to die.

So before it was over, there would be a whole legion of gunmen searching these hills for him. A devil's legion, Frank thought as exhaustion finally claimed him and he drifted off to sleep.

Hunger pangs woke him during the middle of the night. He dug the jerky out of his saddlebag and gnawed on the tough, dried meat until it softened up enough for him to eat it. Getting a little food in his belly made him feel better, though he was far from satisfied. He slept again.

When he woke in the morning, the first thing he was

aware of was the sunlight washing over the hillside beyond the mouth of the cave. The clouds of the day before were gone.

But that didn't mean that today wouldn't have some storms of its own, Frank thought as he stood up and stretched. If this day was anything like the several that had preceded it, it would bring its own particular brand of trouble.

Stormy was anxious to get out of the cave, and so was Frank. He told the horse to wait and stepped to the mouth of the cave, listening intently for the sound of voices or the thudding of hoofbeats. He heard nothing except the normal small noises made by the denizens of this rugged country going about their morning activities. Somewhere nearby a squirrel chattered and a bird sang.

In addition to listening, Frank looked over the part of the range he could see from his position. Nothing moved other than a couple of puffy clouds that drifted lazily through the blue sky. He was convinced that no manhunters were out there anywhere close.

Yet.

Turning away from the cave mouth, Frank kicked apart the faintly glowing embers of the fire he had built the night before. Then he caught hold of the Appaloosa's reins and said, "Come on, big fella."

They stepped out into the sunlight, and it felt awfully good to do so. Frank rolled his left shoulder and swung that arm around. He felt some stiffness and soreness in the shoulder, but it wasn't too bad. Considering the close call he'd had, he felt grateful to be in as good a shape as he was.

Stormy drank some from a puddle that remained on the ground from the downpour the day before. Frank knelt and scooped up a little of the muddy water in his hand. He was parched, and muddy water was better than no water at all. Stormy began cropping at the grass. Frank was still hungry, but not *that* hungry.

As he looked around at the hills and the dark rim of the forbidding mesa several miles to the northeast, he realized that he didn't know exactly where he was. He figured he could orient himself quickly enough, though, by using the Mogollon Rim as a landmark. If he headed west, which meant keeping the rim roughly behind him, sooner or later he would hit the Verde River.

The best thing for him to do now, he decided, was to get back to San Remo and try to slip into the settlement without anybody seeing him. He had to have some food, and an ally or two would help, too. If he could talk to Jasper Culverhouse or Mayor Donohue, he thought he could convince them that he was innocent of the murder of Howard Flynn, which they had probably heard about by now.

But whether or not he could reach San Remo without being spotted depended on how many men were out scouring the range for him. Probably all the Lazy F crew would join the hunt, and men from the other ranches in the area might come after him, too. Flynn had been pretty well liked by everybody except Ed Sandeen.

Another worry had begun to gnaw at Frank's thoughts. With everybody on the Lazy F up in arms about what had happened to Flynn, the ranch headquarters might be deserted except for Laura and Acey-Deucy. Sandeen and his crew would never have a better opportunity to ride in and take over. Sandeen could even claim that he was doing it to "protect" Laura now that her uncle was dead and she was alone. Folks around here would know better, but it might be a convincing story to outsiders.

But Buckston wouldn't take that lying down. Not the way he felt about the Lazy F . . . and about Laura Flynn. There would be gunplay for sure if Sandeen tried such a move.

Yes, Frank thought grimly as he swung up into the saddle and rode away from the cave that had been his temporary refuge, Howard Flynn's death had lit the fuse on the powder keg that was the Mogollon country, and with the odds stacked against him the way they were, Frank didn't see any way he could prevent the explosion that would blow the whole range to Kingdom Come.

But he was sure as hell going to give it a try.

Chapter Nineteen

Jeff Buckston was all too aware of how close Laura Flynn was sitting beside him on the wagon seat. This was a tragic occasion, he reminded himself, and he shouldn't be thinking about how from time to time her arm brushed his, and certainly not about how their knees bumped when the wagon jolted over a particularly rough spot in the trail.

After all, her uncle's body was lying back there behind them in the wagon bed, only a couple of feet away.

It was a solemn procession that made its way from the Lazy F toward San Remo this morning. Buckston had left only a few men behind at the ranch, and they had protested at being forced to miss the boss's funeral. Buckston wasn't going to leave the spread completely unprotected, though, not as long as that skunk Sandeen was still drawing breath. Buckston was more convinced than ever that Morgan had been working for Sandeen all along, and now that The Drifter had murdered Howard Flynn, Sandeen would surely try to complete his land grab and take over the Lazy F.

He would succeed only over Jeff Buckston's dead body, though. Buckston had made that vow to himself.

Even though the rain was gone and the sun was shining, the day still seemed gloomy to Buckston. How could it be otherwise when Laura was still sniffling from time to time and dabbing at her eyes with the lace handkerchief she clutched in her right hand?

She wore a dark gray dress and a hat of the same shade. It was a traveling outfit, but it was the nicest one she had, and the most fitting for a funeral as well. The day before, Buckston had sent a rider galloping to San Remo to deliver the news that Howard Flynn had been killed and to make arrangements with Pastor Homer Mc-Crory for the service to be held at the Baptist church. That was where they were headed now. Flynn's body rested in a black-draped coffin that Buckston and a few of the other hands had hammered together the night before. Jasper Culverhouse in San Remo might have done a little better job, but Buckston felt like he owed it to Flynn to build the coffin himself.

Flynn would be buried in the graveyard behind the church. That was the way he had wanted it. He had been instrumental in starting the church in San Remo and had served as a deacon there at one time, although he hadn't attended services very often in recent years. His wife and their two sons were already buried there.

"What are you going to do, Jeff?" Laura asked suddenly as Buckston handled the reins and kept the horses moving along the trail toward San Remo.

"Why, drive on into town and see that your uncle is laid to rest properly, I reckon," he said with a frown.

"No, I mean after that. Mr. Morgan is still out there somewhere."

Buckston's frown darkened. "Don't think I don't know it," he said in a hard voice. "I figure I'll see you home after the service, and then some of the boys and I will get started lookin' for Morgan. I promised you I'd bring him to justice, and I aim to do it."

"You don't plan to take all of the hands with you?"

"Can't do that," Buckston answered. "That's what Sandeen's countin' on."

"You're still convinced that Ed Sandeen was behind Uncle Howard's killing?"

They had talked this over the night before, in Flynn's study. Buckston had explained to Laura that she was now the owner of the Lazy F and that she could give the crew any orders she chose to. She had protested that she didn't know anything about running a ranch and asked Buckston to help her, to guide her in any decisions that she had to make. Buckston had hoped she would feel that way, but again, he didn't want to take advantage of her, so he pressed her on the question of whether or not that was really what she wanted.

"Jeff, you *have* to help me," she had said, her voice breaking a little from the strain. "Otherwise, there's no way I can get through this."

He had nodded curtly and said, "Yes, ma'am, you're the boss." She had started to protest about that, and he had held up a hand to stop her, saying again firmly, "You're the boss."

Now, as he kept the wagon moving, he said in answer to her question, "It had to be Sandeen's doin'. Morgan's been workin' for him all along."

"That just doesn't seem right somehow. I don't doubt what you saw, and I want you to catch Mr. Morgan and bring him to justice, but I just have a feeling that there's more to all this than we know right now."

"Maybe so, but the only way we'll get any answers is by layin' hands on Morgan. In the meantime, I'm not goin' to leave you there at the ranch by yourself. I don't trust Sandeen as far as I can throw the—" He stopped himself from saying what he was going to say. "The scoundrel," he concluded instead.

He drove on, and a short time later the wagon and the riders who followed it came in sight of San Remo. Buckston sent the wagon rattling across the plank bridge over the Verde and turned south toward the church. Quite a few people were already gathered in front of the white-washed frame building with its bell tower and steeple. Most of the settlement's citizens had turned out to attend the service for Howard Flynn. Even though Flynn had occasionally rubbed a few folks the wrong way, he was still one of the most respected men in this part of the territory.

Buckston brought the wagon to a halt and pulled the brake lever. Then he stepped down from the seat and turned around to reach back up and help Laura. He didn't own a suit, but he was dressed in his Sunday-go-to-meetin' best and his boots were shined. The same could be said of the rest of the Lazy F cowboys.

When Caleb Glover dismounted, he went straight to join Mary Elizabeth Warren near the doors of the church. She took his hand and squeezed it and gave him a sad smile. She knew how fond he'd been of his boss.

Homer McCrory was waiting at the doors. He shook Laura's hand and said, "You have my deepest sympathy, Miss Flynn. Your uncle was one of the finest men I knew."

"Thank you, Mr. McCrory. I appreciate everything you and the rest of the people here in San Remo are doing for Uncle Howard."

"It's only fitting and proper," McCrory assured her. He turned to Buckston and shook his hand as well. "Jeff. Are we ready to get under way?"

Buckston turned his head and glanced bleakly at the black-shrouded coffin in the back of the wagon. "I reckon so," he said.

Half a dozen of the punchers lifted the coffin from the wagon and carried it into the church.

Down the street, Mitch Kite stood in the doorway of the Verde Saloon and watched the mourners file into the church. He wasn't going to attend the funeral. He didn't have anything in particular against Howard Flynn, but Flynn was Ed Sandeen's enemy, and since Kite worked for Sandeen . . .

Kite supposed that Sandeen was mighty happy about this development. With Flynn dead, that pretty niece of his would inherit the ranch, Kite supposed. The Lazy F crew was a salty one—not as tough as Sandeen's bunch of hired killers, of course, but still not men to tangle with lightly—but without Flynn to give them their marching orders, they wouldn't be able to stop Sandeen from pushing his way in. One way or another, it wouldn't be long before the Lazy F was part of the sprawling Saber spread.

But that wouldn't be accomplished without bloodshed. It was entirely possible that even more gunmen would converge on San Remo and the surrounding area when Sandeen made his move. That meant the Verde Saloon would be doing a booming business, with a lot of money coming into the till. Of course, there would be some added danger, but Kite didn't care about that. The reward would be worth the risk.

For the past six months, Kite had been skimming money from the saloon's take, in addition to collecting the cut that Sandeen had promised him for running the place. Sandeen had no idea the embezzlement was going on. He had been too busy at first trying to court Laura Flynn to pay that much attention to how Kite was running the saloon, and after Laura had rejected him, Sandeen was distracted by his anger at her and his plans to take over the Lazy F. Kite had squirreled away a pretty good nut, and it would only get better over the next few months. Then, when he felt like he had enough loot, he would disappear some dark night and nobody in these parts would ever see him again. It was a nice plan, and it made Kite smile as he thought about it.

"What you grinnin' about, Boss?" Speckler asked as he came up beside Kite. The bartender looked down the street, following the direction of Kite's gaze, and saw the last of the mourners filing into the church. "That's Old Man Flynn's funeral goin' on down there, I guess."

"That's right."

Speckler sighed. "Ashes to ashes and dust to dust, as the old sayin' goes. Reckon everything's got to come to an end sooner or later."

"Yes," Kite said, thinking about the money he had hidden, "but every ending is the beginning for somebody else."

"Every new beginning is some other beginning's end."

Kite glared over at Speckler, surprised by the comment. "I don't pay you to philosophize," he snapped. "Go wipe down the bar."

"Yes, sir." Speckler shuffled away.

Kite turned his gaze toward the hills between the river and the Mogollon Rim. The stranger in black who had ridden into San Remo during the storm the day before had ridden back out again, and Kite had a feeling the man was up there somewhere, searching for Frank Morgan. Morgan didn't know it yet, but with a killer like that on his trail, there was a good chance he was already a dead man.

All it would take was a little time for the hunter to close in on his prey.

Assuming, of course, that none of the other men who would be hunting Morgan with vengeance on their minds found The Drifter first. . . .

The funeral service was as fine as such a sorrowful thing could be. Even though talking in front of a bunch of people scared Buckston more than fighting Apaches or rustlers ever had, the foreman got up and said some words about what a good boss and a fine man Howard Flynn had been. Vincente Delgado played a couple of hymns on his guitar, since the church's pipe organ was broken. Delgado was a Catholic, not a Baptist, but that didn't matter all that much at a moment like this when a pillar of the community was being laid to rest. Pastor McCrory got up and preached a short sermon, and while he was doing that, Laura leaned against Buckston's shoulder and sobbed quietly. Buckston didn't look at her, but kept his eyes fixed straight ahead. After a while, though, he couldn't help but slip his arm around Laura's shoulders and hug her a little, strictly to comfort her in this her time of grief, he told himself. Shoot, his own eyes were a little damp with tears. Howard Flynn really had been a good man and a good boss. Buckston had worked for him for almost ten years, about half of that time as the foreman of the Lazy F. It was the best riding job he'd ever had, and the spread was his home now, always would be.

Finally, the preacher wrapped things up. The pallbearers moved forward to pick up the coffin and carry it out through the back door of the church and on to the graveyard, which was only a few steps away. The mourners all followed, led by Laura and Buckston. She clutched his hand, and he laced his fingers tightly through hers.

The grave had been dug early that morning by Jasper Culverhouse and Vincente Delgado. It lay next to the spot where Flynn's wife Martha was resting, with their two boys beyond her. The marble monument that had been brought from Phoenix when Martha Flynn died had both her name and Flynn's name chiseled on it, along with their birth dates and her death date. All that remained to be added was Flynn's date of death, and Culverhouse would handle that. The big monument was topped by a statue of an angel. It was the largest, most impressive marker in the entire cemetery, which was fitting considering Flynn's status as the biggest cattleman and one of the earliest settlers in the region.

The coffin was lowered into the ground with ropes as the mourners gathered at the foot of the grave. Pastor

McCrory opened his Bible and said a few more words, then led a prayer. When that was done, nothing was left to do except for the mourners filing past and dropping a handful of earth from the mound next to the grave onto the lid of the coffin. Buckston didn't care for that custom—he thought the hollow thudding of dirt landing on a coffin was one of the worst sounds he'd ever heard—but it was tradition. Laura, as Flynn's only remaining relative, went first. Buckston had to keep a hand on her arm to steady her.

His mouth was a grim line as he dropped dirt on the coffin. "So long, Boss," he muttered. With that farewell said, he began to think about his next move. He had told Laura that he was going to take her back to the ranch, but now he was leaning toward entrusting that task to Caleb Glover, who had been at the Lazy F even longer than Buckston. Buckston's saddle horse was tied to the back of the wagon; he could take some of the boys and leave from here, heading up into the hills in search of the killer, Frank Morgan. The sooner they rounded up that lobo wolf, the better.

That was what he was going to do, he decided, even though Laura might not like it. Frank Morgan had better watch his back trail, because Buckston was coming after him.

And the foreman had blood in his eye.

A keen-eyed man on horseback sat in the thick shadows under a stand of pines atop a hill overlooking San Remo. From where he was he could see the mourners gathered around the grave as the preacher spoke the final words. The rider watched as those down below filed past Howard Flynn's grave and dropped dirt on the coffin. He wasn't particularly interested in the burial itself, or the people who attended the service. What he hoped was that someone else would show up, not down there in the graveyard, of course, but perhaps on one of these wooded hills that gave a good view of the cemetery. The watcher lifted his eyes from the burying and slowly scanned all the territory he could see from here, looking for any sign of movement, any telltale clue that someone might be lurking nearby.

Nothing. If Morgan was here, he was doing a damned good job of lying low. And of course, given Morgan's reputation and the fact that he had survived for so many years in such a dangerous profession, that was entirely possible.

It didn't matter, the hunter thought with a grim smile. Sooner or later he would find Frank Morgan. It was just a matter of time.

Chapter Twenty

Frank figured that Howard Flynn's funeral would be held in the morning, or around midday at the latest. So he waited until that afternoon to approach San Remo, when people would be going about their normal business again. He forded the river miles north of the settlement, stopping so that he and Stormy could drink their fill from the cold, clear, fast-flowing stream, and then circled far to the west so that he could approach the town from that direction. He thought he would be less likely to be spotted that way.

Not knowing how many men were already out in the hills hunting him, he hadn't wanted to fire any shots unless he had to, so he'd had to watch regretfully as Stormy spooked several rabbits during the course of the ride. Frank could have drawn the Colt he had taken from Glover and knocked down any of the critters with ease, and they would have tasted mighty good after he had roasted them over a fire.

But the sound of shots might just bring down more trouble on his head, so he let the rabbits go and remained hungry.

It was early afternoon when he neared San Remo. He was following the trail between there and Prescott, paralleling it about two hundred yards to the north and using every bit of cover he could find. He didn't emerge from the shelter of one stand of trees and head swiftly for another until he had surveyed the range all around him without seeing anyone. A couple of times he'd had to wait until riders moved on out of sight and earshot before continuing toward San Remo.

This wasn't the first time Frank had been a hunted man. He hadn't liked the feeling on those other occasions, and he didn't like it now.

But eventually he was able to work his way to within a hundred yards of the rear of Jasper Culverhouse's livery barn. Frank swung down from the saddle and let his gaze rove over the settlement. From there he couldn't see anything except the backs of some of the buildings and a few cabins. Nobody was moving around, though, so after a while he decided it was time to risk making a move of his own.

Leading Stormy, he walked quickly toward the barn, covering the distance in only a few moments. The back door was closed, but Frank swung it open and led the Appaloosa through it. A feeling of relief washed through him when they were both inside the barn, out of sight.

Frank didn't see Culverhouse. He listened for a second and heard the clang of hammer and anvil. Culverhouse was working in the blacksmith shop. Frank turned Stormy into the usual stall and dumped some oats from the bin into the trough for the Appaloosa. Then he went to the barn's entrance, where the big double doors stood open on this warm, sunny day.

Staying back in the shadows, he looked across the yard between the livery barn and the blacksmith shop. The doors in the front and back of the smithy were open to let the heat from the forge escape. Frank saw Culverhouse working at the anvil, sparks flying through the air as he smashed the heavy hammer against whatever he was fashioning.

Dog sat in the back door, his head tilted in interest, watching the burly blacksmith.

Frank smiled. The wind was out of the east, or Dog would have already caught his scent. Frank gave a low whistle. Dog's ears shot up, and the big cur jumped to his feet and whirled around. He bounded across the yard toward the barn and raced inside the building, rearing up on his hind legs to rest his front paws against his master's chest. His tongue lapped against Frank's face.

Culverhouse had noticed Dog's sudden reaction, as Frank had hoped he would. Still holding the hammer, the blacksmith stepped toward the shop's back door and looked across at the barn, frowning. Frank ruffled the fur on Dog's head with one hand and waved the other at Culverhouse, whose eyes bulged in surprise when he saw who was standing there just inside the barn, at the edge of the shadows.

Culverhouse set his hammer aside and started quickly across the yard. He opened his mouth to call out, but Frank made a gesture that silenced him. The blacksmith didn't say anything until he had stepped into the barn.

"Good Lord, Frank, what are you doin' here?" Culverhouse asked. "The whole country's after you for killin' Howard Flynn!"

"I didn't kill Flynn," Frank said.

"Jeff Buckston said—"

"Buckston's wrong," Frank cut in. "It's true enough that he and some other hands from the Lazy F rode up and found me standing beside Flynn's body, holding a gun, but that doesn't mean I shot him."

Culverhouse's frown deepened. "Buckston said you told some story about another man who was there, who happened to be wearing the same sort of slicker you were. . . ."

"That's the truth. I'm convinced it was Vern Riley or one of Sandeen's other hired guns who killed Flynn. I just came along and got the blame for it."

Culverhouse looked skeptical. "I don't like doubtin' you, Frank, but that's a mighty hard story to swallow. If it's true, why'd you jump Caleb Glover and then take off for the high lonesome like you did?"

"Because I knew Buckston would never believe me no matter how many times I told him what happened," Frank said. "Probably most of the other people around here wouldn't have, either. I've got to have proof if I'm going to convince anybody that I didn't kill Flynn, and I couldn't get that if I was locked up somewhere."

Culverhouse rubbed at his heavy jaw and was obviously thinking hard about what Frank had said. After a moment he asked, "Why'd you come back here?"

"Because I need food and supplies. I'm going to have to make myself pretty scarce around the settlement for a while. Also, I wanted to talk to you and maybe Mayor Donohue. I want somebody in these parts to know that I'm innocent, at least of shooting Howard Flynn. That's why I'm asking you to believe me, Jasper."

"Well . . . I reckon it *could* have happened the way you said. Lord knows there are plenty of fellas around here who own yellow slickers. I've got one myself, and I know several others in town who do. Why don't you tell me the whole story?"

Frank did so, backing up to start with his visit to Sandeen's ranch and Sandeen's denial that he'd had anything to do with sending Carl Lannigan to kill San Remo's new marshal. By the time Frank finished telling Culverhouse about the mysterious gunman he had swapped lead with immediately following the shooting of Howard Flynn, the blacksmith was beginning to look more convinced that he was telling the truth.

"I reckon nobody could prove that it *didn't* happen that way," Culverhouse said. "But you got to admit, it looked mighty bad the way Buckston and the others rode up and found you there."

Frank nodded. "Yes, it looked bad. But it's not proof that I'm guilty."

"No, it ain't." Culverhouse took a deep breath and nodded firmly, as if he had reached a decision. "I believe you, Frank. And I'll help you if I can. What do you want me to do?"

"If you've got anything around here to eat, I could sure use some food. My backbone's about to poke out the front of my shirt."

Culverhouse smiled. "Stomach thinks your throat's been cut, eh? Yeah, I got some grub in the room where I sleep next to the shop. I'll fetch it to you. Just stay back here where nobody'll see you. It'd cause a hell of a commotion if folks knew you were right here in town."

Frank nodded in agreement and waited while Culverhouse brought some biscuits and a slab of salt pork and an opened can of beans from his living quarters. Frank tore eagerly into the vittles.

"I put some coffee on to boil, too," Culverhouse said. "It won't be as good as what you'd get down at the café—"

"I don't care about that," Frank said, "as long as it's coffee."

By the time a half hour had gone by, with his belly now full of food and coffee, Frank felt almost like a new man. He and Culverhouse sat on a couple of stools, and the blacksmith asked, "What are you gonna do now?"

"My plan is basically the same one I had before," Frank said. "I still have to get my hands on one of Sandeen's men and make him talk. But now I not only have to get him to admit that Sandeen sent Lannigan after me, but also to reveal who really killed Flynn."

Culverhouse shook his head. "That won't be easy. All those boys who ride for Sandeen are tough hombres."

"I'm tougher," Frank said. "It's *my* life that's at stake."

* * *

Not surprisingly, weariness caught up to him once his belly was full. He and Culverhouse agreed that he would climb up into the hayloft and get some sleep until night fell. They also decided not to bring Mayor Donohue in on this just yet. The fewer people who were aware that Frank was back in San Remo, the better.

"I'll head for Saber once it's dark," Frank said as he paused at the bottom of the ladder leading up to the loft. "That's where the answer to this problem is going to be found."

"I sure hope you're right, Frank. And whatever you do, I hope you can do it without bein' spotted. There are a lot of hombres around here who would be more than happy to shoot you on sight."

"I had the same thought myself," Frank said with a grim smile as he began to climb the ladder.

He bedded down in the hay and slept soundly, not waking until the aroma of coffee drifted up to him. When he opened his eyes and sat up, he saw through the open hayloft door that it was dark outside. He moved to the edge of the loft and cautiously looked down into the barn. The front doors were closed now, and Culverhouse had lit a lantern that hung from a hook on the wall. The blacksmith looked up at the loft and called softly, "Come on down, Frank. It's all clear."

Frank descended the ladder and found that Culverhouse had brought more food and coffee for him, including a bowl of stew and a slab of apple pie from Mary Elizabeth Warren's café. "If eatin' that pie don't raise a man's spirits," Culverhouse said with a grin, "then nothin' will."

"What excuse did you give her for bringing the food back here instead of eating it there at the café?"

"Told her I had a horse about to foal and that I had to keep an eye on it."

Frank nodded. "Good idea."

"I packed you some more biscuits and salt pork, too,

to take with you in your saddlebags when you leave. Anything else I can do for you?"

Frank shook his head as he swallowed a spoonful of the savory stew. "No, because I don't know how long I'll be gone. I may get hold of what I need tonight, or it might take several days."

"Somebody willin' to testify against Sandeen, you mean."

"That's right."

Culverhouse sighed and shook his head. "Still seems like a long shot to me."

"When it's the only shot you've got, it doesn't matter how long it is. You just have to make it."

"Yeah, I reckon."

Frank polished off the food, smacking his lips over the delicious pie, and drank the last of the coffee. Then he shook hands with Culverhouse and said, "I'm much obliged for all your help, Jasper. And I thank you even more for believing me. You don't know how much that means."

"Yeah, well, I like to think I'm a pretty good judge of when a man's lyin' and when he's tellin' the truth." Culverhouse gripped Frank's hand hard. "Don't let me down, Marshal."

Frank glanced down at the badge that was still pinned to his chest. He hadn't even thought about it lately. "I don't guess I'm the marshal of San Remo anymore," he said.

"Nobody's fired you, have they?"

"Well . . . no."

Culverhouse nodded. "Then as far as I'm concerned you're still the marshal."

Frank slapped him on the shoulder and grinned, then brought Stormy out of the stall and began saddling up.

When Frank was ready to ride, Culverhouse blew out the lantern, plunging the barn into pitch darkness. Culverhouse knew the place like the back of his hand and was able to find the rear door and swing it open. Silvery light from the moon and stars demarcated the rectangular opening. With a wave that he didn't know if Culverhouse saw or not, Frank rode out of the barn into the night.

He didn't plan to cross the river here; too much chance that the sound of the Appaloosa's hooves on the plank bridge would draw attention. Culverhouse had told Frank there was another place where the Verde could be forded about five miles south of San Remo. That was Frank's destination, and then from there, Ed Sandeen's Saber spread.

The moon was only a thin crescent, and that was just fine with Frank. There was enough light for him to see where he was going, but not so much that he would be readily visible if anybody was looking for him. He hoped that the search for him had been called off with the coming of night. If there were a bunch of trigger-happy cowboys blundering around in the darkness, somebody would probably get shot before morning—but it wouldn't be Frank Morgan.

He found the ford Culverhouse had told him about with some difficulty, having to cast back and forth along the river a couple of times before he finally located it. The stream widened out a little here, and the level dropped enough so that Stormy could swim across without much trouble. With the legs of his jeans dripping from being soaked in the river, Frank turned the Appaloosa eastward, knowing that would take him onto Sandeen's range.

So far he hadn't seen or heard anyone else abroad in the darkness, but as he approached Sandeen's headquarters, Stormy suddenly lifted his head, his ears pricking forward. Frank knew that something had alerted the Appaloosa, so he pulled back on the reins and brought the horse to a halt. Then he sat there in the saddle, listening intently.

After only a couple of seconds he heard the sound of hoofbeats; a whole passel of them, in fact. Frank estimated that at least a dozen riders were on the move, maybe more.

And they were coming in his direction.

Chapter Twenty-one

Frank reined Stormy into the thick shadows under some trees. He swung down from the saddle and stood close against the horse's side. His hand came up and closed over Stormy's nose. The Appaloosa knew from experience that gesture meant for him to stay quiet and not call out to the other horses that would soon be passing.

In all likelihood, the men were members of one of the makeshift posses combing the hills for Frank Morgan, the notorious Drifter, the gunslinger who had shot down Howard Flynn. They firmly believed that they had right on their side and that bringing a murderer to justice was their only goal.

But Frank *wasn't* a murderer, and he knew how easy it was for a posse to turn into a lynch mob or a firing squad. He stayed where he was in the shadows and waited for the group of riders to pass.

But when they did, a few minutes later, he was immediately struck by something odd about them. He couldn't see them all that well, since the light wasn't very good and the men trotted their horses past at least fifty yards from where Frank was hidden, but he thought something was wrong with their faces. There were more than a dozen riders—Frank now estimated twenty—and they were almost all past him before he realized what had made the hair on the back of his neck stand up.

They were all wearing masks.

Bandannas were pulled up over the bottom halves of their faces, and their hat brims were tugged down low to obscure their features even more. No posse, even an unofficial one, was going to be gallivanting around the range at night with masks over their faces.

So if they weren't looking for the fugitive, where were they going?

Frank didn't have an answer for that, and the question strongly stirred his curiosity. He thought about the directions involved and realized that the masked riders could have come from Saber. And if they kept going the way they were headed, their route would take them pretty close to the headquarters of the Lazy F.

Suddenly, Frank decided that his visit to Sandeen's spread was going to have to be postponed. He was going to follow those mysterious riders and see if he could find out what sort of mischief they were up to.

He was willing to bet that it wouldn't be anything good.

When the riders were out of sight but he could still hear their horses, Frank stepped up into the saddle and started after them. They wouldn't be able to hear Stormy's hoofbeats over the sounds of their own mounts, so Frank urged the Appaloosa into a brisk pace that wouldn't let him lose the trail of the men he was following.

Not surprisingly, the group veered a little east of north a short time later. Now they were riding straight toward the Lazy F ranch house. Frank no longer had any doubt that was where they were going, or that they were up to no good.

Being careful not to get too close, he trailed the men until they brought their mounts to a stop on a knoll overlooking the Lazy F headquarters. A hundred yards behind them, Frank reined in, too, and swung down from the saddle to slip forward on foot, leaving Stormy behind him with the leathers dangling. The Appaloosa knew to stay right where he was until Frank either whistled for him or came back for him.

Skulking like the Apaches who had once roamed this land, Frank catfooted forward, darting from bush to bush, tree trunk to tree trunk. The masked riders had all their attention focused on the ranch headquarters spread out before them and had no idea anyone was slipping up on them from behind. Within moments, Frank was close enough to overhear that they were saying in low voices.

"—kill the girl," a voice that Frank didn't recognize was saying, and the words sent a pulse of anger throbbing through him. Did Sandeen hate Laura Flynn so much that he had ordered her murder?

A second later, the man giving the orders went on, and Frank's nerves eased a little as he heard, "Anybody else is fair game, but she's not to come to any harm, understand?"

That made more sense. Sandeen had sent these killers to raid the Lazy F, but he didn't want anything to happen to Laura. Of course, it was hard to guarantee such a thing once the lead started flying, but that was the job these hired gunmen were charged with.

The mystery deepened as the man ramrodding the raiding party continued. "We'll hit the place hard and fast and then pull back. Do as much damage as you can, but remember, we're not out to take it over."

Muttered agreement came from the other gunnies.

Frank wasn't sure why Sandeen had ordered such a hit-and-run raid on the ranch, but at the moment, the motive didn't really matter. Death and destruction were about to descend on the Lazy F. Frank could see that several lights were burning in the main house and the bunkhouse, but there was no real air of vigilance about the place. Buckston was smart enough to know that Sandeen might try something now that Flynn was dead, so the foreman likely had posted a few guards. But they probably wouldn't be able to raise the alarm soon enough to stop these raiders from sweeping in and killing at least a few of the crew.

"Got those torches?" the leader asked.

Torches! They were going to try to start a fire. They probably aimed to burn down the barns.

Frank didn't wait to hear any more. He backed away from the brush where he had crouched in concealment and then turned to run silently toward the spot where he'd left Stormy. He had to let the people who were at the Lazy F know what was about to happen.

But even as he reached the Appaloosa and vaulted into the saddle, he knew he was too late. He heard the thunder of hoofbeats as the raiders charged down the hill toward the ranch, and the swift rattle of shots as they opened fire.

Buckston fought against the discouragement he felt gnawing away at his vitals. He and a good number of the men had spent all afternoon searching for Frank Morgan. They had started by going back to the place where Howard Flynn had been killed, and then they rode in the same direction Morgan had fled, searching for any sort of trail they could pick up.

Rain had washed out any tracks that Appaloosa of Morgan's might have made, so they had to rely on other signs—broken branches, chipped places on rocks where a horseshoe might have struck them, the sorts of things that only an expert tracker could see. Buckston had lived in Arizona Territory all his life and was an experienced frontiersman, but this sort of task was beyond even his expertise. None of the cowboys with him were up to the chore, either. Inevitably, they had lost what little trail there was.

That meant they were reduced to riding back and

forth through the hills, trying to pick up a trail that might or might not be there and hoping they would stumble over Morgan or some trace that would lead them to him.

And of course, that effort had been futile. Morgan had disappeared like a veritable phantom. Buckston wasn't really surprised. From all accounts, Morgan had spent years—decades, actually—getting into and out of trouble. It was to be expected that he would be one slick son of a bitch.

But that didn't matter. Sooner or later, Buckston would get him. If he had to spend the rest of his life in the effort, he would bring Frank Morgan to justice.

Looking at Laura Flynn lifted Buckston's spirits. When he and the boys rode in, he had come to the main house to report their failure, and Laura had asked him to stay and have supper with her. Buckston had agreed, thinking this would be a good time to discuss the details of how the Lazy F was run. He doubted that Laura would want to make any changes; after all, as she admitted, she didn't know anything about running a ranch. But as the owner, she had the right to know what was going on and to express her opinion of it. And if she wanted to issue orders, whether they were right or wrong, as foreman Buckston would be duty-bound to honor them.

So he'd gone back out to the bunkhouse and told the men who had remained at the ranch during Flynn's funeral to take their rifles and spread out around the headquarters to stand guard. Buckston hadn't forgotten that Ed Sandeen and his men still represented a threat. He told some of the men who had gone with him on the search for Morgan to turn in early, get some sleep, and then relieve the sentries around two in the morning. With that taken care of, he returned to the main house to have dinner with Laura.

As it turned out, she didn't want to talk about the business of running the ranch. Instead, as they ate the fine supper that Acey-Deucy had prepared for them, she asked Buckston to tell her more about her uncle. She said, "He was closemouthed, you know, especially about himself. But it must be quite a story, how he came out here when the only ones around were Indians and outlaws and made a home for himself and his family."

"It was pretty adventuresome, all right, from what I've heard," Buckston said. "You understand, I've only been here on the Lazy F for the last ten years or so, so I can't speak from experience about what it was like back there. When I started ridin' for your uncle, though, Ol' Badger Burris was still here, and Jap Clark and Ned Simms, and all of them were with the boss in the early days. Those old codgers liked to talk, too."

Laura smiled and leaned forward. "So tell me their stories," she said.

"Some of 'em are sort of rough," Buckston cautioned. "In a lot of ways, Arizona is dark and bloody ground, and the tales about the early days are, too."

"That's all right. I want to hear them. I want to learn all I can, not so much about the running of the ranch— I know I can trust you to handle that, Jeff—but about the spirit that motivated men like Uncle Howard to risk everything to make something worthwhile out of such a wilderness. I want to learn what was in his heart . . . so I can find the same strength in mine."

At that moment, there was no doubt in Buckston's mind. He loved this woman. She would do to ride the river with. She would stand at a man's side and make him proud.

So he started telling her all the yarns those old cowboys had spun, about the savage winters and the brutal summers, about the droughts and the floods, about the raids by bloodthirsty Apache renegades and the rustlers who had foolishly thought that they could come in and clean out Howard Flynn's stock. Flynn and those who rode for him had fought the elements, and they had fought ruthless, unscrupulous men. Most of the time they won, and even when they didn't, they battled their way to a draw. In the end they might have scars to show, but those scars were badges of honor, proof that they had fought the good fight. And the fact that they were still here showed that they had never been defeated.

Laura listened intently, hanging on Buckston's every word. Despite all the tragedy, he sensed an even deeper bond growing between them. In the back of his mind, hopes and dreams stirred.

It was a good moment, and as far as Buckston was concerned it could have lasted a lot longer, but suddenly his head jerked up in alarm as guns began to blast outside. He came to his feet, and without even thinking about it, his hand moved to the butt of his gun and closed around the well-worn walnut grips.

"Stay here," he said to Laura. "I'll see what's going on out there."

She stood up, too. Her face had gone pale and her eyes were wide as she said, "It's my ranch. I ought to—"

"Stay here," Buckston said again, and his tone of voice made it clear he wouldn't tolerate any argument. "That's one order *I'm* givin'."

More shots rang out and he heard men shouting in alarm as he hurried toward the front door. He jerked it open, stepped out onto the porch, and saw muzzle flames spurting in the darkness as a dozen or more raiders on horseback swept down the hill that overlooked the headquarters of the Lazy F. Some of them galloped into the yard between the house and the barns and the bunkhouse, firing at anything that moved. As Buckston lifted his gun and tried to draw a bead on one of the hard-riding figures, he realized with a shock that the men were masked.

The masks didn't really matter. He knew they had to be some of Sandeen's hired killers. He squeezed off a shot, but couldn't tell if he hit the man he was aiming at.

The bastard didn't tumble off his horse, that was for sure. The rider kept going, peppering the house with bullets. Buckston heard the lead singing around his head and dropped to a knee to make himself a smaller target. He fired again, the revolver kicking against his hand, as he saw several of the marauders swinging brightly blazing torches over their heads. Horror welled up inside Buckston as he saw those torches go spinning through the air as the masked raiders flung them into the barns and onto the roof of the bunkhouse. Buckston shouted a furious curse as he stood up again and emptied his Colt toward the attackers.

He had just squeezed off his last shot when something slammed against his head and knocked him back several steps. He reeled and tried to lift his gun again, no longer thinking straight enough to realize that it was empty. He fell, but he didn't feel it as he crashed down on the planks of the porch. Blackness surged up around him, threatening to engulf him, and the last thing he heard before oblivion claimed him was Laura Flynn screaming his name.

Chapter Twenty-two

Frank sent Stormy charging after the raiders. The noise of battle already had grown intense by the time he reached the top of the knoll and started down the slope toward the ranch. Frank knew he was only one man, but he had the advantage of surprise and could also hit the attacking gunmen from the rear.

He pulled his Winchester from the saddle boot as he started down the slope. At the biggest of the barns, a Lazy F puncher raced out and started firing at the raiders. He was cut down almost instantly as bullets from several different guns tore into his body. Frank saw that and his face was set in grim lines as he let Stormy pick his own path. The rifle came up to Frank's shoulder. He fired, levered the Winchester, fired again, and was rewarded by the sight of one of the men jerking in the saddle and almost falling off his horse. Frank had scored a hit, even if he hadn't knocked the man completely out of the fight.

The men with the blazing torches made good targets. Frank reined Stormy to a halt and leaped down from the Appaloosa's back so that he could aim better. He drew a bead on one of the torch-wielders and pressed the trigger. The Winchester kicked against his shoulder. The bullet slammed into the back of the man with the torch just as he threw it and drove him forward over the neck of his horse. The torch spun crazily in the air and fell short of the barn to gutter out in the dirt of the yard.

Frank emptied the Winchester in a matter of moments. By the time he was finished, several of the raiders were hunched over in their saddles in pain and a couple of others had limp, dangling arms that had been smashed by Frank's shots. But the attack was still going on. As Frank jammed the rifle back in its sheath, he saw a tall, lean figure on the porch of the big house blazing away at the raiders with a six-gun. Even at this distance, Frank recognized Jeff Buckston.

But then Buckston staggered and went down, the gun dropping from his hand. Frank couldn't tell how badly the foreman was wounded. Laura Flynn appeared in the open doorway of the house, her left arm in a black sling. Her right hand went to her mouth, and Frank figured she was screaming at the sight of Buckston lying on the porch. He couldn't hear her over the sound of all the shooting, though.

Frank leaped back into the saddle. One of the barns and the bunkhouse were on fire by now. Several bodies were sprawled out in the open, probably the guards Buckston had posted who had been caught and gunned down while they were trying to give the alarm or get to cover. A bitter taste filled Frank's mouth. If not for the bad luck that had caused Buckston to blame him for Howard Flynn's death, the two of them might have been able to work together and prevent this violence, or at least meet it more effectively. Now, for some of those men who were down, it was probably too late.

As Frank galloped toward the ranch headquarters, he saw Laura Flynn on her knees beside Buckston, cradling his head in her lap. But that wasn't all she was doing. As Frank watched, she pulled her left arm out of the sling, reached over, picked up the gun Buckston had dropped, and using both hands, pointed it at the masked men and began to fire, squeezing off several shots in rapid succession.

Frank hoped the raiders all remembered Sandeen's orders that Laura wasn't to be hurt. In the heat of battle, with the woman shooting at them, some of the gunmen might lose their heads and return the fire. Frank sent Stormy racing toward the house. As he did so, he began raking the raiders with well-placed shots from his Colt, hoping to keep them so busy they wouldn't have time to turn their guns on Laura.

He heard someone shout, "Fall back! Fall back! Let's get out of here!" Sandeen's men had accomplished their deadly hit-and-run mission. The barn and the bunkhouse were both burning strongly and probably wouldn't be able to be saved. Several members of the Lazy F crew were either wounded or dead, including the foreman, Jeff Buckston. The damage they had set out to do was done, so they were ready to get the hell out.

But they weren't escaping unscathed. Frank knew he had wounded several of them, even though they weren't leaving any dead behind as they sent their mounts charging off into the darkness. He fired a couple of final shots after them, but then the hammer of the Colt snapped on an empty chamber.

Frank swung the Appaloosa toward the porch, intending to check on Buckston's condition. But as he did so, Laura Flynn pointed the gun in her hands at him and fired. The bullet came close enough to his ear so that Frank heard the wind-rip of its passage. The next instant, Laura screamed, "Morgan! It's Frank Morgan! He's their leader! Get him!"

Frank's jaw tightened and he grated a curse through clenched teeth as the Lazy F punchers opened fire on him from the various places where they had sought cover during the raid. Bullets whistled around his head.

He didn't want to fight these men. They were honest

cowboys. Besides, the gun in his hand was empty and he didn't really have time to reload. The only choice he had left was to whirl Stormy around and light a shuck out of here as fast as he could.

Flame geysered from rifle muzzles and lead continued to claw through the night after him as he raced away from the ranch. Luck was on his side for a change, though, and none of the shots found him or the big Appaloosa. In a matter of moments, he was out of sight.

Even though he and Stormy were all right, frustration seethed inside Frank. He hadn't been able to stop the masked gunmen from carrying out their raid. He didn't know whether or not Buckston was dead, or how badly the foreman was hurt if he was still alive. And perhaps worst of all, Laura Flynn had seen him, recognized him, and blamed him for what had happened. By the time twenty-four hours had passed, everybody in this part of the country would believe that Frank Morgan himself had led the deadly raid on the Lazy F.

The hole he was in was just getting deeper, and it seemed that every time he tried to dig himself out, things only got worse. Who was going to believe him now? Even Jasper Culverhouse might not believe in his innocence anymore, once he had heard what Laura Flynn had to say.

He had some supplies now. Maybe he ought to just ride on, he told himself, and leave this part of the territory behind for good. Let the folks here sort out their own troubles.

But if he did that, the killing of Howard Flynn would always be hanging over his head, tarnishing a reputation that wasn't all that sterling to begin with. And even worse, he would know that he had turned his back on people who needed his help.

Like it or not, Frank told himself as he rode through the night, heading once again in the general direction of Sandeen's spread, he was in this fight to the finish.

He couldn't get up from the table until the last hand was played.

Whatever the cards might be.

Laura Flynn fought back tears as Caleb Glover and Acey-Deucy carried Buckston into the house. "Careful with him!" she said as his head lolled and blood dripped from the wound just above his right ear. "Oh, please be careful!"

"We're bein' as easy with him as we can, Miss Laura," Glover assured her. "You sure you want us to put him on the divan? He'll get blood on it."

"I don't give a damn about that!" Laura said, not caring a whit that it wasn't proper for a lady to curse. She still clutched Buckston's six-gun in her hand and had his blood smeared all over the front of her dress, too, and that wasn't really ladylike, either.

Her injured left arm ached like blazes, but she was barely aware of the pain. She had been acting purely on instinct when she grabbed up the fallen gun and began firing it at the masked attackers. The recoil of the shots had jolted her arms, causing the wounded one to throb. She didn't care. All she could think about was Jeff Buckston, and whether he was going to live or die.

He was still alive right now, and she was grateful for that. Anyone with such a gory head wound ought to be dead. But after Glover had bounded up onto the porch and determined that she wasn't hurt, he had slipped a hand inside Buckston's shirt and reported a fairly strong heartbeat.

Then he had looked at her and asked, "What do we do now, Miss Laura?"

The enormity of it had almost overwhelmed her at that moment. With Buckston out of action, the men would look to *her* for leadership now. She was the owner of the Lazy F, after all. But she didn't know what to do.

Still, she had always had common sense, and she had been able to fall back on it then, ordering Glover and Acey-Deucy to carry Buckston inside and put him on the divan in the parlor, and then she had told one of the other hands who came up to the porch to have the men do their best to keep the fire from spreading beyond the two buildings that were already burning. "Salvage what you can later from the bunkhouse and the barn," she had ordered, "but I don't want to lose any more buildings."

"Yes, ma'am!" the cowboy had said as he hurried off to carry out the commands.

Now Laura knew she would have to just trust the men to do the best they could with the fires, because she had more pressing business in here. After Glover and Acey-Deucy had placed Buckston on the divan, she leaned over him and asked, "Can you tell how badly he's hurt?"

"Hard to say for sure with all the blood on his head," Glover replied. "Could be he's just creased, though. The fact that he's still alive is a good sign. If that slug had gone on through, or if it was still rattlin' around inside his brain pan, I reckon he'd be dead by now."

The matter-of-fact way in which Glover spoke of such hideous possibilities made a chill go through Laura. She told herself that this was still a violent land, and those who were going to live here had to grow accustomed to dealing with the effects of that violence. She had to be strong, in other words.

"Acey-Deucy, we need some hot water," she said, forcing her voice to sound crisp and businesslike. "Some clean rags, too. Hop to it."

"Yes, Missy Laura," the cook said as he scrambled toward the kitchen.

Laura lifted the gun in her right hand and looked at it. "Do you have some shells that will fit this weapon, Mr. Glover?"

"Yes'm, I do."

She held it out toward him. "Would you reload it for

me, please? My left arm hurts, and I'm not sure I can manage to do that right now."

She thought she saw a hint of a smile play across Glover's face as he took the gun and said, "Yes'm, I'd be right glad to reload for you."

While he was doing that, Laura moved the sling around and got her left arm back in it, wincing a little as she did so. She slipped her right hand inside the left shoulder of her dress and reached down to check the dressing around the wound. It didn't seem to be wet.

"How's that arm o' yours doin', ma'am?" Glover asked.

"It hurts like hell, but I don't think it's started bleeding again. It'll be fine."

"I expect it will." The cowboy closed the loading gate on the .45 and extended it butt-first toward Laura. "I left the hammer restin' on an empty chamber. Less likely to shoot yourself that way."

"I'm not going to shoot myself," she snapped. She might not be a native Westerner, but she wasn't totally incompetent.

"No offense meant, ma'am," Glover said mildly. "That's the way most folks carry 'em out here. Just a precaution, you understand."

"Oh." She felt a little embarrassed. "Well, thank you, Mr. Glover." She took the gun from him, looked around for a second, and then set it on a small table beside the divan where Buckston lay, still unconscious. The Colt would be within easy reach there if she should need it.

She wondered if from now on she would always have to make sure there was a gun close at hand.

Putting that worry aside, she leaned over Buckston and slid her hand inside the open throat of his shirt. She felt a little awkward touching a man's body like that, but it was for medical purposes, she told herself. She rested her palm over his heart and felt the beating. It seemed strong enough, if a little irregular.

She straightened and said, "He's going to be all right. I know he is."

Acey-Deucy hurried in with a basin of steaming water in his hands and several clean rags draped over his arm. Laura told him to set the basin on the floor next to the divan, and then she knelt there as well. She took the rags from the cook, soaked one of them in the hot water, wrung it out, and then used it to swab at the blood around Buckston's head wound. The rag turned crimson. After a few minutes Laura tossed it aside and picked up a fresh one. She worked quickly but carefully, cleaning away the blood so that they could get a look at the injury. Glover and Acey-Deucy leaned over her shoulders, watching intently.

Finally, Laura had enough of the blood cleaned off so that she was able to use her fingers to part Buckston's thick hair and reveal the long, still-bleeding gash in his scalp. "Just like I thought," Glover said. "That slug didn't do nothin' but give him a good hard lick on the side o' the head. It bled so much because that's what head wounds do. They're worse'n just about anything for lookin' bad when they really ain't."

"You mean he's going to be all right?" Laura asked.

"Hard to say. Sometimes when a fella gets a real hard clout on the noggin like that, it sorta scrambles up his brains so that he ain't ever the same again."

"Oh, my God," Laura breathed, filled with horror at the thought that Buckston might be permanently impaired.

"But I suspect ol' Buck'll be just fine," Glover went on. "He's got a pretty hard head. Prob'ly have a ring-tailed howler of a headache when he wakes up, but that'll be all."

"I hope you're right about that, Mr. Glover. I pray that you're right." Laura dabbed away the blood that had seeped from the wound as they were talking. "I'll stay with him and try to stop the bleeding. Then I assume all we can do is wait for him to wake up and see how he is."

"Yes'm. That's about the size of it."

"Go on back outside and see how the men are doing with those fires. Acey-Deucy will be here to help me if I need anything."

"Yes'm."

Laura took a breath. "And Mr. Glover . . . thank you."

"No need to thank me, Miss Laura," the cowboy said with a grin. "I was just doin' what the boss told me to do."

With that he nodded and went out, and Laura resumed tending to Buckston's wound. She didn't want to press too hard on it since she didn't really know the extent of the injury, but she kept some pressure on the wound in hopes that it would slow down and maybe eventually bring the bleeding to a halt.

Buckston showed no signs of coming to over the next few hours. Laura finally managed to stop the bleeding. She soaked a rag in whiskey and tried to clean the wound that way, but Acey-Deucy suggested pouring the liquor right on the gash. "Burn like blazes," he said, "but it get the job done, Missy Laura."

She took his advice, carefully pouring the fiery stuff right on the wound. Buckston stirred a little, and she knew that even in his unconscious state, he was feeling the pain. But he still didn't wake up.

Laura put a clean dressing on the wound, and Acey-Deucy lifted Buckston's head a little while she tied the bandage in place. Then he pulled one of the rocking chairs over next to the divan so Laura could sit down and still keep an eye on the wounded man.

Laura wasn't sure what time it was—long after midnight, certainly—when Glover came in and reported that the crew had been able to put out the fires and save part of the bunkhouse. The barn was a total loss, though.

"And we got two men dead," Glover went on in grim tones. "Smalley and Catlett. Half a dozen more o' the boys got ventilated, but I don't reckon any of 'em are liable to die. Some of 'em will be off their feet for a while, though."

"Did we lose the wagon?" Laura asked.

"No, ma'am."

"Good. In the morning you can use it to take the men we lost into town and arrange for their funerals. In the meantime, do you need any help doctoring the ones who are wounded?"

"No, ma'am, I reckon not. There are several of us who have quite a bit of experience when it comes to patchin' up bullet holes. We can tend to it. You just stay here and watch over Buck, if that's what you want to do."

"All right." She paused. "How long do you think he'll be unconscious?"

"No way o' knowin'. He might wake up five minutes from now, or it might be sometime tomorrow."

"Or never," Laura said hollowly. "I've heard of such things happening."

"Yes'm, so have I. But it ain't gonna happen here. I got faith in Buck."

Laura hoped that would be enough . . . but she couldn't quite bring herself to believe it.

Glover went back outside. Laura continued sitting beside the divan, and although she wouldn't have believed it was possible, she dozed off some time later, along toward morning. She slept there in the chair as exhaustion took its toll on her, and when she was jolted suddenly out of her slumber by some sort of commotion, she had no idea how much time had passed. The sunlight slanting in through the windows of the parlor told her it was morning, though. Her eyes went to the divan as terrible memories of what had happened the night before flooded into her brain. Jeff Buckston still lay there, unmoving except for the steady rising and falling of his chest. He was alive, but remained unconscious.

With a shake of her head, Laura realized that it had been angry shouts from outside that had roused her.

Now heavy footsteps thumped on the porch, and Caleb Glover flung open the front door and hurried in. His hands were tight on the rifle that he carried, and his face was set in equally taut lines.

"Mr. Glover, what is it?" Laura asked as she started up out of the chair.

"Riders comin' in, ma'am," he reported tersely, "and one of 'em is Ed Sandeen."

Chapter Twenty-three

"Sandeen," Laura repeated. Instinctively, she looked at the table where she had placed the Colt the night before. She reached over and picked it up.

"Yes'm, and about half a dozen o' his riders," Glover said.

"Then he didn't come to fight, or he would have brought more men."

"Prob'ly. He must want to parley, Miss Laura."

She nodded. "I'll talk to him. I want to hear his explanation for what happened last night."

"Whatever he's got to say, chances are it'll be a lie," Glover warned.

"Don't worry, Mr. Glover, I know that." She looked at Buckston one more time, then marched briskly toward the front door. Glover stepped aside for her and let her go first onto the porch.

She stopped at the top of the steps and turned a level gaze on the riders who had just reined their horses to a stop in front of the big house. Not surprisingly, Ed Sandeen was in the lead. He was the type of man who always had to be out in front, no matter what he was doing. He wore a black suit, a white shirt, a string tie, and a dark gray Stetson. His boots were polished to a high shine and his mustache had been trimmed recently. He looked handsome and distinguished, no doubt about that. Laura wasn't just about to let such a thing affect her judgment, though.

The men arrayed just behind Sandeen were some of his hired gunslingers who had been masquerading as cowboys. One of them was Vern Riley, who was almost as big a dandy as Sandeen and hadn't even been trying to keep up a façade of being a working puncher. Instead of a Winchester, he carried his usual shotgun in a saddle sheath.

Sandeen smiled, took his hat off, and nodded politely to Laura. The other men settled for ticking a finger against the brims of their hats. As Sandeen held his hat over his heart as if in a gesture of sincerity, he said, "Good morning, Laura. You look as lovely as ever today."

"That's a bald-faced lie, Mr. Sandeen," she said, not returning the familiarity with which he had addressed her. "I was up most of the night, I have my arm in a sling and blood on my dress, and I'm sure I look terrible." She glanced toward the barn that had been destroyed by fire and the bunkhouse, which had been heavily damaged, and had to suppress a gasp of surprise. This was the first time she had seen the destruction in the light of day. She glanced over her shoulder at the house and saw the bullet holes pocking the walls. She looked at Sandeen again and went on. "But not as terrible as my ranch."

Sandeen stopped smiling and put his hat back on. He nodded and said, "I heard you'd had some trouble up here on the Lazy F. As your nearest neighbor, I thought the right thing to do would be to ride over and see if you need any help."

Laura wondered if that was his way of claiming not to know anything about the attack on the ranch. For that matter, how could he have heard about it this early in the morning?

She addressed that question to him. "Who told you we'd had trouble?"

"One of my night herders noticed a red glow in the sky last night, and this morning he told me that he thought there had been a big fire in this direction. I sent a man up here to have a look, and when he came back, he told me that one of your barns had burned down and that the bunkhouse had been damaged, too. Was it an accident?"

Laura's mouth tightened. She swept the hand holding the revolver toward the wall of the house behind her and noticed that as she did so, several of Sandeen's men tensed, as if they thought gunplay might be about to break out.

"Take a look at those bullet holes," she said. "Does that look like an accident to you, Mr. Sandeen?"

The cattleman's forehead creased in a frown that darkened his face considerably. "I really wish you'd call me Ed, Laura. You did at one time. And to answer your question, no, it looks like your spread was attacked. Do you have any idea who was responsible?"

You, she thought, but she said, "The men were all masked. I didn't see their faces, so I couldn't recognize them." She glanced at Riley and the other gunmen. It was possible some of them had been among the masked raiders. She would never recognize a man simply by the horse he rode, and in the dim light, with all the shooting going on, the last thing she would have been doing was studying the enemy's clothing.

"That's terrible," Sandeen said. "It's a shame there's no real law in these parts, so that someone could put a stop to such outrages. It was probably rustlers, or some other outlaws, trying to intimidate you."

"Perhaps," Laura said coolly.

Sandeen leaned forward slightly in his saddle. "I'd like to help you in this time of trouble, Laura. I've lived on the frontier a lot longer than you have, and now that your uncle is gone . . . now that you're alone in the world . . . you could use the advice, and dare I say, the guiding hand, of someone more experienced."

She took a deep breath and said, "Maybe you're right."

Behind her, Glover let out a little grunt of surprise, so quietly that no one except Laura heard it.

Sandeen was smiling again, probably sensing an opening, a weakening on the part of Laura's defenses. "Maybe if I could come in, we could discuss what you should do next. Maybe even have a cup of coffee while we talk."

"All right," she agreed. "Come on in."

As she turned toward the door, she saw Glover frowning at her. He made a low rumbling sound, as if he were trying to warn her, but he didn't actually say anything.

Sandeen dismounted quickly, throwing his reins to Riley. As he followed Laura into the house, he said, "If I may be so bold as to say so, we've been close in the past, Laura, and I'd consider it an honor and a privilege if you'd allow me to protect—"

He stopped short at the sight of Buckston lying on the divan with the bandage tied around his head. His eyes widened in surprise.

"I appreciate the offer, Mr. Sandeen," Laura lied, "but I don't need you to protect me." That much was true, and so was what she said next. "My men and I can take care of ourselves. Mr. Buckston will be back on his feet soon, and in the meantime . . ." She hefted the revolver in her hand and went on. "I'm giving the orders on the Lazy F."

Sandeen frowned. "But . . . but you're just—"

"A woman? Was that what you were going to say, Mr. Sandeen? Yes, I'm a woman, but I'm also Howard Flynn's niece, and blood runs true in the Flynn family. I won't do *anything* that I think would disappoint my Uncle Howard, and that includes letting you waltz in here with your smooth talk and take over without firing another shot."

Sandeen's voice was chilly as he said, "I'm sure I don't know what you're talking about."

"I'm talking about those masked men you sent over here last night to burn some of my buildings, kill some of my men, and terrorize me into going along with whatever you wanted."

"That's crazy!" he said angrily. "I never—"

"You asked if I recognized any of the raiders," she cut in. "I got a good look at one of them, and I knew him right away . . . your hired gunfighter, Frank Morgan."

"Morgan! But—" Sandeen stopped himself. "You've got it all wrong, Laura. I didn't have anything to do with those men who attacked your ranch. I'm sorry it happened, and despite your offensive and insulting comments, I'll repeat my offer to help you out in this time of trouble." His voice hardened until it was like flint. "But this is the last time. If you don't accept my offer, then whatever happens from here on out will be on your own head."

Laura's chin lifted defiantly. "That sounds like a threat."

"Not at all. Consider it a word of warning."

"How's this for a word of warning?" Laura lifted the Colt higher. "In case you hadn't noticed, Mr. Sandeen, you're in here alone, while your men are still outside. If anything was to happen to you, Mr. Glover and I could claim that you tried to attack me, and no one would ever be able to prove otherwise."

He paled slightly as he glared at her. "My men are right outside. If they heard a shot—"

"How long do you think they'd be *your* men if you weren't around anymore to pay them?" Laura cut in.

As one of the muscles in his tightly clenched jaw jumped and jerked, Sandeen stared at her for a long moment and then said, "You're going to be sorry about this, Laura."

"The one thing I'm sorry about is that once upon a

time I was taken in by your lies and thought that you were a gentleman. And my name is Miss Flynn to you."

"All right," he said with a curt nod. "Have it your way. I'll be leaving now . . . unless you'd care to try to stop me."

"Believe me, Mr. Sandeen," Laura said, "it would be just fine with me if you never set foot in my house or on my range again."

Face flushed with rage, he turned and stalked toward the door. Before going out, he paused and said, "I don't know what happened to you. When you came out here, you were a gentlewoman from the East, as prim and proper as could be. And you knew your place."

She fought against the impulse to chase him out of the house with some hot lead and said, "The West happened to me, Sandeen. It stiffened my backbone and put some sand in my craw, as they say out here. And *my place* is right here on the Lazy F."

Sandeen just shook his head, glowered, and walked out. Laura went to the door, followed by Caleb Glover, and stood watching as he got on his horse, jerked the animal's bit savagely, and snapped at his men, "Let's get the hell out of here."

As they rode off, their horses' hooves kicking up a cloud of dust from the yard, Glover gave a low whistle of admiration and said, "No offense, Miss Laura, but what happened to you? I never heard talk like that from you before. It sure did sound mighty good."

The hand holding the revolver sagged as a wave of weariness struck Laura. She leaned against the doorjamb to steady herself and then laughed softly and shakily. "To tell you the truth, Mr. Glover, I don't know where all that bravado came from. I just tried to imagine what Uncle Howard or Mr. Buckston would have done in a similar situation, and I pretended to be a . . . a tough Western woman."

Grinning, Glover shook his head. "Wasn't no pretendin' about it. Somehow, ma'am, over the past few days you've turned into the genuine article. Life on the frontier's got a way o' doin' that. It either toughens you up or makes you hightail back to where you came from."

"Well, I'm not going anywhere," Laura declared. "The Lazy F is my home now and always will be."

"Unless Sandeen takes it away." Glover's grin disappeared to be replaced with a worried frown. "He didn't take kindly to what you had to say. I reckon it's war now, for sure."

"Sandeen started it. He got clever by sending those masked raiders up here. He thought that if he could force me to turn to him for his so-called protection, it would look better if any outside authorities ever investigated the situation." Laura's brain was busy as she thought about everything Sandeen had said and done. "Did you notice the look on his face when he saw that Mr. Buckston is still alive? He was surprised, very surprised. I think one of those masked gunmen must have told him that Mr. Buckston was shot in the head last night, and Sandeen assumed he was dead. That's proof he was behind the raid."

"Don't reckon it'd stand up in a court of law," Glover mused, "but I'd sure say you're right, ma'am. I noticed somethin' else, too. Sandeen looked really surprised when you mentioned Frank Morgan."

Laura looked over at the cowboy and frowned. "What do you mean?"

"I mean he looked like he didn't have no idea Morgan was here last night." Glover hesitated, but then went on. "To tell you the truth, Miss Laura, I ain't so sure Buck was right about Morgan workin' for Sandeen."

"But Morgan *was* here last night," Laura insisted. "He was riding through the yard and shooting. I saw him with my own eyes. In fact, I took a shot at him, just before Mr. Buckston's gun ran out of bullets."

Glover nodded in agreement but said, "I saw Morgan,

too. In fact, I saw him shootin' at them hombres with the masks on."

Laura stared at him. "What are you saying? That Frank Morgan was fighting on *our* side, instead of against us?"

"That's sure what it looked like to me. And I got to ask myself, ma'am . . . if Morgan was battlin' against Sandeen's men last night, what are the chances we judged him wrong on everything else?"

"You and the others found him standing over my uncle's body," Laura insisted.

"Yes'm, we did. But we didn't see him shoot the boss. I've thought long an' hard about it, and I reckon everything could've happened just the way Morgan said it did."

"But that would mean . . . that would mean I've misjudged him . . . we've all misjudged him . . . and made him a wanted man for something that he didn't do."

Glover shrugged. "Could be. We don't really know."

"But if that's true, why is he still around here? Why doesn't he just leave? And why in the world would he risk his life to try to help us?"

"I ain't sure, ma'am," Glover said, "but maybe that's just the sort o' hombre that Frank Morgan is."

Chapter Twenty-four

The night before, Frank had followed the men who had raided the Lazy F until he was sure they were headed for Sandeen's ranch. They were almost on the doorstep of Sandeen's hacienda, in fact, before Frank veered Stormy off to the east and headed for higher range. He wanted to find a place to spend the night that could be defended easily if he was discovered.

He found such a place in a clump of boulders atop a hill. The big rocks would give him cover if he had to fight, and he had a good field of fire all around. Of course, if he got trapped up there, his enemies could just keep him pinned down and starve him out, but he hoped it would never come to that.

He made a cold camp because kindling a fire would have been just asking for trouble. Rolling up in his blankets, he stretched out on the ground with his saddle for a pillow and relied on Stormy to serve as lookout. The Appaloosa would warn him if any danger came near.

Frank didn't fall asleep immediately. As he stared up at the millions of stars in the sable sky, he thought about what had happened. He was pretty sure he had Sandeen's ploy figured out. By making sure the raiders were masked, Sandeen could claim that someone else had attacked the

Lazy F. He might even be brazen enough to show up on the ranch and offer to help Laura in her time of trouble. After all, he would argue, she was a woman alone in a hostile land, beset by outlaws, who needed a man to look after her.

The question was whether or not Laura would fall for such an approach. Frank honestly didn't know. He sensed that Laura Flynn had the makings of a frontierswoman, that pioneer blood flowed in her veins whether she knew it or not.

But he didn't know how badly Jeff Buckston was hurt or if the ranch foreman was even still alive. As long as Buckston was around, Sandeen didn't have a chance of getting his hands on the Lazy F without a fight. But if Buckston was dead . . . if Laura felt like she really *was* alone, with no one to turn to . . . well, there was just never any way of knowing exactly what a woman was going to do. With age came wisdom, but no man ever got wise enough to figure out the answer to *that* question.

Frank dozed off and slept lightly, resting even though a part of him remained alert for trouble all night. When he woke up in the morning, his left arm and shoulder were stiff from the three-day-old wound, as they always were, first thing like that. They didn't particularly hurt, though, and he was able to work the stiffness out fairly easily.

Suddenly, the Appaloosa lifted his head and gazed off into the distance, ears pricking forward. Frank took notice of Stormy's reaction and immediately pulled the Winchester out of its saddle boot. He had reloaded the rifle the night before, so it carried its full complement of fifteen rounds. Stormy had heard or smelled something unusual, and until Frank was sure what it was, he was going to be ready for trouble.

The sound of hoofbeats came to his ears, and he knew the approaching horse must have been what had caught Stormy's attention. Frank slid between a couple of the boulders and moved forward until he could see down the hill. There was a trail of sorts down there, a game trail more than likely, and plodding along it was a rangy dun carrying an empty saddle. Frank didn't recall ever seeing the horse before.

He frowned as he watched the dun. The saddle proved that the horse had had a rider in the recent past. Frank hadn't heard any shots, and he didn't see any blood on the saddle. But the dun could have spooked for some reason and thrown his rider. The man could be lying somewhere nearby with a broken leg or a busted head, badly in need of help. If that was the case, he might even die if nobody came along to give him a hand.

Frank grimaced as he thought about what he should do. The smart thing would be to just stay out of sight and let the dun wander on. Whoever the horse belonged to, the man's problems were none of Frank's business.

It was difficult for him to turn his back on somebody in trouble, though. That tendency to try to help had nearly been his downfall many times. But he couldn't change the way the Good Lord had made him.

The dun was carrying a pair of saddlebags. By searching them, Frank might be able to find out who the horse belonged to, at the very least. He scanned the countryside all around and didn't see any sign of movement except the obviously weary dun.

Muttering a curse directed at his own stubborn foolishness, Frank turned around, went back to Stormy, slid the Winchester back in its sheath, and swung up into the saddle. He rode out of the clump of boulders and trotted down the hill toward the dim trail.

The dun saw him coming and stopped. The horse stood there placidly and let Frank ride up and take hold of its reins. He leaned over and opened the flap on one of the saddlebags. There was nothing inside except a box of .44-40 cartridges, some jerky, a small frying pan, and a waterproof packet of matches. He checked the other side of the saddlebags and found just a few supplies—flour, salt, sugar, a slab of bacon. Whoever owned the dun traveled light, carrying only the bare necessities, including a canteen hung around the saddle horn by its strap. There was nothing to tell Frank who the horse belonged to. To find that out, he was going to have to backtrack the animal.

"Come on," he said as he started along the trail in the direction the dun had come from, leading the riderless horse. He listened closely in case anybody was crying out for help, but he didn't hear anything unusual.

A few hundred yards along, the trail passed close by an aspen. Frank didn't pay any attention to the tree until he had already ridden beyond it. The sudden rustle of its leaves warned him, though, and he kicked his feet free of the stirrups, let go of the dun's reins, and rolled out of the saddle. He heard a thump as booted feet hit the ground, and knew that somebody had been lurking in the concealment of that tree and had dropped out of it after he rode past. Frank hit the ground himself, rolled over, and came up on one knee with the Colt in his hand, his finger taut on the trigger.

He found himself facing a man he had never seen before. The man had a rifle in his hands, and the weapon was pointed right at Frank. Neither of them could fire without the other one having a chance to pull the trigger, too.

After a tense moment of silence, the man with the rifle drawled, "Well, looks like we got us a standoff here, don't it?"

He was a lean man about the same height as Frank, dressed in rough but clean range clothes and a battered Stetson. The hair under his hat was a sandy brown, as was the mustache that drooped over the corners of his mouth. Frank judged his age to be in the mid-thirties.

"That your dun horse?" Frank asked.

"Yeah." The rifle muzzle never wavered as the man

replied—but then, neither did the barrel of the Colt in Frank's hand. "Thanks for bringin' him back to me."

"You were hoping I'd be curious enough to backtrack him and try to find out where his rider was. You were trying to draw me out."

The rifleman smiled a little. "Figured that'd be easier than tryin' to roust you outta them rocks up there on top of the hill. A man could get killed doin' that. Anyway, I never heard of Frank Morgan passin' up a challenge."

"You know who I am, then," Frank said flatly.

"Yeah." The man added dryly, "I've seen your picture on the covers o' dime novels."

"That was a pretty smart trick with the horse." Frank watched the man closely, ready to take advantage of any opportunity that presented itself, even if it lasted for only an instant. He wanted to keep the stranger talking. "Do you ride for the Lazy F, or are you one of Sandeen's men?"

"Neither. Name's Horn. Tom Horn."

Frank knew the name, but with iron control he didn't show any reaction. Tom Horn had been a civilian mule packer for General Crook during Crook's campaign against the Apaches, and he had also worked as a scout and translator for Chief of Scouts Al Sieber. Unless Frank was remembering it wrong, Horn had even been Chief of Scouts himself for a while, until Geronimo had surrendered, effectively bringing the Apache Wars to an end. Since then Horn had developed a somewhat shady reputation, sometimes working on the side of the law, sometimes rumored to be nothing more than a common, hired killer. Frank had never crossed trails with him before, but in the way of the frontier, he definitely knew who Horn was, just as Horn knew who he was.

"If you're not working for either of those two spreads, what do you want with me? There's no bounty on my head." Frank paused. "Or is there? I've had rewards posted for me before when I didn't even know about it."

"Naw, no bounty," Horn said, "and I ain't a bounty hunter, anyway. Buckey O'Neill sent me into this here Mogollon Rim country. I'm workin' for him as a special deputy."

Frank grunted in surprise. He had also heard plenty about Buckey O'Neill, the former newspaperman turned sheriff of Yavapai County. A few years earlier, O'Neill had set off with a posse after a gang of outlaws that held up a train at Diablo Canyon Station. The other members of the posse had gradually given up, but O'Neill had pushed on doggedly, pursuing the outlaws in a dangerous trek that had eventually covered over six hundred miles before he brought them all to justice.

"O'Neill sent you after me?" Frank asked.

"Not exactly. Don't reckon he even knew you were hereabouts when he sent me in. He's been hearin' rumors that there's a range war brewin' in these parts, and since some of the range involved lies in Yavapai County, he decided to find out what's goin' on and nip it in the bud." Horn chuckled. "I reckon you could say that I'm the nipper."

"He's right about the war. There's been trouble, even bloodshed, between Howard Flynn's Lazy F spread and Ed Sandeen's Saber ranch. But Flynn's dead now, and I figure Sandeen's on the verge of a cleanup. The Lazy F is being run by a woman now, Flynn's niece."

"Yeah, I heard about all that. Heard, too, that you've been in the middle of the big trouble ever since you rode into these parts, Morgan."

"Not by choice," Frank said. "Trouble just seems to find me."

"I know the feelin'," Horn drawled.

It was odd that they could be here like this, conversing calmly while pointing guns at each other, both of them ready to kill if they had to. Each man had icy nerve to spare, though, and they weren't quite ready to trust each other.

"I been pokin' around for the past few days," Horn

went on. "Did some drinkin' in all the saloons in San Remo. Didn't really talk to anybody, but I did a lot of listenin'. Most folks seem to think that you're workin' for Sandeen and that you killed Howard Flynn."

"Neither of those things is true," Frank said. "Sandeen offered me a job at fighting wages, and I turned him down flat. And I'm convinced it was really one of Sandeen's men who killed Flynn."

"Yeah, I've heard that you had some trouble with a few of Sandeen's men. Killed the Hanley brothers and Carl Lannigan, didn't you?"

"I did. None of them gave me any choice."

"Them Hanleys wasn't such a much, but Lannigan was one tough hombre. So are you, from everything I've heard about you. But you never struck me as the sort who'd just work for anybody who met your price. I ain't surprised you turned down Sandeen." Horn sighed. "Hell, Morgan, I'm gettin' a mite tired. What say we put down these guns and finish our talk without threatenin' to shoot each other?"

Frank smiled faintly. "Sounds good to me . . . as long as you go first, Horn."

Horn snorted. "You think I won't do it. I never heard tell of The Drifter gunnin' a man down in cold blood, though, so I reckon I'm gonna surprise you, Morgan." He lowered the rifle, letting the barrel fall until it pointed to the ground in front of him. The tension left his body, too, and a grin creased his leathery face. "See? If you want to shoot me, there ain't a damned thing I can do about it."

Frank was still wary of a trick. He suggested, "Why don't you get your horse and put the rifle back in the saddle boot?"

"Sure." Horn strolled toward the dun, whistling for the horse to come to him. They met, and Horn slid the rifle into its sheath. He faced Frank again and said, "There you go."

Frank nodded and lowered his Colt. Horn wore a six-gun on his hip, too, but although the former scout was a deadly shot at any range with a rifle, Frank had never heard anything about him being fast on the draw with a handgun. He holstered his Colt, knowing that he could beat Horn if the other man decided to slap leather.

"That's better," Horn said. "No need for us to get feisty with each other. Happens I believe your story, Morgan. I don't think you killed Flynn."

"You may be the only one in this part of the territory who feels that way. How come you don't think the worst of me, too?"

Horn shrugged. "I know a little about the sort o' man who kills for pay. You ain't like that, Morgan. Now, what say we go back up in them rocks where I trailed you to, build us a fire, and cook up a little breakfast while we figure out what the hell we're gonna do about this range war?"

Chapter Twenty-five

As they rode back to the boulder-topped hill where Frank had camped the night before, he said, "If we build a fire, the smoke is liable to draw trouble to us."

Horn laughed. "Now, just what sort o' trouble do you think that Frank Morgan and Tom Horn can't handle, eh?"

Frank supposed he had a point.

"Fact of the matter is," Horn went on, "you and me would make a good team, Morgan. I can drop a fella at a thousand yards with this long gun o' mine, and you can take care o' all the closeup chores with a Colt. There are gents who'd pay handsomely to have the two of us workin' for them. What do you say?"

"I ride alone most of the time."

"Yeah, well, I didn't really figure you'd take me up on it," Horn said casually, "but I figured the offer was worth makin'."

They reached the knoll and rode up the slope to the clump of boulders. Both men dismounted. Horn walked a short distance down the hill to gather some wood for the fire and came back with an armful of broken branches. Frank kept a close eye on Horn as he got to work building the fire. Frank still wasn't sure if he completely trusted the so-called special deputy. Horn was probably telling the truth, but Frank would be betting his life on that.

Once the fire was going, Horn broke out his frying pan and sliced some bacon into it. The aroma that soon rose from the sizzling strips made Frank's mouth water. "I've got some biscuits," Frank said. "They're getting a little stale by now, but they're not too bad."

"Bring 'em out," Horn said as he hunkered by the fire. "Reckon they'll go right fine with this bacon. Got a coffeepot?"

"I do," Frank said. "And some Arbuckle's, too."

Horn licked his lips. "We're gonna be eatin' like kings in a few minutes."

When the food was ready, they sat on opposite sides of the fire and ate. Maybe it wasn't fit for royalty, despite Horn's comment, but it wasn't bad.

Horn asked Frank for his version of everything that had happened over the past several days, and Frank complied, leaving out none of the details and filling Horn in on his theory about Sandeen's plans, too. Although Horn wasn't an educated man, Frank sensed that he had plenty of natural cunning, especially when it came to the shady side of life on the frontier.

When Frank was finished, Horn sipped his coffee and nodded. "Sounds to me like you're right about this fella Sandeen," he said. "You think he used to ride the hoot-owl trail?"

"I'd take odds on it. That was Buckston's impression, and he seemed like a good judge of character." Frank smiled. "Well, up until the time he decided that I'd killed Howard Flynn, anyway."

"Everybody makes a few mistakes. Don't mean they're wrong about everything." Horn took another sip of Arbuckle's. "What were you plannin' on doin' next?"

"I want to get my hands on one of Sandeen's men. I think that under the right circumstances, one of them might confess that Sandeen is behind all the trouble. If he made that confession to you, you could go back to Buckey O'Neill with the story and get plenty of law in here, enough to round up Sandeen and his gun-throwers."

"That might be a war in itself," Horn observed.

Frank shrugged. "Yes, but it would keep the Lazy F from being wiped out."

"You have anybody in mind to grab?"

"I was thinking of Vern Riley," Frank said.

Horn frowned. "I've heard of Riley. Don't think we've ever met. He's supposed to be pretty tough, though. Why'd you pick him?"

"Because he's Sandeen's *segundo* and probably knows more about his plans than anybody except Sandeen himself. And I think I can convince him to talk."

"I might be able to help out a mite there," Horn mused. "I been around the Apaches quite a bit. Ain't nobody knows more about torture than those red devils."

Frank drank his coffee and didn't comment. He didn't plan to actually torture anybody—but if whichever of Sandeen's men he captured wanted to believe that was going to happen, then so much the better.

"We might ought to move pretty fast on this," Horn went on. "If Sandeen thinks that he's got the upper hand now because Flynn's dead and that niece o' his is on her own, he won't wait very long to strike."

"That's what I thought," Frank agreed. "We'll clean up here and then head for Saber. The sooner we lay our hands on Riley, the better."

"If everything I've heard about Vern Riley is true, we won't get him without a fight," Horn warned.

Frank nodded, his expression hard as rock. "Riley won't do us any good if he's dead, so we can't kill him. But there's nothing that says we have to treat him gentle as a baby, either."

Horn grinned and said, "I like the way you think, Frank Morgan."

* * *

Caleb Glover flicked the reins against the backs of the horses pulling the Lazy F's ranch wagon. Behind him in the bed of the vehicle, as he was all too aware, lay the blanket-wrapped bodies of Hiram Smalley and Wilbur Catlett, the two hands who had been killed in the raid on the ranch the night before. Miss Laura had given Glover the grim task of taking the bodies into the settlement so that Jasper Culverhouse could see to the burying.

Some big ranches had their own cemeteries, but Howard Flynn had always laid his riders to rest in the graveyard in San Remo when something happened to them. And of course, Flynn himself was buried there now, along with his wife and sons.

Miss Laura was the last of the Flynns. As such, she had all of Glover's loyalty. He had ridden for the Lazy F for most of his adult life, and the boss had never been bothered in the least by the fact that Glover's skin was black. Howard Flynn hadn't believed in punishing a man for something that was beyond his control—but neither had he believed in giving that man any special rights and privileges because of it. All that had ever mattered to Flynn was whether or not a fella made a good hand.

So Glover wasn't just about to desert Miss Laura. In fact, he would have rather been out at the spread now, keeping an eye on things. But she said she trusted him to see to it that Smalley and Catlett were buried fittin' and proper, so he had gone along with what she wanted. She had split the crew, sending about half the men to town with Glover while the other half stayed at the ranch in case of more trouble. She herself remained at the Lazy F, of course, to watch over the wounded Jeff Buckston.

Worry gnawed at Glover's brain over that very issue. He thought Miss Laura should have kept more of the men close to home, to protect her. If Sandeen attacked with all of his gunslingers, the dozen or so able-bodied

men at the ranch might not be able to fight them off.
She had wanted the Lazy F to be well represented at the
funeral, though, so she had sent ten men with Glover
and the wagon. Four rode on either side of the vehicle
and a couple behind it.

The trail started down a hill between a pair of fifteen-
foot-tall banks. At the bottom of the slope was a wide
stretch of grassy flatland that reached all the way to the
Verde River and San Remo just beyond.

As the trail entered the cut, it narrowed so that the
flanking riders had to drop back and join the ones behind
the wagon. Glover had been over this route hundreds of
times before, so he didn't think anything about it.

Until the first shots rang out and one of the men trailing behind the wagon grunted in pain and toppled out
of his saddle in the loose sprawl of death.

Glover's instincts betrayed him then. He hauled back on
the reins and brought the team to a stop, rather than whipping them into a gallop as he should have. He snatched his
rifle from the floorboards at his feet and twisted on the
seat, looking around to see what was happening.

Shots came from the banks on both sides of the trail.
Pistols cracked, rifles blasted, and there was even the
roar of a shotgun. It was instantly obvious to Glover that
bushwhackers had been hidden up there, waiting for the
group from the Lazy F to come along. The cowboys were
trying to fight back, but the ambush was brutally effective. In the opening seconds of the fighting, two more
Lazy F punchers were blasted out of their saddles by the
storm of lead, one of them practically blown in half by a
load of buckshot.

And even as Glover brought the rifle to his shoulder
and snapped a couple of shots at one of the spots where
powder smoke spurted at the edge of the bank, he realized that his companions didn't have anywhere to flee as
long as the wagon was blocking the trail.

He acted as fast as he could, turning around again and

dropping the rifle at his feet. But as he reached for the reins, a bullet slammed into his right shoulder and drove him forward, off the seat. More slugs chewed into the wagon body as Glover landed on the floorboards. He heard grisly thuds, too, that told him some of the bullets were striking the bodies of Smalley and Catlett.

At least the dead men couldn't feel any more pain. Glover was filled with a vast sea of agony that washed from one end of his being to the other. He gritted his teeth and sweat popped out on his face as he struggled to push himself upright and reach for the reins. He knew he still had to get the wagon moving, before all of his friends were massacred.

His strength deserted him, though, as he slumped down again, gasping in pain from his bullet-shattered shoulder. The reins he had dropped were right before his eyes, but he was too weak to reach out and grasp them.

However, the continuing roar of gunfire, the screams of wounded men and horses, and the smell of blood and powder smoke in the air did what Glover had failed to do. The horses hitched to the wagon danced around skittishly for a moment, spooked by the violence all around them, and then suddenly bolted, stampeding down the trail with the wagon careening along behind them.

Glover bounced around on the floor of the driver's box, and each jolt sent even more agony smashing through him. He felt his grip on consciousness slipping. But at least the wagon was moving again, he thought, and maybe some of the men could get out of that bottle-neck and escape from the ambush. It was beyond his power now to do anything except hope that was so, and even that was fading.

Once the horses stampeded, they had no place to go except straight down the sloping trail toward the flat. When they reached the end of the cut, instinct kept them on the trail. Glover roused a little when he realized the wagon was traveling over level ground. The trail was rough, though, and it still bounced wildly. He lifted his head and peered blearily over the footboard, over the backs of the lunging, straining, scared-out-of-their-heads horses. He saw a bend coming up and knew the team was moving too fast for the wagon to take the turn safely. If the horses left the trail and took off across the open country, that would probably be better, although such a course held its own dangers. But if they followed the accustomed path, the wagon might not be able to handle the speed it was moving at now. Grimacing in pain, Glover reached again for the dangling reins. His fingers touched them, tried to gather them in. . . .

Then the wagon jolted again and the long strips of leather slipped over the footboard to drop out of Glover's reach. The horses were truly running wild now, and there was nothing he could do to stop them or even slow them down. He fell back with a groan of despair.

At least his wounded shoulder was numb now. In fact, his whole side had lost its feeling. Despite the morning sun, Glover was cold. He was dying, he thought wildly.

But he was too stubborn to give up without a fight, and as his pain-wracked gaze happened to fall on the wagon's brake lever, he summoned up what little strength he had left and tried to lift his leg. If he could get his foot against the lever and knock it back, that might slow the runaway horses a little. He gasped from the effort as he strained to get his foot up to the brake lever.

He was too late. The fear-maddened horses swept around the sharp bend at a full gallop. They were able to make that turn, but the wagon swung far out to the side behind them. The wheels on the left side drifted off the trail and slid down the slight embankment at its edge. The wagon leaned precariously in that direction.

For a second Glover thought the vehicle was going to make it, was going to right itself and pull back onto the

trail. But then he felt the jolt and heard the sharp sound
as the front axle cracked and the left front wheel folded
up, shattering from the impact with the ground. Glover
opened his mouth to scream, but there was such a huge
grinding crash as the wagon tipped over and began to
roll that he couldn't even hear himself yell. Earth and
sky changed places, and the wounded cowboy felt himself flying through the air.

Then the whole world seemed to crash down on top
of him with a crushing weight that drove all the awareness out of Glover's mind and body.

Chapter Twenty-six

Frank and Horn reined in as the sound of gunshots drifted to their ears—a lot of gunshots, in fact.

Horn grunted. "Sounds like a big fracas. Think we ought to go have a look?"

Frank was already turning Stormy's head. As he heeled the Appaloosa into motion again, he said, "I damn sure do."

The shots were a long way off, well up the valley of the Verde River, in fact. Frank had intended to reconnoiter around the headquarters of Sandeen's ranch and hope for a chance to grab Vern Riley. But in order to check out the sounds of battle, they would have to swing wide around Sandeen's place and ride hard toward the Lazy F.

Frank wondered if Sandeen was already making his move against Laura Flynn. Would the man be brazen enough to simply ride in with his hired gunmen and try to take over the Flynn ranch?

Frank didn't know Sandeen well enough to rule out the possibility entirely. Sandeen might feel that he could do whatever he wanted to with impunity, now that Howard Flynn was dead and Jeff Buckston might well be, too. Frank had seen the overarching arrogance in the man's eyes. When an hombre like that kept getting away with things, sooner or later he came to believe that he was above the law, above even any restraints of common decency. That was when he was the most dangerous, because he thought he was untouchable.

Because of his worry about Laura Flynn's safety, Frank was willing to postpone his attempt to capture one of Sandeen's men. He and Horn could always come back to that later, after they had determined the cause of all the shooting.

The gunfire continued long enough for Frank to pretty well determine that it wasn't coming from the vicinity of the Lazy F ranch house. The directions were wrong for that. The battle was taking place somewhere between there and San Remo, though, and for all Frank knew Laura could have started toward the settlement with some of her men and been jumped along the way by Sandeen's killers. The tense lines of his face became even more taut when the shooting suddenly stopped and an ominous silence fell.

"Don't much like the sound o' that," Horn said.

"Neither do I," Frank agreed. He pushed Stormy to an even faster pace, and soon both men were galloping over the wooded hills and across the lush pastures.

The frontiersman's instincts that they possessed led them unerringly to the spot they sought. They struck a trail that Frank knew was the main route between the Lazy F and San Remo and turned toward the settlement. Moments later they approached a long cut that slanted down between high banks to the flats along the river. Frank let out a curse as he pulled Stormy to a halt. Beside him, Horn reined in, too, and whistled softly in surprise.

"Ain't seen anything quite this bad since the Apaches gave up," the special deputy said.

The trail inside the cut was littered with bodies, mostly those of men, but a few horses were down, too. Several other mounts wandered around aimlessly, their saddles splashed with blood. The scene told Frank plainly what had happened. Killers had been hidden up there on the banks, and as this group of men had ridden unknowingly into the ambush, they had been cut down brutally and mercilessly by the gunfire from above. What happened here had been cold-blooded murder, not really a fight at all.

"Cover me just in case any of the bastards are still skulking around," Frank said to Horn. He swung down from the saddle and let Stormy's reins drop to the ground as he started forward on foot. Behind him, Horn pulled his rifle from the saddle boot and let his keen eyes swivel back and forth from bank to bank, watching closely for any sign of a further ambush.

Frank reached the first body, that of a young cowboy who lay on his back, staring sightlessly up at the blue sky. Judging by the bloodstains on his shirt, he had been shot through the chest three times. At least he had probably died quickly, Frank thought, but that was a grim comfort at best.

Frank was reasonably sure that he remembered seeing the young puncher on the Lazy F. When the face of the next dead man looked familiar, too, he was more certain of it than ever. Then he came to a horse that had fallen so that the brand on its hindquarters was visible, and the letter F lying on its side was unmistakable. For some reason, this group of Lazy F punchers had come riding along here, only to meet their deaths in the craven ambush.

Sandeen, Frank thought. The boss of Saber had sent his hired killers out to do their deadly work, and these bloody corpses scattered along the trail were the result.

It was just possible that some of the men were still alive. Frank moved quickly from body to body, checking each one, knowing the chances that any of them had survived were mighty slim but unwilling to give up hope until he was sure they were all dead.

He saw more faces he recognized and others he

didn't, but he had never been around all of Howard Flynn's crew so the unfamiliar ones didn't surprise him. Unfortunately, all of the men were dead. As Frank straightened from where he had been kneeling beside the last one, he counted quickly. Ten bodies. Ten men who would never again defend the brand they rode for.

Laura Flynn was in deeper trouble than ever before, and she might not even know it yet.

A frown creased Frank's forehead as he asked himself what these men had been doing out here. From the looks of it, they had been on their way to San Remo, but why? Frank thought back to the battle at the Lazy F the night before. If some of the punchers had been killed in that raid, Laura would have sent their bodies to town so that Jasper Culverhouse could see to the burials. But that would have required a wagon. . . .

Frank's eyes narrowed as he spotted the tracks of iron-rimmed wheels in the dust of the trail. The marks looked fresh. There *had* been a wagon with the group of riders, and that fact supported his theory. But where was it now?

He turned his head and looked out across the flats at the bottom of the slope, and he bit back a curse as he spotted what looked like some sort of wreckage a few hundred yards away. Turning, he hurried back to where Stormy waited, along with Tom Horn.

"All dead?" Horn asked.

Frank nodded curtly. "And it looks like the wagon that was with them crashed down yonder. Come on. We'll see if there's anybody alive there."

He mounted quickly and sent Stormy down the trail through the cut, letting the Appaloosa pick his own way through the welter of dead bodies. Horn followed.

When they reached the flats, Frank heeled Stormy into a trot. It took them only moments to reach the bend in the trail. The wrecked wagon lay upside down just beyond the turn. The team had broken free and stampeded on down the trail for a couple of hundred yards before stopping. Frank spotted them just standing there, still spooked but no longer in the grip of panic.

A couple of long, blanket-wrapped bundles lay on the ground near the overturned wagon. Frank recognized them for what they were and knew his theory was correct. The wagon had been carrying a couple of dead punchers from the Lazy F into San Remo so they could be buried. He wondered if one of the rough shrouds contained the corpse of Jeff Buckston.

He wondered, too, where the driver of the wagon was. Maybe he had been shot off the seat and was one of those unlucky men lying back up there in the cut, at the site of the ambush. That was the most likely explanation—

But then a groan of pain told him it was the wrong answer. The driver was down here, underneath the wrecked wagon.

Frank was out of the saddle in a flash, running forward to see if he could help the injured man. Horn was right behind him. They reached the wagon and saw a man lying just beyond it, with his legs trapped underneath it. Frank recognized Caleb Glover. The black cowboy's face was now an ashen gray with agony. The right side of his shirt and jacket were soaked with blood, probably from a bullet wound. And the way he was lying told Frank that the wagon had landed on his legs when it flipped over, probably crushing both of them.

"We got to get him out from under there," Horn said.

Frank nodded. "There's a rope on my saddle. We'll tie it to the wagon and see if we can use the horses to lift it enough to pull him free."

"Yeah, I got a lariat, too," Horn agreed. "We'll use 'em both."

He hurried back to the horses to see about that while Frank knelt next to Glover. The cowboy was unconscious, but he moaned from time to time, feeling the overwhelming pain even though he was senseless at the moment.

"Glover," Frank said. "Glover, can you hear me?"

The man didn't respond. Frank hadn't really expected him to. Between the loss of blood from the bullet wound and the injuries he must have suffered in the wreck of the wagon, it was amazing that Glover was even still alive.

Horn ran back trailing two ropes. One of the lariats was tied to Stormy's saddle, the other to Horn's horse. Horn handed one of the ropes to Frank and took the other himself. Without wasting any time, the men tied the ropes to the body of the wagon at front and back of the vehicle, running them across the bed to the side where Glover lay.

"You start the horses backing up," Frank told Horn. "I'll be ready to pull Glover clear as soon as the weight's off him."

Horn nodded in understanding. He ran back to the horses, caught hold of their reins, and walked backward, clucking to the horses and urging them to follow suit. Stormy and Horn's dun both cooperated, backing up so that the ropes pulled tight against the weight of the overturned wagon.

The sideboards on the other side from where Glover was pinned dug into the ground and acted as a fulcrum as the ropes tautened. The side that lay on Glover began to lift. Frank grabbed him under the arms and pulled him back about five feet. "That's good!" he called to Horn.

Horn let the horses step forward again, and the wagon sank to the ground. Leaving the horses hooked up to it, the special deputy trotted around the overturned vehicle to join Frank in kneeling next to Glover.

"You know this fella?" he asked.

Frank nodded. "Yes, his name's Caleb Glover. He rides for the Lazy F. One of the old punchers who was with Flynn for a long time. Looks like he was driving into San Remo with the bodies of the men who were killed in the raid last night. Laura Flynn must have sent the other men along with him. But then they rode into an ambush set up by Sandeen."

"How do you know it was Sandeen's men who were up there on those banks?"

"I guess I can't prove it," Frank admitted. "But nobody else in these parts has any reason to want to wipe out a group of Lazy F cowboys. With that many men lost, Laura doesn't have enough now to fight off any real attack on her place."

"Maybe somebody better go warn her about what's probably comin', then."

"Yes, but we need to get Glover on to the settlement, too. Maybe something can be done for him."

"So we split up?" Horn suggested.

Frank thought about it, but only for a second. Then he nodded and said, "We don't have any choice. You take Glover to San Remo, and I'll head for the Lazy F."

"Why not the other way around?"

"Nobody in town is going to believe me after everything that's happened," Frank said. "But maybe they'll believe you, since you're working for Buckey O'Neill. Get help for Glover, and tell people what's going on. Maybe you could get some men together and ride back out to the Lazy F, to help protect the place from Sandeen."

"A posse, you mean?"

"You're a special deputy, after all," Frank pointed out. "I reckon that gives you the authority to deputize folks to help you."

Horn chuckled humorlessly. "Well, if it don't, we'll say it does. But you're facin' the same problem either way, Morgan. The folks on the Lazy F aren't gonna believe you any more than the townspeople would. And those wild cowboys are liable to start shootin' at you as soon as they lay eyes on you."

"I'll just have to run that risk. If I can get to Laura Flynn and talk to her, I think I can convince her that she's in a lot more danger from Sandeen than she is from me."

"Maybe . . . if you can stay alive that long."

On the ground between them, Glover suddenly stirred. He let out another groan, and his eyelids fluttered. "Get my canteen," Frank told Horn. He got an arm under Glover's shoulders and lifted the injured man a little while Horn fetched the canteen from Stormy's saddle.

Frank took the canteen from Horn and dribbled a little water into Glover's mouth. The cowboy choked some but swallowed most of the water. His eyes opened all the way. For a few seconds his pain-wracked gaze wouldn't lock on anything, but then his eyes settled on Frank's face.

"M-Morgan?" Glover husked.

"That's right," Frank said. "Just take it easy, Glover. We're going to take you to town and get you some help."

"H-how bad . . . am I hurt?"

"I don't know," Frank told him honestly. "You've been shot, and that wagon landed on your legs when it turned over." Frank glanced at Glover's mangled limbs and added, "They're probably both broken. I can't tell whether or not you're busted up any inside. But you're still alive, and that tells me you want to live. I know Miss Warren wants you to live, too, so you just think about her and hang on, hear?"

Glover closed his eyes and nodded weakly. "Th-thanks . . . Morgan." He opened his eyes and looked up at Frank again. "The boys . . . with me . . . we was . . . ambushed . . . did any of 'em . . . make it?"

"How many riders were with you?"

"T-ten."

Frank's mouth was a thin, grim line as he said, "I'm sorry, Glover. They're all up there in that cut, dead."

Glover's face turned a little more gray. "Th-that bastard . . . Sandeen . . . it was his men . . . who done this . . ."

Horn leaned forward, suddenly more interested. "You know this for a fact?"

Glover licked his lips, and Frank gave him a little more water. That seemed to strengthen him. He said, "Yeah, I . . . I seen that son of a bitch Riley . . . and his damned shotgun . . . just caught . . . a glimpse of him . . . but it was . . . enough."

Horn looked across Glover's broken body at Frank and nodded. "It's enough, all right. There's the testimony you been lookin' for, Morgan. I heard it with my own ears, and on my authority as a special deputy, I can arrest Sandeen now."

"Not with forty gunslingers around him, you can't," Frank pointed out.

"Well, I didn't say it'd be easy, now did I?" Horn asked with a grin. "Anyway, I'm countin' on you to whittle down them odds a mite first."

Frank nodded. "I'll do my best. Let's get Glover on your horse, so you can get on to San Remo."

Horn took the lariats loose from the wagon and coiled them, replacing them on the saddles. Then, as carefully as possible, he and Frank lifted the injured man to the back of Horn's dun and tied him into the saddle. Horn climbed on behind him and said, "I'll hang on to him. Won't be the first time I've got some blood on me."

"Just follow this trail," Frank told him. "It'll take you right to San Remo. When you get there, take Glover to Jasper Culverhouse, who owns the blacksmith shop and livery stable. He's the closest thing the town has to a doctor. Miss Warren at the café is Glover's friend, and I'm sure she'll want to help, too."

Horn nodded. "I'll take care of this fella as best I can, Morgan. Just you be careful, too. Better keep your head down when you ride up to the Lazy F, or they're liable to try to part your hair with lead."

"Like you said about the blood," Frank replied, "it won't be the first time."

Chapter Twenty-seven

Laura didn't want to leave Jeff Buckston's side even for a moment, because she planned to be there when he woke. But Acey-Deucy finally persuaded her to go to her room and clean up a little. He promised he would watch Buckston like a hawk and call her right away if there was any sign that he was about to regain consciousness.

She had to admit that she felt a little better after she had washed her face, brushed her hair, and gotten out of the bloodstained clothing she'd been wearing since the night before. She put on a clean dress and went back downstairs, hoping that there might have been some change for the better in Buckston's condition while she was gone.

But as she entered the parlor, Acey-Deucy looked up at her and just shook his head glumly. Buckston still lay there on the divan, out cold. The gentle rise and fall of his chest was the only sign that he was still alive.

"He wake up soon, Missy Laura," the cook said. "You not worry."

Laura summoned up a smile. She knew that Acey-Deucy was just trying to cheer her up. In truth, none of them knew when—or if—Buckston would ever wake up again.

"I'll sit with him," she said. "You go on about your cooking. The men will be wanting some dinner pretty soon."

Acey-Deucy bowed his way out of the parlor and headed for the kitchen. Laura sat in the rocking chair next to the divan and watched Buckston.

She had never been fully aware of the depth of her feelings for him until he had been hurt. Now she knew she loved him and wanted to spend the rest of her life with him. And it wasn't just because she needed him to help her run the Lazy F, either. Like all top hands, he had a great deal of loyalty to the brand for which he rode. He would have stayed on here as foreman and done his absolute best to run the ranch properly whether or not there was ever anything personal between the two of them. She was sure of that, because that was just the sort of man Jeff Buckston was.

But she knew now she would have loved him no matter what the circumstances were, simply because he was a good man and something within her responded to him. She liked and admired him, and at the same time she longed to feel his hands on her body, his lips on hers. She knew she was being brazen to even have thoughts like that, but she couldn't help it. She loved him.

If only he would wake up . . .

She sighed and thought that she would be glad when Mr. Glover and the other men she had sent to San Remo with the bodies of the two dead punchers returned to the ranch. They ought to be back by nightfall, she told herself. She thought the Lazy F would be safe until then. It seemed unlikely to her that Ed Sandeen would attack the place in broad daylight.

But then, she had to admit that she really didn't know what Sandeen was capable of. When she first met him, she wouldn't have dreamed that he was actually the sort of man he was. But the more time that passed, the more she saw the truth. He was a ruthless man who would stop at nothing to get what he wanted . . . and what he wanted was the Lazy F and, she feared, her. He hadn't gotten over her rejection of him and was still determined to have her, one way or another.

Sooner or later, he would come to take what he wanted. Laura could only hope that Glover and the others would be back by then, and that she would have enough men to fight off Sandeen and his killers.

She was musing grimly about that when one of the hands came up onto the porch and knocked on the open front door. "Miss Laura?" he called.

Her head jerked up as the words broke her reverie. "What . . . what is it?" she asked as she stood up and turned toward the door.

"Better step out here for a minute," the cowboy advised her.

She glanced at the unmoving Buckston, then went to the door and walked out onto the porch. The cowboy held his hat in his hand as he said, "Listen."

Laura listened, and right away she heard the distant sounds that had been inaudible inside the house. "That's gunfire, isn't it?" she asked.

"Yes'm," the puncher said. "It's shootin', and a lot of it. Sounds like it's comin' from somewhere between here and town."

Immediately, Laura thought of Glover and the riders she had sent along with the wagon. "Have our men had time to reach San Remo yet?"

The cowboy shrugged. "Hard to say, but prob'ly not."

"What does this mean?" Even as she asked the question, Laura was afraid she knew the answer, and the thought made her stomach clench sickly.

"Well, it could be that those shots don't have anything to do with the fellas you sent to town," he said, turning his hat over nervously. "But it could be that somebody jumped 'em, too. That many shots means a big ruckus."

"An ambush, you mean?"

"Could be."

The man's refusal to give her a straight answer was maddening, but Laura understood it. He just didn't *know* what had happened. But under the circumstances, the chances were that the shots didn't mean anything good.

Damn that Sandeen! He would have known that she would have sent the bodies of the men who had been killed the night before into town. He could have sent his killers to set up a trap for her men. She never should have sent so many riders with the wagon. She realized now that she was facing a cunning enemy who might have just cut her forces almost in half. She had played right into his hands.

If only Buckston had been in charge, he never would have made such a mistake, she told herself bitterly. If only . . .

But there was no point in such self-recrimination. The past couldn't be changed, and she had to deal with the situation the way it was, not the way she wished it could be.

"You want me to send a rider to take a look . . . ?" the cowboy began.

Laura shook her head. Despite the fear she felt that something might have happened to Mr. Glover and the others, she couldn't afford to split the ranch's defenders any more, not even by one man.

"All the remaining hands are here at headquarters, aren't they?" she asked.

The puncher grimaced. "Yes'm. Ain't nobody out ridin' the range today. Sandeen's men may be roundin' up all our stock, right this minute."

She knew the decision to abandon the cattle didn't sit well with the men, but there was nothing that could be done about it. The ranch headquarters had to be defended. They could try to recover any stolen stock later, when this whole range war was settled.

"I want every man armed with a rifle and pistol, and make sure they have plenty of ammunition in their pockets," she ordered. "Stay out of sight as much as possible. Everyone is to find some good cover that can be easily defended."

"Yes, ma'am. You reckon Sandeen's gonna hit us again?"

"I think it's only a matter of time," Laura said.

If not for the smoke that curled thinly from the main house's chimney, Frank would have thought that the headquarters of the Lazy F was deserted when he rode up some time later. He didn't see anyone moving anywhere as he approached. When he came closer, he spotted quite a few horses in the corral. It looked like the remaining punchers were staying close to home today, rather than riding the range. That jibed with the observations Frank had made as he rode toward the ranch. He had seen Lazy F stock but no one tending it.

Laura Flynn had hunkered down to wait for trouble. That was a wise move, Frank thought, because she was bound to get it as soon as Sandeen decided the time was right to make the final move in this deadly game.

Frank rode openly along the trail that led to the ranch. Since it was obvious that he was only one man, he hoped the spread's defenders would hold their fire when they saw him, even if they recognized him. And if they didn't . . . well, he hoped their aim wasn't any too good.

Stormy's hooves thudding against the hard-packed dirt of the trail was the only sound. Other than that an eerie silence hung over the landscape. Frank was five hundred yards from the house, then four and three and two hundred, and finally he was within easy hailing distance. No one called out to him, though. His instincts told him that he was being watched. He felt the hostile eyes on him. But still, no one tried to stop him as he rode right up to the porch of the main house.

The front door was open, but the inside of the house was too shadowy for him to be able to see much. As he shifted his weight as if he were about to dismount, Laura Flynn's voice came from inside, accompanied by the metallic ratcheting sound of a gun being cocked.

"Don't move, Mr. Morgan," she said. "I can see you just fine where you are, and I'll shoot you if you try to get off that horse."

Frank settled back in the saddle, still calm. He had been threatened with a gun too many times to let it bother him now. "Take it easy, Miss Flynn," he said steadily. "I'm not looking for trouble. I came to help you, and to deliver some news."

"Good news?" Laura asked skeptically from inside the house.

Frank sighed and shook his head. "Not hardly, I'm afraid. Some of Sandeen's men bushwhacked your wagon and your riders as they were on their way into town."

For a long moment, Laura didn't say anything. Frank sensed he wasn't telling her anything she hadn't already been afraid of. The sound of the massacre could have been heard easily here on the ranch.

Finally, Laura asked, "Are any of my men alive?"

"Just Glover, and he's hurt pretty bad. A fella I know took him on into town to get help for him."

"One of Sandeen's men, you mean? Why would he do that?"

Frank took a deep breath and suppressed the annoyance he felt. "Not hardly. The man I'm talking about is named Tom Horn. He's a special deputy sent into the Mogollon range by Sheriff Buckey O'Neill to get to the bottom of all the trouble in these parts."

That information prompted a surprised silence from Laura. Frank waited a moment and then went on. "I've told you before, Miss Flynn, that I'm not working for Sandeen. I know you saw me here last night and thought that I was with those masked raiders, but I was actually trying to stop them."

"That . . . that's what Mr. Glover said." Frank heard a step, and Laura Flynn moved into the doorway where he could see her. She was holding a Colt in her right hand. The barrel pointed at Frank and didn't waver as Laura said, "He told me that you were shooting at Sandeen's men last night."

Frank nodded. "That's right, and I winged a few of them. I give you my word, I didn't kill your uncle and I've been trying to stop Sandeen, not help him."

The revolver in Laura's hand lowered. "But I . . . I shot at you."

Frank smiled thinly. "That wasn't the first time I've been shot at by somebody who made a mistake. I don't take any offense from it. I'd still like to give you a hand, if you're willing to accept my help."

She stared at him, clearly torn by the decision facing her. She said, "Mr. Buckston was so sure. . . ."

"Buckston made a mistake, too." Frank paused. "I saw him get hit last night. Is he still alive?"

"Yes, the bullet just creased his head." Laura hesitated, as if unsure whether to say anything else. Then she continued. "But he's still unconscious. We . . . we don't know if he's ever going to wake up again."

Frank nodded solemnly. "I've seen the same thing happen. For what it's worth, nearly everybody I've known who got hurt like that came to eventually."

"*Nearly* everybody?"

Frank shrugged. "A few never did," he said. Right now, Laura needed honesty more than she needed to have punches pulled.

After a moment, Laura asked, "How badly is Mr. Glover hurt? Will he pull through?"

Again, Frank was honest. "It'll be touch and go. He

was shot through the shoulder, and that wagon turned over while he was trying to get away from Sandeen's men and landed on his legs. Both of them were broken, that's for sure. Whether or not he had any other injuries, I just don't know."

"My God," Laura said in a hollow voice. "To think I could have prevented all this death and misery if I had just . . . just gone along with what Ed Sandeen wanted . . ."

Frank shook his head and said, "Don't start thinking like that. There never would have been peace between Sandeen and your uncle, no matter what you did. Sooner or later Sandeen would have tried to take over the Lazy F, and your uncle would have fought back. The trouble was bound to happen as soon as Sandeen moved into this part of the country. His sort of man brings it with him, wherever he goes."

"What sort of man is that?" Laura asked.

"Ruthless," Frank answered. "Ambitious. Hungry for money and land and above all, power. Call it whatever you want, but it comes down to the fact that Sandeen and men like him think they can take whatever they want and nobody can stop them. It's up to the decent folks, the honest folks, to show those men that they're wrong."

Laura smiled faintly. "Well, if nothing else, you've convinced me that you *don't* work for Sandeen, Mr. Morgan. What do I do now?"

Frank returned the smile. "You could invite me in. I don't like to sit back and wait for trouble to come to me, but in this case I don't see that we have any choice. Sandeen has us outnumbered, so we'd be foolish to take the fight to him. Tom Horn's going to try to bring some help back from San Remo. Until then, we hunker down and wait."

"You're right, of course. Come in, Mr. Morgan. Welcome to the Lazy F. I apologize for the inhospitable welcome at first."

Frank had already spotted rifle barrels protruding

from windows in the house and several of the outbuildings. As he swung down from the saddle he grinned and said, "As far as I'm concerned, any welcome is a hospitable one as long as folks hold their fire."

Chapter Twenty-eight

Glover had lost consciousness again by the time Tom Horn reached San Remo with him, but the cowboy was still alive. Horn had his left arm around Glover's torso and could feel the wounded man breathing. The dun's hooves clattered on the plank bridge as Horn rode across. He spotted the livery barn with the smaller building in front of it that had to be the blacksmith shop Frank Morgan had told him about, and headed straight for the place.

A short, burly, mostly bald man stepped out, obviously having seen him coming. The fact that two men were riding double and one of them was hanging on to the other meant trouble most of the time, and the blacksmith acknowledged that fact by greeting Horn with a rifle in his hands. A big, wolflike dog followed the man out of the shop and watched the newcomers with a keen wariness.

"Good Lord!" the blacksmith exclaimed when he got a good look at the man riding in front. "That's Caleb Glover! What happened to him?"

"Got shot in an ambush and then had a wagon turn over him," Horn replied as he brought the dun to a stop. "You Jasper Culverhouse?"

"That's right." Culverhouse lowered the rifle. "Do I know you?"

"No, but Frank Morgan told me to find you." Horn noticed how the big cur's ears pricked forward at the mention of Morgan's name and wondered if the dog belonged to The Drifter. "My name's Tom Horn. I'm workin' as a special deputy for Sheriff O'Neill. Now, are we gonna keep jawin', or are you gonna help me with this fella?"

Culverhouse set the rifle aside and reached up with brawny arms to take hold of Glover. "Easy now," he said. "We'll take him in and put him on my bunk."

Carefully, the two men carried Glover into Culverhouse's living quarters. The blacksmith's bed was little more than a rope bunk in a narrow room, but they lowered the injured man onto it and then as they stepped back, Culverhouse said, "Would you mind goin' down to the café to fetch the lady who runs it? She keeps company with Glover, and she can lend me a hand takin' care of him."

Horn nodded. "Yeah, Morgan said something about her. I reckon she's a colored lady?"

"Yeah, but we don't pay much attention to such things around here," Culverhouse said in a warning tone.

"It don't make no nevermind to me. I'll bring her right back."

Horn turned to go, but Culverhouse stopped him with a hand on his arm. Horn tensed and looked icily down at the blacksmith's hand. Culverhouse let go.

"You say you're a special deputy?"

"That's right. Buckey O'Neill sent me to get to the bottom of all the trouble in these parts. I ran into Morgan, got most of the story from him, and then him and me found this fella and some others who'd been ambushed by Sandeen's men."

"Sandeen! You know for sure he was behind it?"

Horn gestured toward the bunk. "He said he saw

somebody named Riley who works for Sandeen. Sounds like enough proof for me until I hear something better."

"And Morgan . . . Morgan's not part of it?"

Horn smiled. "He ain't workin' for Sandeen, if that's what you mean. He says he didn't kill Howard Flynn, and that's good enough for me."

"Me, too," Culverhouse agreed. "Some folks may not want to believe it, but I do."

"We'll hash it out later," Horn said. "For now, see what you can do for that fella, and I'll go get his lady friend."

He left the blacksmith shop, only to find that several people were already headed in that direction. Somebody must have noticed him and Culverhouse carrying Glover into the building, and the word had spread that there was a wounded man up here.

A scruffy-looking gent in a suit and a bowler hat, with a graying beard and an eye that tended to wander, came up to him and said, "Mister, who might you be?"

"I could ask the same question of you," Horn drawled coolly.

The man hooked his thumbs in his vest. "I'm Willard Donohue. Happen to be the mayor of San Remo. I'm told you just brought in an injured man."

Horn thought the man looked more like a tramp than the mayor, but he ignored that and jerked a thumb toward the blacksmith shop. "Yeah, I left him down there. Culverhouse is workin' on him. Fella name of Glover, rides for the Lazy F."

"Caleb Glover!" Donohue said. "My God, somebody needs to tell Mary Elizabeth!"

"Lady who runs the café?" When Donohue nodded, Horn went on. "I'm on my way there now."

"Much obliged." Donohue started past him, then stopped. "Say, you never did tell me your name."

"Tom Horn."

The look on Donohue's face told Horn that he had heard of him, but Horn didn't hang around to explain what he was doing here. He strode toward the café, his long legs covering the ground quickly.

It was mid-afternoon by now, a slack time for any eatery. The café was empty when Horn walked in. A woman's voice came through an open doorway that led to the rear of the building. "Be right with you." Judging from the appetizing aroma that drifted through the door, she was baking back there.

"Miss Warren?" Horn called.

She stuck her head out the door, a good-looking black woman on the cusp of middle age, and began, "I said I'd be—" She stopped when she saw the look on Horn's face. The fact that he was a stranger probably alarmed her a little, too. "What is it? What's wrong?"

"I just brought in a fella named Glover. He's down at the blacksmith shop, hurt pretty bad."

The woman's hand went to her mouth as her eyes widened in horror and fear. "Caleb!" she cried. She rushed out of the kitchen, still wearing her apron and with flour dusting her hands, and left the café on the run.

Horn followed at a more leisurely pace. Before he reached the blacksmith shop, he noticed a buggy rolling into San Remo from the other end of town, along the trail that meandered to the northwest and eventually reached Prescott. He might not have paid as much attention to the vehicle if not for the fact that there were two women in it, and the one handling the reins was pretty and had long red hair. She brought the buggy to a stop in front of one of the mercantiles.

The women weren't any of his business, Horn told himself. He resumed walking toward the blacksmith shop. By the time he got there, quite a crowd had gathered. They parted to let Horn through, and when he stepped into Culverhouse's room, he saw the blacksmith and the colored lady bent over the bunk, working on the injured man.

"How bad is he?" Horn asked Culverhouse. He had heard Glover's statement that the bushwhackers were led by the gunman named Riley, who evidently worked for Ed Sandeen. That was enough legal proof for Horn to act upon, but it would better in the long run if Glover was around to testify against Sandeen if matters ever came to court. Which they probably wouldn't, Horn mused, since dustups like this usually resolved themselves in powder smoke and blood, but just in case . . .

"Bad enough," Culverhouse answered grimly. "The bullet busted his shoulder and he lost a lot of blood, but at least it went on through so he's not carryin' a chunk of lead in him. Both legs are broken. He'll never ride again, and he'll be damned lucky to walk."

"But he *will* live?"

Culverhouse grunted. "The fact that he's still alive is a blasted miracle, so yeah, I'd say he's got a chance. If losin' that much blood didn't kill him, us cleanin' him up and tryin' to set those legs in splints probably won't. But we'll know more in a day or two."

"Do what you can for him," Horn said. "I got to have a talk with the rest o' the citizens."

He stepped out of the blacksmith shop and raised his hands to quiet the clamor among the crowd. As they looked at him curiously, Horn reached inside his shirt pocket and pulled out a badge. He pinned it to the front of his shirt and said in a loud voice, "My name is Horn. I'm a special deputy workin' for Sheriff Buckey O'Neill of Yavapai County and empowered by him to take action for the purpose o' quellin' the range war that's supposed to be brewin' in these parts." Quelling, that was a good word. He liked that. "Earlier today, gunmen workin' for Ed Sandeen ambushed a party of Lazy F riders and wiped them all out except for the man I just brought into town."

That brought angry mutters from several of the townies. Horn raised his hands again.

"There's a good chance that Sandeen is goin' to attack the Lazy F itself," he went on, "and I'm callin' for volunteers, here and now, to form a posse and ride back out there with me to help defend the place."

"How do you know Sandeen was responsible for the ambush?" one of the men asked.

"That fella inside, Glover by name, said he saw one of Sandeen's hired killers amongst the gunmen. Somebody named Riley."

"That'd be Vern Riley," Mayor Donohue said. "He's one of Sandeen's men, all right, and damn sure a killer. But what makes you think Sandeen's gonna strike directly at the ranch?"

"That's what Frank Morgan thinks, and that's good enough for me, too."

"Morgan!" another man said. "But he works for—"

Horn shook his head wearily. "Don't say Sandeen. You folks got the wrong idea about him. There's nobody around here who wants to stop Sandeen more than Morgan, and nobody Sandeen would like to see dead more than him."

Donohue scratched his grizzled beard. "Morgan always did strike me as an honest fella, even when it looked like the evidence was against him. Shoot, I'm the one who hired him as town marshal before Howard Flynn got killed and all hell broke loose."

"Yeah, well, hell's due to get a chunk shoved under the corner if Morgan's right about Sandeen ridin' against the Lazy F," Horn said. "The girl who owns the place, Flynn's niece, doesn't have enough men left out there to fight off a bunch of raiders. That's why I want to take a posse out there, and we don't need to waste any time, otherwise there may not be anything left to save."

"You said you're a deputy," one of the townies said.

"Can't you get word to Sheriff O'Neill and have him send in more men?"

"By the time a rider could get to Prescott and Buckey could send a posse back here, the Lazy F might be wiped out," Horn snapped. "I do intend to send word to the sheriff, but we can't expect to see any reinforcements from him get here in time." Horn looked around at the citizens of San Remo. "It's up to you folks. I know some of you have done business with Sandeen in the past, and you don't want to get on his bad side. But if you'd seen what I saw out there on the trail between here and the Lazy F, you'd know he's gone kill-crazy. If he gets away with grabbin' that spread, he'll go after all the other ranches in these parts next, and when he gets his hands on those, he'll turn his attention on the town. I've seen range hogs like that before. If you don't stop him, he won't quit until he controls everything in the Verde valley, all the way to the Mogollon Rim."

"But . . . but such things can't happen!" one of the men sputtered. "This is a civilized country. We have laws!"

"Laws are just words, and they don't mean a damned thing unless somebody's willin' to stand up and make 'em stand for something," Horn said as he rested a hand on the butt of his gun. "I'm goin' back out to the Lazy F. The rest of you do what you want."

The scorn in his voice was plain to hear. He started to push his way through the crowd, but Donohue blocked his path. "Wait just a minute, fella," the mayor rumbled. "We didn't say nobody was goin' with you. We've stood up to Sandeen before, and we can do it again." He looked around. "Ain't that right, boys?"

There were grim nods of agreement from most of the men in the group.

"Just give us a few minutes to go get our guns and our horses," Donohue went on. "Then we'll be back, and we'll all ride out to the Lazy F together."

"All right," Horn said with a nod. He looked at the sky. "Just don't take too long about it. It's liable to be night before we can get there, and I've got a hunch Sandeen won't wait very long to strike once darkness falls."

As the crowd dispersed, the stocky, fair-haired man at the rear of it walked quickly back to the Verde Saloon. Mitch Kite was a man in turmoil. From the sound of everything Kite had heard, Sandeen had reverted all the way back to his hoot-owl ways and was ready now to take what he wanted by force. This might be a good time for Kite to take the loot he had stashed in a carpetbag under a loose board in the storeroom and light a shuck out of these parts. The law was in on this now, in the person of that special deputy, Horn. Kite had heard of Tom Horn and knew the man was no more honest than he had to be, but like most Westerners, Horn had a code and stuck to it. Right now, he was working on the side of the law and nothing would sway him from that path. Next month, Horn might sign on with a man every bit as bad as Sandeen and would then be loyal to *him* until the job was done. Tom Horn was the sort of man most folks *thought* Frank Morgan was.

Yet Morgan and Horn had one thing in common— they were both very dangerous men, and now that they were working on the same side, Sandeen wasn't fully aware of what he was getting into by taking them on. Somebody ought to warn him, Kite thought, and he considered saddling up a horse and riding for Saber as hard as he could, in hopes that he could get there before Sandeen gathered up his army of gunslingers and rode on the Lazy F. In the future, Sandeen might be very appreciative of somebody who brought him a warning like that.

So that was the dilemma facing Kite as he stood at the

bar of the Verde Saloon and poured himself a drink. He tossed the fiery liquor down his throat and tried to figure out what to do. Cut and run, taking what he could—or keep betting on a Sandeen victory and play the game out to the end?

"You all right, Boss?" Speckler asked from the other side of the hardwood.

Kite reached a decision. He thumped the empty glass down on the bar and said, "I'm fine. Go out back to the shed and slap the saddle on my horse."

"Sure, Boss. You goin' somewhere?"

"Yeah," Kite said.

And he hoped it wasn't straight to hell.

Chapter Twenty-nine

Frank didn't really want to give Laura Flynn the details of the tragic scene he and Horn had discovered on the trail between the Lazy F and San Remo, but she was insistent. Anyway, the men who had been ambushed were her riders and had been following her orders when they were killed. She deserved to hear the truth about what had happened to them.

"Then . . . it really is my fault that they're all dead," she said with a catch in her voice as she and Frank sat in the parlor of the ranch house with the still-unconscious Jeff Buckston.

"Some people might blame you," Frank said, "but they'd be wrong. Whenever something bad happens, some folks are always quick to jump on whoever it happened to and try to claim that it was their own fault, that they brought whatever it was on their own heads. But that lets the varmints who actually did the bad thing off the hook. Nobody forced Riley and the rest of Sandeen's men to pull the triggers on their guns. They made that choice all on their own. When somebody does something evil and folks say it's not their fault and try to blame the victim . . ." Frank shook his head in incomprehension. "Well, that's just crazy."

Laura smiled weakly. "I don't know if you're just trying to make me feel better or not, Mr. Morgan, but I appreciate your kind words. I'll always carry the deaths of those men in my heart."

"It's all right to mourn them," Frank said. "But when you get done with that, it's time to strike back at the evil bastards who are really responsible."

"Yes. I can see that. But you said we can't take the fight to Sandeen, that we don't have enough men."

"I've been thinking about that," Frank mused. "How attached are you to this place?"

She looked at him in surprise. "The Lazy F, you mean? Why, it's become my home. And it was my uncle's home for thirty years, too, so that means something to me as well."

"I'm not talking about the ranch itself. I mean this house, the barns and corrals and the smokehouse, all the things like that."

"Well . . . of course, the ranch house itself means a great deal to me because of Uncle Howard, but . . . if something ever happened to it, I suppose it could be rebuilt. . . ." She frowned at him. "Exactly what do you have in mind, Mr. Morgan?"

Frank glanced out the window at the yard in front of the house. The light was fading now. In another hour, it would be dark outside. And not long after dark had fallen, Sandeen would strike. Frank was convinced of that.

"We're easy targets here," he said. "Sandeen will have us outnumbered probably four to one. And there's no guarantee that Horn will get back from San Remo with a posse in time to help. In fact, we don't know for sure if he'll even be able to raise a posse."

Laura said, "I think he will. Uncle Howard was well liked in the settlement, and people are starting to understand just what sort of man Ed Sandeen really is."

"That's true," Frank agreed, "but you still can't count

on folks picking up a gun and risking their own life until they actually do it."

"Then what do you suggest?"

"If we got out of here, along with the men you have left, we could hit Sandeen from behind when he attacks the place. The odds would still be against us, but at least we'd have the element of surprise on our side. We'd be able to move around, too, instead of being pinned down in the buildings."

"Would that be enough to . . . to make a difference?"

Frank smiled. "You never know until you try. Besides, I don't like just sitting and waiting for trouble."

"No, you'd rather go out and stir it up," Laura said with a smile of her own. "I'm no strategist, Mr. Morgan, but I like the sound of your plan. As far as I'm concerned, there's only one thing wrong with it."

"What's that?"

"I can't leave. Mr. Buckston is still unconscious, and he shouldn't be moved until he wakes up. We can't risk injuring him even more, and I won't leave him."

Frank frowned. That was a problem, all right.

"When Sandeen gets here, if he finds the place deserted he's liable to torch all the buildings. That's why I asked how attached you were to them. And if you're here, he'll take you and use you as a hostage to get what he wants."

"Then it'll be up to you and the rest of the men to see that he doesn't get the chance to do any of those things . . . won't it?"

Frank had to chuckle at her cool demeanor. "I guess so," he said.

She reached over and touched the butt of the gun that lay on a small table beside her. "Besides, I'm armed. Ed Sandeen won't take me without a fight. Or should I do as I've heard the women did in the days of the Apache raids and save the last bullet for myself?"

"I wouldn't go that far," Frank advised. "Sandeen's

pretty bad, but he's not an Apache. Besides, no matter what happens tonight, his days are numbered. I imagine Tom Horn has already sent word to Sheriff O'Neill about what's been going on in these parts. Sooner or later the law will stop Sandeen, even if we don't."

"All right," Laura said. "I'm in agreement with your plan, as long as you agree that I'll stay here with Mr. Buckston. I'll keep Acey-Deucy with me, too. He wouldn't be of much help to you in a running gun battle."

Frank nodded. "I'll fetch in the other men and let you talk to them. I've got a hunch they won't take orders from me unless you tell them to."

"Of course. I'll make sure they understand what they're to do."

Frank waited until the shadows of dusk had gathered and thickened even more before he slipped out of the house and began making his way around the remaining outbuildings of the Lazy F headquarters, passing the word to the men who were forted up inside them that they were to gather in the main house so that Miss Laura could talk to them. They cooperated, although some of them were a little reluctant and obviously still distrustful of Frank. They had lingering doubts about whether he was responsible for Howard Flynn's death.

Frank was cautious about moving around in the open and warned the punchers to do likewise, because it was possible that Sandeen had a man up in the hills watching the ranch through field glasses. In order for his plan to be effective, he and the Lazy F crew had to leave headquarters without Sandeen being aware of what they were doing. All the lamps had been blown out in the house, and one by one, the men slipped in and gathered in the parlor.

In the gloom of the parlor, Frank made a head count and found that he had fourteen men at his disposal. Several of them were wounded, but swore they could ride and hold up their end in a fight. He had no choice but to believe them. Laura told them the plan, then said, "You'll take orders from Mr. Morgan. He's the most experienced at this sort of thing."

That was right, he thought. He had probably risked his life against well-nigh impossible odds more than any of these cowboys, tough and rugged though they might be.

One of the men objected. "How do we know this fella Morgan is tellin' the truth?" he questioned. "He's a gunfighter, just like the polecats who ride for Sandeen, and I still ain't sure he didn't gun down the boss."

"*I'm* sure," Laura said firmly, "and those are my orders." She paused. "However, I'm *not* going to order any man to go along who doesn't want to. You can draw your time and ride out right now, and chances are you'll be well away from here before Sandeen attacks. The choice is up to all of you."

An embarrassed silence fell over the men, and after a moment the cowboy who had spoken up mumbled, "Aw, heck, Miss Laura, I didn't say nothin' about drawin' my time. If there's gonna be a fight, I sure don't want to miss all the fun."

"Me, neither," another man said, and there was a chorus of agreement. All of the ranch hands were going to stick, just as Frank had thought they would.

"All right, then," Laura said with a satisfied nod. "I'll turn things over to Mr. Morgan."

"Thanks," Frank said as he faced the men. He couldn't see them very well in the shadows, but he could sense their rapt attention. "We need to move fast, but we can't rush things and get careless. One by one, saddle your horses and lead them away from here, but don't mount up just yet. Move as quietly as you can, and don't light any lamps or even strike a lucifer to light a quirly. We need a place to rendezvous. You boys know the country around here better than I do. Any suggestions?"

After a moment one of the men said, "There's a bald

knob about a mile and a half north of here. I reckon we all know where it is and can find it in the dark."

Again, the men muttered agreement.

Frank nodded. "That'll do. I remember seeing it when I was looking over the range, so I can find it, too. We'll drift up there, and as soon as we're all together, we'll circle around so that we can guard the trail from Saber that leads up here. If Sandeen and his men ride by, we'll let them go and give them a little lead before we fall in behind them. When the trouble starts, we'll hit them from the rear, just as hard and fast as we can. If luck is with us, we'll drop enough of them fast enough to even up the odds a little."

"I don't much like leavin' Miss Laura here with just the cook and Buck," a puncher said.

Without hesitation, Laura said, "That's my decision to make. Mr. Buckston can't be moved. And besides, the place has to look like someone is here, doesn't it, Mr. Morgan? That will draw Sandeen in and make him concentrate his attention on the house instead of what might be behind them."

"That's good thinking," Frank said with a nod. "Once we're all gone, have Acey-Deucy light some of the lamps in here, as if it's a normal evening on the Lazy F."

Laura laughed humorlessly. "As if anything around here will ever be truly normal again."

"You never know," Frank told her. "As long as there's hope to hang on to, anything can happen. We'll see how things play out tonight."

"Yes, of course." Laura faced the men again. "Before you go, I . . . I just want to say thank you for everything you've done and for sticking by me. I know it can't be easy working for a woman—"

"You ain't just a woman, Miss Laura," one of the punchers said. "You're Howard Flynn's niece. You're the boss of the Lazy F now, and we ride for the brand, by God!"

Again the men spoke up, voicing their agreement.

"Let's go," Frank said. "Remember what I told you . . . move quick, but make sure nobody sees you, either, if Sandeen has watchers posted."

It was an even bet whether or not they could actually get away from the ranch without Sandeen being aware of it and turn the tables on the rogue cattleman. But it was the best chance they had, and the odds would still be against them.

But not if Tom Horn was able to bring help from San Remo and reached the Lazy F in time. Frank knew it was a long shot, but if a posse hit Sandeen's raiders from one direction while Frank and the punchers were attacking from another . . .

Like he had told Laura Flynn, as long as there was hope to cling to, anything could happen.

In his life, Mitch Kite had spent plenty of time in a saddle, often fleeing at a gallop from a posse or an outraged husband or a vengeful relative. But it had been quite a while since he had ridden this hard and fast, and the pace was taking a painful toll on his body. Clearly, living the life of a saloon keeper had softened him up some.

But he made a lot better time than a bunch of townies from San Remo would, and it was only dusk when he rode up to the hacienda at Saber. He saw right away that something was going on. Men were leading saddle horses out of the barns and corrals, and other men were standing around checking the loads in their rifles and six-guns. A grim but anticipatory atmosphere hung over the place.

Sandeen was getting ready to go to war.

A stocky, bearded hard case named Devereaux was standing in the open wrought-iron gate that led into the big house's courtyard. Kite reined his mount to a stop and asked the man, "Where's Sandeen?"

"Right here," came the answer from inside the court-yard, and Sandeen himself strode past Devereaux, fol-lowed by the dapper and deadly Vern Riley. "What the hell are you doing here, Kite?" Sandeen demanded. He was wearing range clothes instead of his usual suit, and a gun belt and holstered six-gun were strapped around his waist. "You ought to be in San Remo, looking after my saloon."

"You may not have a saloon come morning if you don't listen to me, Ed." Kite suppressed the flare of anger he felt at Sandeen's contemptuous tone of voice. Sandeen might be the big skookum he-wolf around these parts now, but once upon a time Mitch Kite had been a man to stand aside from, too. He continued. "The law is on to what you're doing."

Darkly, Sandeen frowned up at him. "What the devil are you talking about? What law?"

"Buckey O'Neill sent a special deputy in to poke around when he heard rumors about a range war up here. It's that fella Tom Horn."

"Horn!" Vern Riley exclaimed. "Hell, he's not much better than an outlaw himself."

"Maybe not, but right now he's wearing a badge," Kite said. "And it gets worse. He met up with Frank Morgan, and he believes Morgan's story about him not killing Howard Flynn." Kite looked at Riley. "You got lucky Morgan came along when he did that day, Vern, so you could pin the killing on him, but luck doesn't always last."

"Damn it!" Riley grated. "Morgan was the one who was really lucky that day. He was the one I planned to bush-whack after I circled around and got ahead of him. But then Flynn came ridin' along, and I thought, why the hell not?"

Sandeen snapped, "And you acted without my orders when you killed him, too."

"You didn't seem to mind when Flynn was dead and it looked like Morgan was going to get the blame," Riley bristled.

Impatiently, Kite said, "None of that matters now. Morgan and Horn have teamed up. They found those Lazy F punchers you and the boys wiped out, Vern."

Riley shrugged. "Dead men can't talk."

"Yeah, but that darky Glover isn't dead."

"What?" Sandeen burst out. He swung around to face Riley again. "You told me—"

"Hell, he was shot, and then that wagon turned over on him!" Riley defended himself. "How the hell was I supposed to know—"

"You could have ridden down there and put some more bullets in him to be sure!"

"Horn heard Glover say that he saw you among the bushwhackers, Vern," Kite said as Sandeen and Riley glared at each other. "That means the law will be coming after *you*, Ed."

Sandeen shook his head. "No one can prove I ordered that ambush, any more than Morgan could prove that I sent Lannigan after him. I can always claim that Vern acted on his own—"

"Throw *me* to the wolves, you mean!" Riley objected. "The hell you will! If it comes down to it, I'll tell the law everything I know about you, Sandeen, about all those banks you robbed back in Kansas and those trains you held up and those killings in Montana—"

The gun that Mitch Kite had slipped out of his coat suddenly roared as flame lanced from its barrel. Riley was driven backward against the adobe wall by the slug that tore into his chest. He tried to lift his shotgun, but Kite fired twice more. The bullets made Riley bounce off the wall and pitch forward on his face, dropping the scattergun as he fell. He kicked once and then lay still.

Sandeen looked down at him impassively. "Damn fool. He should have known better than to threaten to spill his guts to the law." He gave Kite a curt nod. "Good work, Mitch. You saved me the trouble of killing him."

"I knew that's what you'd want," Kite said casually as he began to reload the expended chambers in the revolver he held.

"I'm glad you're here," Sandeen went on. "You'll ride with us tonight against the Lazy F."

Kite's head jerked up in surprise. "You're going through with the attack on the ranch? You can't, Ed! You still don't know the whole story. Horn's gathered up a posse to take out there from San Remo."

"You think I give a damn about that? I'm not worried about eight or ten of those piddling townies. They won't be enough to make a difference. I'll be surprised if Laura Flynn has more than a dozen able-bodied men left to defend the place. Throw in that so-called posse, and it's still not enough to keep me from taking what I want."

"But . . . but you don't have to!" Kite sputtered. "Riley's dead. He was the only direct link between you and that ambush. Without him, the law can't prove anything. You can just deny everything and sit back and wait. The Lazy F's not going anywhere. You can always get control of it later, after things have quieted down some."

Sandeen chuckled coldly. "You don't understand, Mitch. I've never been a man who likes to wait. When I see something I want, I take it. Then and there. I let Howard Flynn and that niece of his get away with too much for too long. The Lazy F is the best range around here, so it's mine by right. And so will the rest of the Mogollon Rim country be mine before I'm through."

Kite stared at him. Blinded by ambition and arrogance, Sandeen had lost his mind, and Kite suddenly found himself wondering if the man had been insane all along, just holding it in check.

"You're making a mistake, Ed," he said. He started to turn his horse. "I'm going back to San Remo—"

The harsh click of a gun being cocked stopped him. "Are *you* turning on me, too, Mitch?" Sandeen asked in a quiet but deadly menacing tone.

Kite stiffened in the saddle. He hadn't even seen Sandeen draw, but the gun in his hand was rock-steady. Kite didn't doubt for a second that Sandeen would use it, either.

He had no choice. He said, "No, Ed. I'm not turning on you. I'm with you, you know that. I'll back your play all the way."

"I thought so." Sandeen lowered the hammer and leathered the iron. "We'll be ready to ride in a few minutes." He laughed happily. "Just think, Mitch. By morning the Lazy F will be mine, and it's just the beginning. I'm going to rule this whole part of the territory like it was my own private kingdom . . . and who knows? Maybe someday you'll be working for Governor Sandeen, or even Senator Sandeen. Nobody can stop me now!"

Kite wiped the back of his hand across his mouth. Crazy or not, he hoped Sandeen was right.

But with a sick feeling in the pit of his stomach, Kite told himself that Sandeen had forgotten all about the man called The Drifter.

Chapter Thirty

Tom Horn gritted his teeth to hold back impatient, frustrated curses. The citizens of San Remo meant well and he supposed they were better than no posse at all, but they were damned sure as slow as molasses in January!

It had taken them what seemed like forever to fetch their guns, saddle their horses, mount up, and move out. Now that they were finally riding toward the Lazy F, they still weren't hustling along fast enough to suit Horn. The sun was already down, and night was falling rapidly. At this rate, they wouldn't reach the Flynn ranch until an hour or more after dark. Depending on how impatient Sandeen was, that might be too late to do any good.

But no matter what happened tonight, Horn told himself, the jig was up for Mr. Ed Sandeen. Before leaving San Remo, Horn had written out a note for Sheriff Buckey O'Neill and sent the Mexican saddle maker's oldest boy galloping off to Prescott with it. The youngster would get there sometime the next morning, and by the end of the next day, O'Neill would probably reach San Remo with a real posse. Even if Sandeen succeeded in grabbing the Lazy F tonight, he wouldn't have it for long.

Jasper Culverhouse and Mayor Donohue flanked Horn. The big wolflike cur loped alongside Culverhouse's horse. As Horn had suspected, the dog belonged to Frank Morgan, and Culverhouse figured he would want to come along for the fun.

Trailing along behind the three men were eight more—Wilson and Desmond, the two storekeepers; Hightower, McCain, and Williams, who owned the three saloons in San Remo that Sandeen didn't own; Vincente Delgado, the saddle maker; and Pearsoll and Higgins, who worked as bartenders for Hightower and McCain, respectively. They all seemed like good men, brave enough, and like all frontiersmen they knew at least a little about handling guns, but none of them had ever been part of a fight like this. None of them would be a match for even the least skilled of Sandeen's hard cases and gun-throwers.

But the country had a history of common men banding together and going out to oppose evil, Horn reminded himself. It was a tradition that went back over a hundred years, back to the days of the revolution that had freed the colonies from England's despotic grip. And hadn't the Texans ultimately defeated the much larger army fielded by that Mexican dictator, Santa Anna? Time and again, Americans had taken up arms against seemingly impossible odds and somehow emerged triumphant. Maybe all it meant, Horn thought, was that sometimes El Señor Dios smiled on courageous fools.

That might be enough.

"How much longer will it take us to get there?" Donohue asked.

"Half an hour, maybe," Horn said. "That's just a guess, though. I ain't as familiar with this part of the country as I am with some others."

"Sounds right to me," Culverhouse put in. "What do we do when we get there?"

"Well, if everything's peaceful, we ride in and add our numbers to those defendin' the place. If it ain't . . . if the ruckus is already goin' on . . . I reckon we'll figure that out when the time comes."

"I'd give a lot for a shot at Ed Sandeen," Donohue growled. "He's sure caused plenty of trouble in these parts."

"Better be careful what you wish for, Mayor," Horn drawled. "Before the night's over, you might just get it."

Frank found the bald knob without any trouble. The moon was rising, and it made the rocky knoll shine a little in the night, like the hairless skull of an old man.

He had been the last to leave the Lazy F, waiting until the cowboys had slipped away one by one, almost as quietly as Apaches. Standing in the open door of the darkened house, in the shadows of the porch, he had listened intently but hadn't heard any hoofbeats. That had brought a satisfied nod from him. The men had done as he'd told them and waited until they were out of earshot of the house to mount up and ride toward the rendezvous point. All he could do was hope that if Sandeen had any watchers posted nearby, they were unaware of the men leaving the ranch headquarters.

Before taking his own leave of the house, he had asked Laura, "You're sure you want to stay here?"

"I'm certain," she had replied without hesitation. "I have a feeling that Mr. Buckston is going to wake up soon, and I want to be here when he does."

"All right," Frank had told her. "Maybe next time we see each other, this will all be over."

She had smiled at him and taken his hand, and then impulsively hugged him. "I'm sorry I misjudged you, Mr. Morgan. And I'm awfully glad that you're really on my side."

Now as he approached the bald knob, Frank recalled the warmth and strength he had felt in Laura Flynn's slender body as he briefly returned that hug, and he thought that Jeff Buckston was a lucky man. At least he would be, if he ever woke up from that bullet crease on his head.

Frank reined in as he heard the whistle of a night bird. That was the signal he'd been listening for. He whistled in return, and a moment later more than a dozen riders emerged from the shadows under the trees at the base of the knoll and came toward him.

"Everybody accounted for?" Frank asked as the men rode up and stopped.

"Yeah, we're all here," one of them replied. "What do we do now, Morgan?"

"We'll swing around to the east, over close to the rim," Frank said, "and then circle back toward the trail between Saber and the Lazy F. If one of you boys who knows this range better than I do wants to lead the way, that would be just fine with me."

"I can do it," one of the men said. "I grew up around here. Reckon I know just about every foot of the range."

Frank nodded. "Good. We'll follow you. Now let's get moving."

They rode out, the young puncher taking the lead as Frank had suggested.

Frank had never been the sort of man to be bothered by uncertainty. He was in the habit of sizing up a situation the best he could, deciding on a course of action, and then following that course without looking back or brooding about what else he might have done.

But he had to admit that he was a mite nervous tonight. There were too many things going on that he couldn't control, too many groups moving around in the night, too many hands that could play out differently than he expected. It was almost like sitting down at a poker table blindfolded and trying to figure out what cards you had by feeling them. That was fine if the cards were marked, but if they weren't, and if you were gambling with people's lives . . .

Even the iciest nerves would twinge a little under those circumstances.

The young cowboy did indeed seem to know where he was going. He led the group almost into the dark shadow of the Mogollon Rim, then turned back to the west and rode hard. The others kept up with him, and about half an hour later he drew his mount to a stop on top of a thickly wooded ridge.

"Down yonder is the trail," he said in a low voice as he pointed.

"That's how Sandeen will get to the Lazy F?"

"Well, I reckon he could always go some other way," the puncher said with a shrug, "but that's the quickest and easiest trail to follow."

Frank nodded. He leaned forward in the saddle, some instinct warning him that not everything was as it should be. Something was wrong, and it took him a moment to realize what it was. Then he sniffed the air and knew.

The young waddy beside him caught on at the same time. "Dust!" he said. "There's dust hangin' in the air. A bunch o' horses went by here not long ago."

"Sandeen and his men have already ridden past," Frank said. "We have to head for the Lazy F."

"Wait a minute," one of the other men said. "What if you're wrong, Morgan? What if somebody else kicked up that dust? You wanted us to surprise Sandeen, and now you're maybe throwin' that edge away."

Frank knew the man was right. He was gambling again, staking lives on the turn of an unseen card. But he knew from experience to trust his hunches, in both poker and life, and he knew that Sandeen's raiders had already ridden past on their deadly mission.

"I'm heading for the Lazy F," he said as he heeled Stormy into motion down the slope. He didn't ask who was with him, and he didn't look back to see if any of the cowboys were following. He would take on Sandeen by himself if he had to.

Then he heard the hoofbeats behind him and knew they were coming with him. He reached the trail, turned north, and urged Stormy into a ground-eating lope. They might not have any time to waste.

Less than five minutes later, gunfire began to pop and rattle in the distance, and Frank knew that time was up.

After Frank Morgan and all the other men were gone, Acey-Deucy padded into the parlor and asked, "You want me to light the lamps now, Missy Laura?"

From the rocking chair beside the divan, Laura nodded and said, "Yes, please. Mr. Morgan said to make the house look as normal as possible."

The cook lit the lamp in the parlor and then hurried off to do Laura's bidding. Over the next few minutes, a warm glow began to fill the sprawling ranch house as Acey-Deucy lit several lamps.

In the parlor, Laura studied Buckston's haggard face. His skin was so pale that his dark mustache and the beard stubble that had grown over the past couple of days stood out starkly. He was not really what one would call a handsome man, even under the best of circumstances, Laura reflected. His features were too rough-hewn for that.

And yet when he smiled, she always thought he was very handsome, probably because that was when his gentle nature was the easiest to see in his eyes. The poets said that the eyes were the windows of the soul, and Jeff Buckston had a good soul, Laura thought. She looked at his eyes . . . his eyes that were . . .

Open.

Her breath froze in her throat as realization jerked her body forward in the chair. She leaned toward him and peered down into his eyes. She hadn't even noticed him opening them, but she wasn't imagining it. "Jeff," she whispered, then louder, "Jeff!"

He blinked vacantly, and for a horrible second she thought that he wasn't right in the head, that he didn't know her and would never be the same again. But then his unsteady gaze fastened on her and she saw awareness blossoming there, awareness and memory and all the things that made him who he was.

"L-Laura . . . ?" he rasped through dry lips.

She slid from the rocking chair and fell to her knees beside the divan, clutching his shoulders but being careful not to jostle him too much as she leaned over him and said, "Jeff, you know who I am? You're all right?"

"Sure, I know . . . who you are . . . and I reckon I'm . . . all right . . . 'cept my head hurts . . . like I got kicked by . . . a Missouri mule."

Tears of relief and love fell from her eyes to land on his lean, grizzled cheeks. She bent over him and brushed her lips gently against his. "Oh, my darling," she said. "I thought I had lost you."

"Nope, I'm still here . . . but where—" He stopped short as more memories obviously came back to him. "Sandeen!"

"Don't even think about that," Laura told him. "You've been hurt, and you need to rest."

"Feel like I been . . . restin' . . . for a long time." He lifted a hand and shakily reached toward his head. "What's this?"

"There's a bandage around your head. A bullet grazed you and knocked you out."

"For . . . how long? Those masked . . . bastards . . ."

"They're gone," Laura told him, without mentioning that the same gunmen, along with just as many others, were probably on their way here right now. "That was last night. You've been unconscious for almost twenty-four hours."

"That's a . . . long nap." Buckston raised his arm again, but this time he slipped it around her and brought her down so that her head rested on his chest as she leaned over the divan. "Pardon me for . . . bein' forward," he whispered. "Just feel like . . . I want to hold you for a spell. . . ."

"That's all right," she said as more tears spilled from her eyes and dampened his shirt. "You can hold me for as long as you want. Forever if you want."

But even as she wept for joy at the fact that she hadn't lost him after all, she remembered the deadly threat that loomed over the Lazy F tonight. Surely she hadn't had the man she loved returned to her only to have everything snatched away again by Ed Sandeen.

Without lifting her head from Buckston's chest, her eyes went to the gun lying on the table next to the divan. If Sandeen were to step into the room right now, she would kill him. She had no doubts about her ability to pick up that gun and empty every bullet in its cylinder into Sandeen's brutal, arrogant face. Just let him try to take away what she had been given!

As that thought went through her head, she caught her breath. Gunfire sounded in the night, heart-stoppingly close by, and as it continued, Laura knew what it meant.

The showdown, the final battle in this short-lived range war, had begun.

Sandeen had sent one of his hired gunmen, a former cavalry captain named Lawton who had been drummed out of the service for drunkenness and graft, to keep an eye on the Lazy F. He wanted to know what sort of odds he would be facing when he got there—not that it would really matter. Sandeen knew he was destined to emerge victorious. He could feel it in his bones.

Kite wasn't so certain of that, but he felt a little better when Lawton gave a whippoorwill's call and then rode in to report that the dozen or so ranch hands left on the Lazy F were still forted up in the remaining outbuildings.

"I've been watching all afternoon and evening, just like you told me to, Mr. Sandeen," Lawton said. "Nobody's moving around down there. They're probably holed up thinking about how they're going to die."

"What about the main house?"

"I spotted the girl and that chink cook through my field glasses. Wasn't sure what was going on at first because they didn't light the lamps right away when it got dark, but they did a little while later. Saving coal oil, maybe." Lawton gave an ugly laugh. "Like it's going to matter."

Uneasiness crawled along Kite's spine. It seemed to him that something wasn't quite right here, but he had to admit that from the sound of it, the Lazy F was ripe for the plucking. Sandeen and his army of more than forty gunslingers could ride in there, kill the few defenders, and take over the ranch house. Then, with Laura Flynn in his power, Sandeen could insist that he was just protecting her and her ranch from rustlers and outsiders. Nobody would really believe that, but who could prove otherwise in a court of law, especially if the girl went along with the story? Which she would have to if she wanted to live.

Through sheer boldness, Sandeen might just win. And if he did, like he said, there would be no stopping him.

"There may be a posse on its way from San Remo," Sandeen said to Lawton. "Any sign of it?"

The former cavalryman turned hired gun shook his head. "Nope. You don't have a thing to worry about, Boss. Just ride in and take over."

Sandeen lifted his reins. His lips pulled back from his teeth in a triumphant grin. "That's exactly what I'm going to do."

He heeled his horse into a walk and started down the slope toward the ranch house. In the moonlight, he was making himself a clear target for any rifleman who wanted to draw a bead on him. But just as clearly, he didn't care about that. He wasn't worried. An air of supreme confidence hung over him. Like a conquering general with his army right behind him, he rode down the hill.

And from the west, with a swift, sudden rataplan of hoofbeats, riders swept toward Sandeen and his men, the guns in their hands spouting flame. Sandeen whirled his horse, saw the small number of men attacking him and his forces, and knew that the posse from San Remo had arrived.

But they could be destroyed as easily as anyone else who dared to oppose him.

"Kill them!" Sandeen howled. "Kill them all!"

Chapter Thirty-one

Horn cursed as he saw the imperious rider high-stepping his horse down the hill toward the Lazy F headquarters. Even though he had never seen Ed Sandeen before, there was no doubt in his mind that he was looking at the former outlaw and rogue cattleman. Accompanied by a small army of gunfighters, Sandeen had come to claim what he thought of as his rightful prize.

And Horn had less than a dozen inexperienced townies to stop him.

It would have been easy at that moment to turn and ride away. Horn even considered the idea—for about two seconds. He knew he had a growing reputation as an amoral bastard. But there had been a time when he was an honorable man, and for damn sure nobody had ever accused him of being a coward. He just wished he was a little better with a short gun.

He drew his pistol anyway and looked over his shoulder at the tense faces of his unofficial posse. "Let's go," he said, and he spurred forward before any of them had a chance to argue with him. The gun in his hand bucked against his palm as he fired the first shot of the battle.

Thankfully, he wasn't charging Sandeen alone, as he had worried for an instant that he might be. More shots blasted as the men from San Remo spread out in a line and galloped toward the gunmen on the hillside. Even over the roar of guns, Horn heard somebody shouting orders. That would be Sandeen. Horn kept his eyes fixed on the man and rode straight toward him, holding his fire for the moment until he got closer. If he could kill Sandeen, the rest of that murderous gun crew might not be inclined to fight quite so hard.

Suddenly Horn felt a shiver go through his horse as a bullet thudded into the animal's body. The dun's front legs folded up, and as the horse collapsed, Horn was catapulted into the air. Only the fact that he had instinctively kicked his feet free from the stirrups as soon as the horse was hit saved him from having the dying animal roll over on him. Instead he slammed into the ground several feet in front of the horse, losing his hat to the impact. He rolled over and came to his knees, his chest heaving as he tried to catch his breath. Somehow he had managed to hang on to the revolver in his hand.

It might not do him much good, though, because as his eyes widened, he stared at the line of killers charging toward him, flame geysering from the muzzles of their guns. Bullets sang around Horn's head.

It was pretty much a toss-up, he thought grimly, whether they would shoot him or trample him first.

But either way he would die fighting. He jerked the gun up and fired.

Buckston tried to struggle up from the divan as he heard the shooting, too. "Wh-what—" he gasped.

Laura held him down. "Stay there, Jeff," she said. "You're in no shape to fight."

"Damn it, Laura—" She was right; his strength deserted him, and he sagged back against the cushions, weak as a kitten, his head spinning madly.

She stood up and lunged toward the table that held

the lamp. A quick puff of breath extinguished the flame and plunged the parlor into darkness. She didn't want the two of them showing up as plain targets through the front windows. Spinning back toward the divan, she picked up the gun and crouched beside Buckston, ready to fight if need be.

His hand reached out in the darkness and brushed her sleeve. Feebly clutching it, he said, "L-Laura, is it . . . Sandeen?"

"That's right," she replied. "He's come to take the ranch. But he's not going to do it." An edge composed of equal parts of anger, determination, and hysteria crept into her voice. "He's not!"

As she waited there, she slipped her injured arm out of the sling. It was still stiff and sore, but she could use it. She stripped the sling from around her neck and then wrapped both hands around the Colt.

"Come on, Sandeen," she breathed through tightly clenched teeth. "Just try to come in here, you son of a bitch."

Stormy stretched his legs and pulled ahead of the horses ridden by the Lazy F punchers. They trailed well behind Frank as he and the Appaloosa almost flew over the trail. It wasn't far to the ranch, but the shooting was fierce and he didn't know for sure what was happening. His best guess was that Horn had made it back from San Remo with a posse and gotten to the Lazy F just about the same time as Sandeen.

But the chances were that Horn and his companions would be heavily outnumbered, and Sandeen's men might wipe them out in pretty short order—unless Frank and his bunch got there in time to turn the tide of battle.

Just as on the previous night, Frank raced through the trees and came out on the ridge overlooking the ranch. In the wash of silvery moonlight, he saw the gang of

killers that had been bound for the Lazy F. Those
gunmen, led by Ed Sandeen, had swung toward their left
flank to meet the charge of a much smaller group. That
would be Horn and the men from San Remo, Frank
thought. As he galloped down the hill, he looked for the
special deputy, but didn't see him.

Then his eyes were drawn to the fallen horse and the
man kneeling on the ground nearby, gun in hand spouting orange flame as he fired at the charging killers.
Frank recognized Horn and knew the man had only seconds to live unless something distracted Sandeen's men.

Looked like it was up to him to provide that distraction.

Shots slammed from his Colt as he attacked the
gunmen from the rear. He saw one man fall, knocked
out of the saddle by a bullet. Other riders reined in and
whirled their horses to meet this new threat. Bullets
began to whistle around Frank's head, but he never
slowed down.

Instead, gun blazing, he plunged straight into the
heart of chaos.

"It's Morgan!" Sandeen exclaimed as he saw the lone
rider racing toward them from the rear, snapping off
shots as he came. "But he's by himself, the damned
fool!" Sandeen forgot about the posse from San Remo
for the moment as he jerked his mount around. They
could be dealt with easily. It was that bastard Morgan he
wanted. And if Morgan was crazy enough to attack by
himself—

"Wait!" Mitch Kite cried from where he rode beside
Sandeen, reaching out to grab his boss's arm. "Look up
there!"

More riders had just topped the hill and now began to
gallop down the slope toward the ranch headquarters.
Spurts of flame winked in the darkness as they started
shooting.

Sandeen had no idea who these newcomers were, but he realized that their identity didn't really matter. What was important was that suddenly he and his men were caught between two opposing forces, and they were being raked by a deadly cross fire. They might still outnumber the ranch's defenders, but their position was no longer nearly as strong as it had been only moments earlier.

There was only one answer. Power lay in the ranch house. Whoever captured it was going to win this battle because that was where Laura Flynn was, and with Laura in his hands, the Lazy F men would have no choice but to surrender. Sandeen whirled his horse yet again and cruelly jabbed his spurs in its flanks. "Come on!" he shouted to Kite. "Let's get to the house!"

Trailed by several of the gunmen, they headed for the Lazy F ranch house.

All of a sudden, Tom Horn wasn't facing the charging killers by himself anymore. The members of the posse caught up to him and swung down from their saddles to form a skirmish line, as directed by powerfully shouted orders from Willard Donohue. Horn was shocked by the authority and command in the trampish-looking man's voice, and wondered fleetingly if Donohue had once been an officer in the Army. He sure sounded like it.

But there was no time to ponder that. Horn came to his feet, flanked once again by Culverhouse and Donohue, and added his shots to the volley after volley ripping out from the men of San Remo. The storm of lead scythed through Sandeen's men and knocked several of them from their saddles. Some of the horses collapsed as they were hit, and riders flew through the air or screamed as the fallen horses rolled on them, breaking bones and crushing organs.

Not that the posse was escaping unscathed. A couple of men fell as Sandeen's men returned the fire, and two more staggered but stayed on their feet and kept fighting. The hammer of Horn's gun clicked on an empty chamber. Coolly, he punched fresh shells from the loops on his belt and began to reload, paying little or no attention to the slugs whistling around his head. A man's time was up, or it wasn't, and there wasn't a whole hell of a lot he could do about it. Horn snapped the Colt's cylinder closed, raised the gun, and started firing again.

The Lazy F punchers slammed into Sandeen's force from the rear. Guns blared, muzzle flashes lit up desperate faces, horses collided, and men grappled hand to hand. The big cur called Dog, who had been brought to the ranch by the posse from San Remo, flashed here and there, pulling down gunmen and savaging them with his teeth until they screamed and curled up into a ball. Sandeen's "army" was split, trying to cope with danger from two directions at once, and as more and more of them fell, the odds drew closer to even.

Frank spotted Sandeen and several other men making for the house and gave chase. He knew that Laura, Buckston, and Acey-Deucy were probably still in there. Despite the fact that Sandeen's men were disorganized and perhaps fighting a losing battle, everything could change in the blink of an eye if Sandeen got his hands on Laura Flynn and used her as a hostage. Frank had to prevent that.

Stormy leaped through the hellish fighting, hooves barely touching the ground. Frank leaned forward over the Appaloosa's neck and shouted, "Sandeen!" A couple of the rogue cattleman's companions whirled around, but Sandeen kept going.

Frank recognized Mitch Kite, who ran the Verde Saloon in town for Sandeen. The gun in Kite's hand spurted flame as he triggered a couple of shots. Frank heard the wind-rip of the bullets as they passed by his ear, and then his own Colt blasted. Kite cried out as the slug tore into his chest and lifted him from the saddle. He thudded to the ground, pawing at his chest as blood welled between his fingers. Then Frank and Stormy flashed past him.

Another of Sandeen's men took Frank by surprise by jerking his horse directly into Stormy's path. The Appaloosa tried to dart nimbly aside, but there wasn't time or room to completely avoid a collision. The horses slammed together and both went down. Frank tumbled from the saddle and rolled across the ground, coming to a stop on his stomach. Bullets kicked up dirt as they thudded into the ranch yard only inches away from him. He tipped up the barrel of his gun and fired twice, the Colt barking savagely as he triggered it. Both of the other men who had been with Sandeen jerked under the impact of the well-placed bullets and pitched from their saddles.

Frank scrambled up, biting back a curse as he saw that Sandeen's horse was at the porch of the ranch house, its saddle empty. That meant Sandeen had to be inside. As he ran toward the house, Frank thumbed fresh cartridges into his empty revolver.

Then suddenly, just as he reached the steps, a shot rang out inside.

Laura brought up the gun as the figure loomed menacingly in the doorway. She was ready to pull the trigger, but at the last second her resolve betrayed her. She couldn't see the man's face, and suddenly realized she didn't know for certain who he was. She might be about to shoot a friend, perhaps even Frank Morgan. So she cried, "Stop! Don't move—"

The man leaped forward, arm swinging. His hand

crashed brutally against Laura's head and drove her to the side. The gun flew out of her hands as she fell to her knees.

"You damn bitch!" a voice that she recognized as Ed Sandeen's grated above her. "I would have given you everything! Now, because of you, I have to *take* what I want!"

On the divan, Jeff Buckston forced himself to roll onto his side, even though his limp muscles still didn't want to work and agony pounded through his skull and the world spun crazily around him. He thought he had heard something strike the floor beside the divan, and instinct made him reach down with a shaking hand and search for whatever it was. His fingers brushed something smooth. He realized a second later it was the walnut butt of the gun Laura had been holding.

Buckston glanced toward the spot where she had fallen when Sandeen struck her. Sandeen still loomed over her, reaching for her with one hand while the other held a gun. Buckston found the strength somewhere deep inside him to close his hand around the Colt and lift it. He swung the barrel toward the two figures across the room. Sandeen had hold of Laura now, and she was struggling desperately against him.

"Sandeen!" Buckston rasped.

Sandeen froze for a second, then viciously shoved Laura away from him, sending her skidding across the floor. He took a step toward the divan. "Buckston?" he said. "You're still alive, you bastard?" The gun in his hand started to come up. "I'm gonna enjoy this."

"So am I," Buckston said, and he pulled the trigger.

Frank bounded onto the porch as the echoes of the shot fired inside the house died away. He came to a tense stop there at the top of the steps as a dark figure loomed in the front door. The man stepped forward, gun in hand, and as he came into the slanting moonlight, Frank recognized Ed Sandeen.

The two of them fired at the same instant, flame lancing from the barrels of their guns and almost touching. Sandeen's shot missed, but Frank's bullet crashed into the man's body and drove him backward. Frank's brain caught up to his instincts then, and he realized that there had already been a dark stain on the breast of Sandeen's shirt before he pulled the trigger. Sandeen was already wounded, maybe even dying, but sheer hatred had driven him on to take one last shot at The Drifter.

But now Sandeen lay on his back in the doorway, his gun slipping from limp, nerveless fingers at his side, and as his final breath rattled grotesquely in his throat, the threat that he represented to the Mogollon Rim country came to an end.

"Mr. Morgan!" Laura cried from inside the parlor. "Mr. Morgan, is that you? Look out for Sandeen!"

"No need," Frank said as he stepped over the corpse in the doorway. "He's dead. Are you all right?"

A match scratched into life, its glare lighting up the room. Frank saw Laura standing by the divan as she lit a lamp. Buckston still lay there, but he was conscious now, propped up a little on one elbow. He held a gun in his hand, and Frank knew the foreman of the Lazy F had fired the first shot to strike Sandeen.

"We're all right," Laura said breathlessly. "Jeff . . . Jeff saved us."

Frank smiled and nodded curtly. "Good to see that you made it, Buckston. I'd appreciate it if you didn't try to shoot me. In case you haven't figured it out by now, I'm on your side, not Sandeen's."

"Yeah," Buckston said in a weak voice. "I reckon I can see that. And I think I've . . . done all the shootin' I can do . . . for now." He let the revolver slide from his fingers to lie on the divan beside him.

Frank turned back toward the porch, and as he stepped out he realized that the battle was over. Bodies littered the ranch yard, but most of them belonged to Sandeen's hired gunfighters. Some of them had realized that the odds were turning against them and had surrendered. They stood now in a dispirited group, surrounded by a mixed force of Lazy F cowboys and armed citizens from San Remo.

Tom Horn limped toward the house, a dark stain on the right leg of his trousers. Jasper Culverhouse and Mayor Donohue were with him. Donohue's left hand clutched his right arm where a bullet had torn through it. Frank grinned as he saw that Dog was with them. The big cur was licking his chops, as if he had just feasted on a bad hombre or two.

"Everybody all right in there?" Horn asked as he nodded toward the house.

"Just fine," Frank said. "Except for Sandeen. He's dead."

Horn grunted. "So are most of his men. He rode over here tonight for a cleanup, but he's the one who got cleaned."

Frank gestured toward Horn's leg. "How bad are you hit?"

"Aw, hell, this is just a scratch. Nothin' to worry about. The mayor got ventilated worse'n I did."

"A mere flesh wound," Donohue proclaimed. "I'll be fine."

Horn turned toward him. "The way you were shoutin' orders and movin' men around, it sounded to me like you've got some military experience, Mayor."

"Him?" Culverhouse snorted. "He was just a Union general back durin' the Civil War and won a few medals for it, that's all."

Frank laughed. Donohue had told him once not to judge him entirely by appearances. That had certainly turned out to be good advice.

Dog nuzzled Frank's leg. Frank reached down and petted him, roughing up the fur on the wolflike cur's head.

"Looks like I'm gonna have my work cut out for me the next few days," Culverhouse went on. "Lots of coffins to build and plenty of buryin' to do."

"Maybe so," Frank said, "but when the sun comes up in the morning, it'll be shining on a lot more peaceful range than it went down on tonight."

Chapter Thirty-two

The menace that Ed Sandeen had represented to this part of the territory had not been ended without paying a price. Two more of the Lazy F punchers were dead, as were Alonzo Hightower and Ben Desmond from San Remo. Several men from both groups had been wounded, a few of them badly. It would take a while for everybody to get over what had happened, Frank knew.

But get over it they would. He was equally sure of that. These were frontier folk, and they had the sort of steel in them that might bend occasionally but never break.

The next day after the big dustup at the Lazy F, Frank was sitting in the Mogollon Saloon with Tom Horn and Mayor Donohue. Hightower's widow had already said that she was going to keep the place open, in honor of her husband's memory. Down the street, the Verde Saloon was locked up. Somebody had seen Jonah Speckler, who had worked there as a bartender, riding out of town before dawn with a good-sized carpetbag lashed to his saddle. Nobody knew when or if he would ever be back.

"I was just down at Jasper's place," Donohue said. He had come into the saloon a few minutes earlier and joined Frank and Horn at the table. "It looks like Caleb

Glover is going to make it. He's gettin' stronger now instead of weaker. Of course, his cowboyin' days are over. But Jasper plans to make him some special crutches and maybe a wheelchair, so he can still get around. Mary Elizabeth says once they're married, he can help her run the café."

"What about that fella Buckston?" Horn asked.

Frank took a sip of the coffee he had ordered instead of a drink. "I rode out to the Lazy F this morning to check on things. Buckston's doing fine except for an aching head. Laura Flynn is going to make him take it easy for a few days, but I suspect he'll be up and around before too long, running the ranch for her again."

"Reckon there's gonna be weddin' bells for them, too?" Donohue asked with a twinkle in his eye.

Frank chuckled. "I wouldn't be a bit surprised."

Horn downed the whiskey in his glass and said, "Well, Buckey O'Neill ought to be here with a posse sometime late this afternoon, and since the range war's over I reckon that'll be the end o' my job as special deputy."

"Sheriff O'Neill would probably keep you on as a regular deputy," Donohue suggested.

Horn shook his head. "Not interested. I've done enough lawin' to suit me for a while. Thought I'd drift on up Wyoming or Montana way. Always lots goin' on up there."

"A lot of trouble, you mean," Frank said.

Horn smiled. "You and me, it seems to follow us, don't it, Morgan?"

Frank just shrugged. He had long since come to accept his destiny. He was one of the last of the truly fast guns. It was something he would never escape until he drew his last breath.

"So," Horn said, turning to Donohue, "you used to be a general. . . ."

Two figures in the doorway caught Frank's attention as his companions continued to talk. A pair of women stood there, looking over the batwings into the saloon as if searching for someone. One was in her forties, the other around twenty, and both had red hair, long and flowing on the younger one, short and touched with gray on the older one. The resemblance between them was such that Frank knew right away they were mother and daughter.

And to his surprise, he realized that they were both looking straight at him.

"Excuse me, boys," he muttered as he got to his feet and left the table. He walked over to the saloon entrance. The women moved back onto the boardwalk. Frank stepped outside and joined them, removing his hat as he did so. He said, "Good afternoon, ladies. Something I can do for you?"

"Are you Mr. Frank Morgan?" the older woman said. Frank thought she was very attractive, although her daughter was more spectacularly beautiful. "Mr. Culverhouse told us we might find you here."

"Yes, ma'am," he said. "Have we met?"

"No. My name is Alma Blake. This is my daughter Tess. We just came down here from Flagstaff."

The names were familiar, but it took Frank a second to place them. Then he said to Alma Blake, "That young cowboy Rufe . . . he was your son."

She smiled sadly and nodded. "And Tess's brother. We received a letter from Howard Flynn about what happened to Rufe, and how you were the last one to speak to him. We came down here to visit his grave, and to talk to you."

"Mrs. Blake, Miss Blake, I'm mighty sorry for your loss," Frank said solemnly as he held his hat in front of him. "If it's any comfort, I can tell you that Rufe was thinking of both of you there at the end. He seemed like a mighty fine young man."

"He was," Tess Blake said. "He was the finest brother anybody could want."

Her mother held out a hand to Frank. "Thank you, Mr. Morgan. I'm grateful that my boy didn't have to be alone when he . . . when he died." Frank took her hand gently. "If you ever find yourself in Flagstaff," Alma Blake went on, "please stop and say hello. We run a boarding-house there."

Frank nodded. "I'll sure do that, ma'am," he lied. He had no intention of ever stopping in to see the two of them, despite the fact that Tess was lovely enough to take the breath away from any man and Alma's more mature beauty was even more attractive to a man of Frank's years. But to them he would always be the man who was there when Rufe was killed, and he didn't figure they would need reminding of that.

He shook hands with Tess, too, and then put his hat on and stood there to watch them walk away. They got into a buggy that was parked in front of Jasper Culver-house's blacksmith shop and drove off, heading out of San Remo on the trail that led to Prescott and on north to Flagstaff.

"Lovely ladies," a voice said from Frank's right.

He turned his head and saw a man he had never seen before standing on the boardwalk about ten feet away. The stranger was tall and lean and dressed in black, and he had a small, black, leather-bound book of some sort in his left hand. He wrote something in it with a stub of pencil, and as the pencil moved, the man spoke the words aloud.

"Frank Morgan."

"That's my name," Frank said with a frown. "What business is it of yours, mister?"

"Just making a note of it." The man closed the book and slipped it and the pencil into a pocket inside his long black coat. "I like to keep track of these things."

Frank's nerves tingled. He knew instinctively that this hombre was trouble. "What things?" he asked.

"Oh—" The man's hand swept the long coat back. "Just the men I've killed."

The same hand that had swept the coat back dropped to the butt of the gun on his hip with blinding speed. The gun was out and up in less than the blink of an eye.

But that wasn't fast enough. Frank's Colt was already leveled. It roared before the stranger could pull the trigger. He had never even seen Frank draw.

The bullet slammed into the stranger's chest, lifting him off his feet. He crashed down on his back on the boardwalk, his unfired gun skittering away. A deep cough wracked him. Blood welled from his mouth.

As Horn and Donohue burst out of the saloon to see what the shot was about, Frank stepped to the stranger's side and stood over him. He had never seen this hombre before, but he knew what sort of man he was—a hired killer. Keeping the Colt trained on him, Frank said, "Who sent you after me? Who wants me dead?"

The dying man's mouth worked and more blood came out, and for a second Frank was afraid that life would flicker out before the man could answer. But then the stranger rasped, "D-Dutton . . . Charles . . . Dutt—"

That was all he got out before he died, but it was enough. The name hit Frank like a punch in the gut. Charles Dutton had been one of Vivian Browning's attorneys. Vivian, Frank's first wife and his son Conrad's mother. The woman who had been cut down by an outlaw bullet because she'd been betrayed by a man she trusted, her own lawyer, Charles Dutton.

Dutton was back East somewhere. Frank had intended to find him someday and settle the score for Vivian, one of the few women he had truly loved in his life. But other things had gotten in the way and Dutton was still alive.

Alive, and obviously worried enough about Frank Morgan seeking vengeance to hire a killer to go after him. Frank leathered his iron and knelt beside the dead man, reached inside the coat, and dug out the small, leather-bound book. The man had bled on it as he died. Frank flipped through it, finding page after page of names, mostly men but a few women, too. And these were all people the stranger had killed, Frank recalled. At least, that was what the snake-blooded bastard had claimed.

"Who was he, Morgan?" Horn asked as Frank straightened.

"I don't know," Frank answered honestly. He dropped the book on the planks next to the dead man. "He didn't tell me his name." The stranger had taken pains to list all his victims, yet he had died with his own name unknown.

"But why did he try to kill you?" Donohue asked.

"To remind me that some chores are best not left undone," Frank said. His hand lifted to the breast of his shirt and unpinned the marshal's badge he was still wearing. He handed it to Donohue and then turned away and headed for Culverhouse's stable. It was time to saddle Stormy, gather up Dog, and move on. It was time for a showdown too long postponed.

And behind him a gust of wind blew across the boardwalk, fluttering through the bloodstained pages and the names in the black book.